The Resurrection of James Temple

A Work of Historical Fiction By
Arlon Davis

The Resurrection of James Temple

A Work of Historical Fiction By
Arlon Davis

Copyright © 2018

**Additional copies of this book
are available from the author:**

Arlon Davis
684 Palmer Drive
Orange, TX 77632
409-883-0074
texasmanproductions-com.webs.com
texasman4@yahoo.com

Published in the United States of America by
Wise Publications
809 East Napoleon St. - Sulphur, Louisiana 70663
337-527-8308 - wisepublications@yahoo.com
Visit our online bookstore: www.wisepublications.biz

Marvel not at this: for the hour is coming, in which all that are in the graves shall hear his voice,

and shall come forth; they that have done good, unto the resurrection of life; and they that have done evil, unto the resurrection of damnation.

John 5:28,29

King James Version

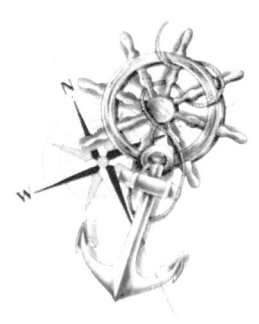

Prologue

"Hit him again Johnny while he's still off balance!" yelled Gil Tobin from the sidelines to his friend .

Quick as greased lightning, Johnny Temple struck his man again staggering him back on his heels towards the feed sacks that lay against the bow of the ship. As Lyle Bartlett struggled to free himself from Johnny's onslaught , his hand fell into the open end of a grain sack and he scooped up a handful. Flinging the grain into Johnny's face gave him the advantage he had hoped for as he struck out hard with a straight jab bringing blood from Johnny's nose.

"Boooooo!" the gathered crowd jeered their disapproval at Lyle's underhanded tactics, but all their booing didn't help Johnny get the grain out of his eyes any faster. Without being able to see clearly, he momentarily lost sight of his sparring partner forcing him to strike out at shadows in all directions in a desperate attempt to stay in the game. He made brief contact with one of his shipmates accidentally hitting him rapid fire in the gut.

"Lookout,...he's behind you!" another shipmate yelled at Johnny, but it was too late. Lyle Bartlett struck Johnny in the kidney with a mean right hook forcing Johnny to wince in pain. As Johnny spun around from the painful blow to face his man again, Lyle decided to lunge at Johnny using his broad shoulder as a battering ram. Although Johnny's vision was cloudy, he could certainly feel the full locks of his opponent hair as Lyle rushed in low. Grabbing a handful of brown curls, he yanked backwards for all he was worth because his father had once taught him that 'wherever the head goes, the body goes too.' It wasn't pretty seeing Lyle make such a drastic stumbling course correction in mid step like he did, but it worked beautifully as Johnny took control of the fight once again deflecting the brunt of Lyle's attempt at breaking his bones.

All at once the two combatants were rolling around on the floor again with Johnny's fingers still entwined in Lyle's hair. Johnny began bouncing his antagonist's head off the floor as he tried desperately to straddle him. Lyle was flailing about trying to get a clear shot at Johnny's head, but each time he swung, his own head was rewarded with a solid thump on the floor. He knew he couldn't keep this up for very long for fear of losing consciousness, so he decided to try and roll Johnny over. However, as hard as he tried, it was not to be. Johnny was anchored fast now as he continued to slam Lyle's head onto the deck.

"Let him up you dirty rat!" someone in the crowd goaded as he kicked Johnny hard in the side allowing Lyle to turn the tables on his unfortunate circumstances. This was not pleasing to the crowd as they took their turns pummeling the offending bystander for interfering.

Up on his feet again, Lyle began to dance around with new vigor taking random shots at Johnny with his long arms and of course, that wicked jab. Johnny did his best to keep his distance and block the incoming pokes while waiting for an opportunity to counterattack. He had to find an opening and get on the inside of his taller opponent's defenses to offset the advantage Lyle held over him with his reach. Suddenly, an opportunity presented itself as Lyle lowered his arms for a split second to relax the tired, sore numbness from his limbs. Johnny stepped in quickly with an uppercut to the bottom of his chin sending shockwaves through Lyle's body. He didn't see it coming as the lights started to dim around him, and he knew one more of those and it would be all over. He attempted to push Johnny away, but it was too little, too late as Johnny was now on the inside pounding Lyle in the gut over and over again forcing the air from his lungs. As Lyle's legs buckled under him, Johnny knew victory was within his grasp just as a very deep and coarse voice sang out loudly behind him.

"See here, what's the meaning of this! Break it up,...let me in there you swabbies, I said," the quartermaster growled as he waded through the other youngsters to get at the two warring combatants.

Johnny felt the quartermaster's rough hand grab the back of his collar as he was pulled off Lyle's limp body. It didn't matter to him that they had been caught, and it didn't matter the punishment because he had confronted his demon and licked him fair and square in front of all his fellow shipmates. From this day on Johnny Temple would walk head and shoulders taller than Lyle Bartlett no matter where they went on board this ship even though he was four inches shorter in actual height.

"You two mutton heads are in a heap of trouble," the older man growled as he reached down and pulled Lyle up by the arm. "You know the captain don't allow fighting on this tub without his consent. Let's go topside and see what he has to say about all this."

Up the stairs they went from the forward cargo hold to the uppermost deck. Upon reaching daylight, Quartermaster Galen Sims dropped both boys on deck and grabbed a bucket of soapy water from one of the sailors who was scouring the deck and poured its contents on them. Both boys wiped the blood and soapy water from their faces as best they could and stood patiently awaiting the next volley from the headstrong quartermaster.

From the far end of the ship came Captain Henry Boles who wanted to see what the commotion was all about. As he stood next to the quartermaster assessing things, the captain looked ten foot tall to the two weary combatants. The boys knew they were in a mess of trouble when the quartermaster began explaining what he'd found.

"Well, what are you going to do with them Galen?" the captain queried. "They are your responsibility as far as I'm concerned."

"I'm thinking about making them walk the plank Cap'n sir for disobeying your direct orders about fighting on board your ship."

"Can we spare them? At this rate, we may not have any sailors left by the time we reach our destination," the concerned captain asked. "It seems a little harsh to throw good, able bodied seamen overboard, no matter how small in stature they might be. Besides, they don't exactly look like dangerous mutineers. Did you bother to ask what the dust up was all about Mr. Sims? Maybe you will have to throw only one overboard if the other was justified in his actions."

The quartermaster turned and growled at the two boys.

"Alright you two scalawags, what were you fighting about?"

"It was my fault sir," Johnny Temple started abruptly, catching Lyle Bartlett off guard before he had time to concoct his own version of a lie. "I challenged Mr. Bartlett for his spot as top cabin boy to the Captain and it kind 'a got out of hand from there." It was all a lie. Mr. Bartlett had been bullying him ever since he'd come on board, and even more so knowing Temple's dad was a top rigger on this very ship. Johnny was hoping for leniency from the quartermaster since it was his first voyage and first offense. He knew that Lyle Bartlett would be in a lot more trouble since he'd been here longer and knew better the unbending rules of life aboard ship.

Lyle Bartlett cocked his head as he looked over at Johnny in disbelief. This young guppy had just whupped him fair and square and now he was standing in punishment for both of them. He certainly had misjudged the miscreant. As Lyle cleared his throat to speak, Johnny spoke again trying to head him off.

"I ask your pardon for breaking the rules Mr. Sims, but I beg you please don't throw me overboard as I don't see any land nearby where I might swim to," Johnny pleaded.

Everyone on deck broke out laughing at the imagery of ten year old Johnny Temple swimming to a nearby island as part of his punishment. Even the Captain ducked his head to hide a smile.

"Well what do you propose I should do with you?"

"I'll tell you what I'll do. I'll stand in double duty for myself and Mr. Bartlett for a week. What do you say Mr. Sims?" Johnny replied sticking out his hand hoping for an end to it all. It seemed more than fair to his young mind.

"Throw in a good flogging along with your double duty Mr. Temple and I'm all in. What do you have to say to that?" the Quartermaster growled back.

Johnny didn't see that coming, but he was committed as he nodded his head slowly in the affirmative.

"Alright then, make way there and tie young Mr. Temple to the center mast as he accepts punishment for fighting aboard ship. Since you're young and new to the ways of the sea, I'll only give you five lashes instead of the usual thirty," the old Quartermaster scowled as he unfurled his whip. As he pulled his hand back to strike the boy, a peculiar thing happened.

"Hold up there Mr. Sims," James Temple requested as he grabbed the whip from behind with his open hand. "I'd like to know what's going on here if it's not too much trouble." Ordinarily a stunt like that would have gotten a normal man in big trouble with the quartermaster, but James Temple was not an ordinary man and Galen Sims was not his equal regardless of his position aboard this ship.

"Seaman Temple, you'd better go back topside, because this doesn't concern you."

"The boy is my son Mr. Sims, and what happens to him aboard this ship concerns me. I'd still like to hear from him about why he's being tied to the mast for a flogging," Temple responded.

"Very well, suit yourself."

After a few moments of conversation alone with his son, James Temple understood clearly what his son was trying to do for the other boy. Dad was very proud of his actions, but still didn't think it warranted a lashing. There was only one thing left to do.

"Mr. Sims, might I have a word."

After explaining things to the quartermaster about what really happened out of earshot of everyone, the boy's father struck up a bargain of sorts with Mr. Sims. With all eyes still on James Temple, he backed away and began to speak where everyone could hear him.

"Since the boy is my responsibility, I am prepared to take his place on the mast. Untie him."

Johnny was shocked, never expecting this from his father as he begged him not to interfere. James looked down into his son's eyes and spoke softly to him.

"I've never been more proud of you than I am right now. I taught you how to fight for what's right and today you've taught me and the quartermaster a thing or two. The quartermaster doesn't want to whip you or me after hearing the whole true story, but he's got his ugly, bumbling self landlocked with no way out. He's got to save face and deliver the punishment you both agreed upon, or there will be nothing but discipline problems aboard ship from here on out. Do you understand?"

"Yes father, but I never intended for you to take my punishment. Please forgive me."

"There's nothing to forgive son. It's just what has to be. Now stand over there with your back to me so you don't have to watch. Since it's only five lashes, we'll both get through this without too much trouble I suspect. Now do as I say and stand over there and don't look."

Young John Temple walked forward and placed his hands on the forward rail as the whipping of his father commenced in earnest. With each stripe, his own shoulders shook until the lashes were meted out. As he turned and raced back to his father, he saw not only the fresh stripes across his back, but others that looked much, much older. He helped his father cross the deck and enter their quarters. Since he only received five lashes, it wasn't too much for a strong hard seaman to endure. James had seen men pass out and die from thirty lashes delivered from the hand of the right man, but he was lucky today since the quartermaster was his friend.

"Alright, back to work you mangy swabs,...the show's over. and furthermore, there'll be no more fighting aboard this ship, says I."

"Send the surgeon down to tend his wounds Mr. Sims, and no more duty this day for either of our Temple seamen. From the looks of them, I think they have contributed quite enough to the entertainment of the ship's morale for the day," the captain commanded as he turned to leave the deck.

"Yes Cap 'n."

"And one more thing for the record Mr. Sims, there'll be no more whips used on children aboard this ship. If you had stayed home and had a few of your own, you might actually understand why. Young Mr. Temple's offer of double duty was a fair one, but you managed in your own clumsy way to turn a simple fight among children into a capital offense. Figure out how to dispel the correct discipline aboard my ship Mr. Sims, or you might find yourself tied to the same mast some dark and dreary night," the captain warned. "You're no longer working a slave ship sir, so learn some manners and civility when working with this crew or by Jove, I'll have you thrown you to the sharks. Do we have an understanding?" he asked.

"Perfectly clear Cap 'n, and I'm sorry for offending you. I've worked on so many slavers these last twenty years, that I've almost forgotten how to act among civilized men," Mr. Sims conceded. "Thanks Cap 'n for reminding me of my duty."

"Just make it work Mr. Sims. Less strife and more harmony," the captain said as he turned and left the Quartermaster to mull over what he had instructed.

"Yes Cap 'n, less strife and more harmony."

As James and his son entered the bunk area, the ship's surgeon arrived shortly thereafter with some soothing salves for James Temple's backside.

"Jim my boy, I thought you had given up fighting for causes. The last time I wrapped you in bandages you almost died," Tom Greely the ship's surgeon remarked as he surveyed the fresh wounds and opened a jar of precious salve to help soothe them. "Ah...these ain't all that bad Captain."

"I asked you not to call me that Tom especially in front of the boy. On this ship I'm just a rigger and nothing more."

"Sorry sir, I'm forgetting my manners. The older I get, the more addled I'm becoming. Some days I wake up and can't even remember me own name. Now that's addled," he remarked as he began spreading the healing salves on his stripes and rubbing them in.

Young John Temple looked confused by the remark the ship's surgeon made concerning his father, 'the Captain'. Being the inquisitive type, he asked his father the meaning.

"Why did he call you Captain, father?"

"See what you did Tom?"

"He don't know about what happened to you Jim, and everything you went through?" Tom queried.

"No, and for right now I'd like to leave it at that. I'll tell him when the time is right. Now finish your doctoring and get out, you blubbering old sea turtle," James teased. Now that the genie was out of the bottle, he figured this was as good a time as any to have a conversation with Johnny about his past.

"There, there Jim my boy, you'll be alright in a day or two. Those stripes didn't even break the skin. It looks as though our Mr. Sims was taking a nap when he laid those on you. Maybe he went easy on you for old time's sake. After I get you taped up, I want you to take two of these and get some sleep. I'll check on you tomorrow," Tom whispered as he patted the top of James' head like a son. In a few more moments he was finished with the wrap.

"Thanks Tom," James remarked as he sat up and slipped his shirt back on over the surgeon's gauze wrap . After adjusting his shirt properly, he looked at his son who was sitting opposite him like a puppy waiting for his master to throw him a bone. If nothing else, he could explain a little more clearly about what had happened this morning.

"Can I get you some water or rum father. You must be thirsty by now," Johnny suggested.

"Some water would be nice, and you might take a moment to clean your own self up a little. You still have blood in your hair and up your nose. Was it a good fight?"

Johnny grinned as he turned to look at his father with some of the residual victory still glowing on his face.

"I whipped him fair and square just like you taught me, but I sure thought he had me there a couple of times. It's like you always say, 'Fight on a little longer cause he's getting tired too, and when he lets his guard down, you'll know what to do.' Before I knew it, he dropped his arms to shake off the tiredness and I put one up under his chin just like we'd practiced."

"You did what you had to do, and I just wish I could have been there to see it. Now do your best not to have any more fights while we're at sea. It'll go better for both of us if can keep our business out of the ship's gossip. Okay?" James asked.

"Yes father, I'll try," Johnny agreed.

James knew curiosity was about to make his boy burst wide open, so he jumped in with both feet.

"I guess you were wondering why Tom Greely called me Captain?"

"Yes sir, but I didn't want to pry. Can you tell me now since there's no one around?" Johnny asked puzzled by all the secrecy.

"Alright son, I guess it's about time you know at least some of it, and I'd rather it came from me than one of the ship's rats," James began after taking a long drink of water to quench his thirst. "Before you were born, I once was a real Captain in the United States Navy. I grew up aboard ship just like you are doing now, and I loved every minute of it. I went aboard my first ship at ten years old and grew to love the sea, and all the grand adventures she offered up on a silver platter. The sea quickly became my mistress and the only time I ever left her was to go ashore on leave. It was on one of those shore leaves that I met and married your mother. In time, I decided to leave the sea for her, but I had one more mission to complete before I left the service for good. That final mission cost me a court-martial."

Johnny blinked and swallowed hard. How could this be? His father was the most honorable man he knew, no matter what a court-martial verdict had declared.

"Why were you court-marshaled father? I've never heard you talk of it before."

"I didn't want to burden you with all this, since it happened about the time you were born. It went so hard on your mother that it finally broke her heart, and she never recovered from the shame," James continued. "It seems she merely lost the will to live I reckon, and one day while I was gone, she died."

"But why were you court-marshaled? I can think of no good reason for anyone to do such a thing to you, if they knew you at all."

James bit his lip not wanting to tell the boy more than the youngster could handle, because it was a lot to take in. After some thought, he decided to tell him some of it.

"There are powerful forces that live and operate in our world son. Some of those forces are good and some are evil. I made the mistake of running headlong into one of those evil forces when I was captain aboard a ship of war. Despite my pleas for help, no one dared come to my defense for fear it would ruin them too. Even the lawyer the Navy gave me turned tail and ran when they turned up the heat. My life was sailing along in good wind and smooth waters until I hit the reef that scuttled it. If I had been engaged in battle on the high seas against an armed enemy I could identify, I'm certain I could have won a victory over them because of my skills as a sailor. However, I found myself engaged in a new kind of warfare I was ill equipped to fight, and it took place on land against an enemy using a different kind of weapon."

Johnny sat very quiet as he listened. He knew how his father's mind worked, and how he formulated information he wished to dispense at times like this. His father was a great orator and a highly skilled teacher, and he knew this was going to be one of those teachable moments he was so familiar with if he could just get him to keep talking.

"What happened father? Will you please tell me? Aunt Lorna never told me any of this. Don't I have a right to know? Tell me who your enemy was."

James had been dreading this moment. How could he tell what happened without souring his son's stomach for the very country he loved so much, and he certainly didn't want the boy to grow into a rebel filled with hate. There were already enough Temple's on that list who filled the bill. He also couldn't tell him who some of the people were that sent him packing because of a promise he made to his dying wife Lena.

"Do you remember how I've always taught you to be fair in your dealings with people?" James asked.

"Yes father."

"That's why I was so proud of you earlier. Your honest attempt at protecting the other boy after the fight showed me that you understood the importance of duty and honor. You whipped your man fair and square without any underhanded dealings or desire for revenge later down the road. Had you wanted to hurt the boy, you could have done it then and his career would have been over, but you chose not to. Only a man of real integrity would have done that. The enemy I fought had no sense of duty or integrity," James trailed off remembering those somber, despicable times.

"Please tell me who your enemy was, so I can make him mine!" little Johnny Temple demanded as he jumped to his feet with clenched fists at his side.

James reached out to control the boy as he grabbed both his arms and held him there.

"If you can't control your anger, then I can't tell you anything more. Remember how Proverbs 16:32 reminds us that, 'He that is slow to anger is better than the mighty, and he that rules his spirit than he that takes a city.'"

Johnny took a few deep breaths and sat back down at his father's direction. His father always seemed to have the right thing to say when he needed it most. That was just his way.

"Sorry father. I'll try and keep my mouth shut," Johnny declared.

"Good boy," James affirmed as he took a drink of water before continuing. "Now here's what happened. I was doing rotation relief for a ship's regular captain who had taken ill when I bumped into one of those forces of evil I was telling you about. Do you remember the Bible telling us that Satan goes about the earth as a roaring lion seeking whom he may devour?"

"I do," Johnny nodded. "Was it Satan you bumped into father?"

"If it wasn't son, it most certainly was one of his kin."

Johnny laughed at his father's description of trouble in that way. He knew his father's Christian view of the world colored everything he did or said. That's why he adhered to the old fashioned ideas of duty and honor with truth above all as his guiding light, and among the sailors, James Temple's word was strong as a rod of iron.

"Did you punch him in the nose?" Johnny curiously wanted to know.

"In a manner of speaking I did, and I kicked over a hornet's nest for my trouble. It caused such an awful fuss when it made the papers, you would have thought I was the boogie man. Let me tell you what happened and you can decide for yourself. I think you're old enough to understand what I did and why."

Johnny was pleased his father was finally opening up to him man to man.

"It was nighttime, and we came upon a ship in trouble in the midst of a terrible storm. From what we could see, it had a busted main sail that looked for all intents and purposes as if it might sink. We stayed close as we could trying to avoid being scuttled by the black hulk. A couple of times when the lightning flashed, I saw what appeared to be men and women being thrown overboard in the darkness, but couldn't quite fathom what was happening. By morning's light, I discovered we had been sailing alongside a slaving ship with a cargo hold full of those poor black devils bound for America," his father began. "You got to know how I detest slaving."

Johnny sat mesmerized with eyes a bulging.

"What did you do father?"

"As soon as it was safe, I went aboard to discern the nature of things only to find I wasn't exactly welcome," he continued. "When I asked about the people being thrown overboard during the storm, I was rebuffed and told it was none of my business. That captain was a mean one, and reeked of rum. What I discovered was a hundred slaves had been thrown into the sea to lighten the load because the bilge pumps were having a hard time keeping up."

"How many slaves do you think were on board father?" Johnny asked. He could hardly believe what he was hearing. Though he knew of slavery's presence back home with Aunt Lorna's slave Etta, he didn't see her as such, and he most certainly didn't how they had come to America until now.

"I reckon there were about three hundred on board that ship at the beginning. Some had died of starvation and disease a month into their voyage, and they were discarded over the side as necessary. However, these living men and women had simply been tossed overboard like firewood during the storm. I tell you true son, it was the most horrible sight of misery I had ever seen in all my years upon the sea. You couldn't breathe the air on deck because of the stench of urine and feces reeking from every plank of that lower deck. When I told the captain to relinquish his ship to me, he refused and laughed in my face. 'On what grounds Captain?' he asked. When I accused him of murder he said, 'You can't kill property and that's all these black devils are to the people who own them. Until they find new homes, these boogies are property of some big investors from New York City."

"Can people really belong to someone as property like that father?" Johnny asked openly disturbed by the story at this point.

"That's a good question son, and therein lies my trouble. I declared they were 'people' and put the captain in irons aboard his own ship. He was illegally bringing in slaves at this time, but with the right judges in place, things like that were overlooked for the right money. We did our best to help relieve the misery of those poor souls by rationing our supplies with them and tending to their sicknesses until I got them safely to port. Their place of storage was washed and cleaned out by the slavers own hands, and they didn't like the smell of it any better than the people who had previously occupied those quarters. Those actions would soon be some of the charges leveled against me. I sent one of my lieutenants aboard to take command of the ship with a small squad of marines, and in a couple of weeks we landed at a safe harbor in the Carolina's."

"Was the captain the Devil father?" Johnny asked curiously.

"No son, but he worked for the Devil's offspring who were the fat business tycoons of New York City who made their ill gotten gain from slavery. Instead of making money the old fashioned way through real capital enterprise, they chose to make theirs off the backs of human misery. Because of them, I soon found myself before a maritime military court martial having to explain why I took command of a ship out in open seas away from a legitimate captain hired in the lawful enterprise of transporting 'goods'. When I explained how miserably he mistreated the 'goods' in his care and what he had done, the courts said I had no legal right to interfere. They said, 'the Captain never declared the slaves were going to America.' As such, they were still considered property of the ship's owners, and subject to the law of the sea under that ship's captain to do with as he willed. He merely saw fit to throw some of the company's 'property' overboard in order to save the ship which was the greater investment. His actions were hailed as heroic and justified by his lawyers."

Johnny reached out to his father who was beginning to tremble under the weight of the story.

"Do you need to rest some father? I won't mind if we finish this later."

"I'm alright son. The most important part of the story is here with us now, and I want you to know what happened lest it's lost in history," James insisted.

"Alright, as you wish," Johnny said as he sat back and listened carefully. The whipping and the story were certainly starting to take a toll on James Temple inside the cramped quarters .

"After the jury reached their verdict, I was stripped and flogged in the public square as a warning to others who dared cross them. Our very own Mr. Sims from the slave ship laid down the lash in good fashion as was required, and I do believe they tried their best to kill me that day. By shining the light of public opinion on all of them, I single handedly brought too much attention upon slavery's dark underbelly and the obscene profits some were making off it. It also exposed plenty of pompous, church going, Wall Street hypocrites for what they were. Were it not for the fact I wanted you to know the truth someday, I probably would have given up and died alongside your mother. I consequently lost all rank and was drummed out of the Navy in disgrace, forbidden to ever sail on a Navy vessel again, or captain a ship as a civilian. Your mother became so sick from all the attention that she died shortly after you were born. It was a bad time all around," James slowed losing the desire to continue.

"Here father, lay back and rest for now. We can finish the story another time. Take these pills and sleep like Mr. Tom said," Johnny pleaded as he gently wiped his father's brow once again with a damp cloth. "I'll go find the ship's cook and get us something to eat."

"One thing more son," James sputtered at the last, "always watch your backside if you ever find yourself in a room full of politicians once you're grown. Some of them are two faced and slippery as a moray eel like the ones who had me drummed from the Navy. You see son, the politicians who oversee the Navy are the same ones who were bought and paid for by the slavers who wielded the real power. Without a doubt, they are the Devil's offspring! Never trust any of them."

"Are all politicians evil?" Johnny asked innocently.

James had to concede that not all were.

"Watch what a man is willing to fight for and you'll see him for what he is. That goes for any man or woman as well. Evil is not always easy to discern, but it will always reveal itself given enough time."

"Lay back and sleep, while I go fetch our food," Johnny said as he scampered off to visit the cook.

As young seaman Temple took his leave trekking his way to the galley, he was met by seaman Bartlett as he was about to enter through the doorway.

"A moment of your time Mr. Temple?" he requested as they stepped inside out of view.

"Alright, but be quick. I have a wounded father to take care of thanks to you," Johnny snapped.

"I'm right sorry for causing you so much grief. I believe for certain I have misjudged you. Is there anything I can do to make it up to you?" he asked, honestly trying to make amends.

"Yes. Please tell me why you set your sights on persecuting me so?" Johnny requested. "I've borne you no ill will since coming aboard, but all I've received from your hand is trouble. I'd like an answer."

Lyle Bartlett hung his head in shame, unable to look his defender in the eye. What he had done was way out of line, so he decided to come clean and tell it all. With some trepidation he began.

"Some of the boys despised you at first because you came off so high and mighty when you came aboard. You can read and write better than most grownups on board, and you already know how to navigate a ship because of your old man," he began slowly. "This old tub has ears and we hear things. We picked up the gossip about your father the minute you two signed on in New York harbor. Since nobody knows the whole story about him, you became the whipping boy everyone needed to get at him. Is it true he was court-martialed as a captain and drummed from the Navy because of something bad he done?"

"It's wasn't like that," Johnny answered reluctant to tell too much.

"Then what was it like?" Lyle questioned honestly hoping Johnny might toss him some crumbs.

"Do you want another poke in the nose?" Johnny responded. "I won't stand up for you the next time."

"Easy sailor, I'll let it go for now. But if he doesn't tell what happened pretty soon, I can't be responsible for how people are going to treat him," Lyle countered.

Johnny decided to throw Lyle a few crumbs. Sometimes, that's all it takes for the gossip hounds to feel like they've had a full meal.

"My dad is the smartest and bravest man I know. He was punished because he done his Christian duty while at sea, and he stepped on a lot of toes in the process. He made some powerful enemies, and they had him drummed out of the Navy. That's about as simple as I can make it for you," he replied without saying too much. "We didn't come on board to make trouble. This ship's captain was once a friend of my dad's and he allowed us to come aboard so he could teach me about the sea firsthand. My dad loves the sea and hoped I might love it too, but at the moment, I'm losing interest."

"Will you give me another chance Johnny. I do want to be your friend. You licked me fair and square today, and I'm beholding to for what you did with Mr. Sims. I'll do everything I can to make it up to you somehow, you'll see. Will you shake my hand, man to man?" Lyle asked.

Johnny was leery of this bird of prey, but he knew things couldn't go on as they were. Deciding to take a chance, he stuck out his hand.

"Alright, I'm giving you my hand man to man," Johnny responded as he held it out to Lyle. "I'm willing to take a chance on you, but don't you dare try to mess me over. The next time we go at it, I'm going to get really angry."

"You mean you weren't angry when we tussled earlier?" Lyle mused.

"Nah! I was just funning around back there trying to find out what you're made of," Johnny responded trying to run a bluff.

"How'd I do?" Mr. Bartlett asked anxious to know.

"You got the makings, I reckon," came the young seaman's answer. Though the answer was vague, it seemed appropriate at the time to force Lyle into a mental game of chess with his new friend. He had just made the first move, and now it was time to see if Mr. Bartlett's next move would make good on any of his promises.

Chapter I

Lyle Bartlett was as good as his word as life aboard ship got a whole lot better for the two Temple seaman. James went about his duties as before during the day and by night he continued to teach Johnny the wonder of the stars and the use of the Dolland sextant in navigating a ship. Johnny enjoyed his time with his father for a host of reasons. Prior to their great adventure together, he saw his father only sparingly. Since he had no prior knowledge of anything, he merely understood his father was plying his trade at sea as a sailor and not as a captain. There was no way Johnny could have known that his father had been forbidden by maritime law to ever work again in that capacity for any American owner. The courts may have deemed his father a reckless marauder, but he now knew the truth and that's all that mattered.

"Good day to you Mr. Temple," Captain Boles said as he strolled by. He had seen Johnny busy polishing the brass nameplate inside the spokes of the wheel and decided to test him. "What's our heading sir?"

Johnny was stunned that the captain had asked him such thing, but stood and answered nonetheless.

"We are on an east by northeast heading sir, traveling at eight knots," he chirped out.

"What's your estimate of our arrival time in Liverpool Mr. Temple?" he asked as he raised an eyebrow.

Johnny closed his eyes and began mental calculations.

"Barring any unseen circumstances sir, I calculate we'll be in Liverpool in three and a half to four days. Without something to write it all down with and check my cipher, that's as near as I can figure it," Johnny answered matter of fact.

"Did the helmsman tell you any of that in passing conversation before I arrived?"

"No Captain, I've just barely arrived and Mr. Lionel and I have barely had time to say good morning. Isn't that so Mr. Lionel?" he asked looking up at the helmsman.

"Is this true Mr. Lionel?" the Captain asked.

"Tis true Captain. The lad arrived and had a look at the compass before sitting down to polish the brass when you walked up. Sometimes he does ask about such things in the course of his duties, but not a peep since he arrived," the helmsman responded.

"Well done then Mr. Temple. I see your numbers are an exact match of mine own. How did you know our speed?"

"To be honest sir, I didn't. I remember the speed we traveled at yesterday and the day before. The winds seem about the same today," he answered.

"I see your father has an exemplary student on his hands. Do you have ambition to be a captain yourself one day?"

"I'm not sure Captain Boles. I want a good education and father says I can learn much of it on board a ship if I apply myself. He's a very good teacher as you know," Johnny beamed.

"I do know," the Captain retorted. "Did your father ever tell you we were once cabin boys together on our first ship?"

"No sir, but he did tell me you've been friends for a long time and that I wasn't to use that knowledge for any advantage while we were aboard your ship."

"Your father is a remarkable man Mr. Temple. You are very lucky to have him chart a course for your life. As you were seaman," he said turning to walk away. "Oh, I almost forgot to ask. Would you like to take the helm some night with your father? A young man with ambitions should want to know the feel of a ship all the way down to her rudder. Would you have an interest?"

"Of course sir," Johnny answered in amazement. "We are at your disposal anytime."

"Very good. I'll pass along the news to your father," he said as he eased along the deck to the next group of sailors who were busy painting whitewash on the bottom side of a skiff and tending her sail.

Johnny stood beaming and jumped back into his work with more gusto than ever. The helmsman looked down at Johnny and grinned.

"I couldn't have done what you just did Mr. Temple. I'm just glad Captain Boles asked you instead of me. How did you know?"

"My father has been teaching me how to chart our course since we left port six weeks ago. He said, 'it's important to know where you are on the ocean at all times, or you could wind up on someone else's doorstep by mistake.'"

Mr. Lionel laughed fully understanding what was meant.

"You keep up the good work Laddie. Sometimes I feel mighty lost on this big ocean myself, but I'm glad to know that somebody like you knows where in the blazes we are most of the time. It used to be a lot easier for me to keep up when the world was flat."

"You're too funny Mr. Lionel," Johnny giggled.

"So I'm told," laughed Mr. Lionel.

****

Liverpool, England was Johnny's first stop on the year long odyssey that would become his training ground to bigger and better things. Ordinarily, a young cabin boy would not be permitted to leave the ship on his first stop, but with his father as escort it was made possible. Captain Boles even went so far as to insist James and his son stay at the same hotel as his with adjoining rooms. The two Temple sailors had asked for no favors, but the captain desired they have a few just the same. Their first breakfast together next day was interesting.

"What are you two going to do while you're in port," Captain Boles asked as they sat downstairs eating together.

"I thought we might go to the library for starters. I wanted to show the boy what a proper library is supposed to look like," James replied.

"Do you and your son like to dance?" the Captain asked.

"I'm a bit rusty, and I doubt Johnny does. Do you know someplace where I might take the boy? I would like for him to learn, but not in a pub or any kind of a setting like that," James countered.

"Don't worry about me father, Aunt Lorna taught me plenty about how to dance," Johnny piped up as he took another bite.

"Very well then. I know of a very splendid party tonight at someone's house I know. I'm quite certain you two would be welcome, and I insist you come. I'll have a carriage sent round about six o'clock to pick you both up here at the hotel."

"That's fine," James replied. "There is one more thing Henry."

"What would that be old friend?"

"It's not your responsibility to entertain us. We're old friends, but you don't have any burden to bear because of what happened aboard ship. There's no need to hold my hand throughout our shore leave. "

"I just asked you to accompany me to a party. It's not exactly like I placed you in my will. Now you two be off and see the sights. He's going to love the city," Henry grinned as he stood and walked away. "Take him out to Princes Park while you're out and let him ride one of those hot air balloons."

Johnny whirled to look up at his dad.

"Is that true? Can a person really go up in a balloon?"

"I suppose so. I've never seen one either, so let's make that our first stop. What do you say?"

"Boy oh boy!" Johnny moaned in pleasure just thinking about the possibilities for the day.

The two seamen made good on their promise to have a most enjoyable and interesting day, including the ride of a lifetime in a hot air balloon. Before going to Princes Park, they had stopped at a tailor's shop to find some appropriate clothing for the party tonight. James might not have been a captain any more, but he always fancied himself as a man of good taste.

At six o'clock sharp, their cab arrived.

"Calling James and Johnny Temple. Calling James and Johnny Temple," the bell boy declared making his rounds throughout the hotel lobby.

"Here boy. What is it?" James declared flipping the youngster an American dime.

"Your carriage is here sir, at the front door."

"Thank you young man," he declared as the boy disappeared from sight. "Well, are you ready to go see how the other half lives son?" "I suppose so father. How do I look?" Johnny chirped.

"Like a man of means," he laughed as he bowed at the waist towards his young son. "Your carriage awaits."

On the ride out, the two seamen gawked at the sights around them. James had not been to Liverpool for more than ten years, and could hardly believe the changes the city's landscape had morphed into. One of the more unpleasant sights was the scores of Irishmen milling about trying to pick up jobs. The potato famine had forced them into the city trying to find work so they could feed their families. He would do his best to stay clear of them for fear of what a desperate Irishman might do for money.

Out into the countryside they went lickity-split until they came upon a fork in the road. Suddenly, the coach veered right down a winding country lane lined with oak trees that led up to a very fine estate. James felt it could just as easily have been a New Orleans plantation for all the pomp and grandeur it displayed, however it was of the old English manor style. When a black man came out promptly from the front and opened their door, it was hard not to reconcile the imagery in his mind with that of any southern estate.

"Welcome sirs. You must be the Mr. Temple's we've heard so much about," the gentleman began with a gentle banter. "If you'll step to the door yonder, someone will announce you."

James reached into his vest preparing to tip the help, but the help had different ideas.

"There's no need for that sir. We live here and serve at the owner's pleasure," he replied shocking James.

"I thought there were no more slaves in England," James confided to the attendant.

"Oh, I'm not a slave sir. I'm a free man since birth who is just fortunate enough to work for this very fine English family. Won't you please go on in."

"My mistake," James said as he looked down at his son awkwardly and shrugged his shoulders.

Inside the door, they could hear the soothing sounds of a waltz, and it reminded James of his late wife who loved fancy gowns and balls. Johnny liked the sounds too, because it reminded him of his aunt Lorna. Inside they spotted their captain across the room and signaled to him. As Henry Boles strode across the floor to meet them, James wondered who in this massive hall did Henry know well enough that would invite wharf rats like the lot of them to such a fancy gala.

"Welcome gentlemen," Henry said as he pumped their hands.

"Hello Henry," James declared. "I'm not quite sure we're dressed according to the standards these folks are used to around here. Our vest are made of cotton, not silk."

"Then you should feel right at home. Most of these people are merchants, not Lords and Ladies of royalty, and they earn their money the old fashioned way through hard work. The investors who own our particular ship are here tonight too, and would like to meet with you when the time is right," Henry began. "I won't tell you who they are for the time being, because I don't wish to spoil your evening. But first, I want you to meet someone very important to me. Follow me."

Crossing the floor to where the refreshments lay, the two Mr. Temple's were invited to pick up food and drink at Henry's direction. Taking them out onto the back terrace where tables had been set up for the occasion, they sat and began to indulge their hunger and thirst.

"I thought you had someone you wanted me to meet?"

"I do, but I thought you might wish to eat first and strengthen your sea legs," Henry laughed. "The person in question has been sent for as we speak."

James and Johnny were both a little confused by all the cloak and dagger, so they went ahead and ate using their best manners, careful not to spill anything on their fellow guests as they dined. After all, they weren't on a sailing vessel with forty other swabs riding out twenty foot swells. James even went so far as to remind Johnny how to hold his fork properly and the proper use of a napkin. Henry sat across the table keeping their attention on him as they talked. Soon Henry saw the person he wanted to introduce coming up, but kept it to himself until she was standing directly behind the Temple duo.

"James, if you can pull yourself away for a moment, I'd like to introduce you to Anne Boles, my cousin," he directed.

James carefully wiped his mouth sensing what Henry was up to and gave him a hard look. Without looking, he rose to meet the woman of mystery and was pleasantly surprised by what he saw once he turned around. She was lovely, about thirty years of age, with a look of real intelligence about her. Though quite tall by English standards, she filled out nicely in all the right places, with jet black hair and the most penetrating eyes he had ever seen. He could sense her uneasiness, and knew at once that good old cousin Henry had forgotten to tell her of their invitation.

"You wished to see me Henry?" she asked.

"Yes cousin. This is a very dear friend I'd like you to meet."

By the surprised look on James' face, Anne also knew at once that Mr. Temple and son were probably lured here under false pretenses in order for Henry to play his little matchmaking game. This wasn't like her cousin to be so bold when introducing her to one of his friends, so she assumed there must be something very special about him.

Anne was not the only one studying the trap Henry had sprung on them. James turned and looked at Henry with a stern face, shaking his head ever so slightly from left to right indicating his disapproval. He let it go for the moment as a gentleman should and spoke to her.

"I'm very pleased to make your acquaintance Miss Boles," James said as he took her extended hand and kissed the back of it.

"And I you Mr. Temple. Is this the young navigator Henry's been telling me so much about?" she asked sweetly displaying no ill will towards either sailor. She was quite certain by now they knew of Henry's deceit by the look James had just given him.

"He is Miss Boles, and a very able seaman he is becoming," James replied making small talk as he patted the top of Johnny's head. "Is this your estate? It is quite lovely."

"Oh no. It belongs to my aunt Mr. Temple. Her husband of many years passed away sometime back and she asked Henry and I to move in with her to alleviate her loneliness. Aunt Mamie and uncle Charles had no heirs," she continued, "and I guess to outsiders looking on, that makes us look like greedy opportunist in the American vernacular, does it not?"

"The thought never crossed my mind. I think I know Henry well enough to know he wouldn't entertain the idea, and I suspect you are much like him, otherwise you wouldn't be here," James answered giving her the benefit of the doubt. "Funny,...James never mentioned you in all the years I've known him."

"It's not his fault really. We only just met last year at one of Aunt Mamie's stuffy ole' ball's she was throwing to introduce me to the local gentry. She was trying her best to marry me off to some Lord or Earl's son, but I set my cap early on to a plan of orderly resistance. I don't like the idea of being bartered over like produce, or worse yet, a merger acquisition. They do that around here, you know," she said matter of fact. "At the ball, I quite literally stumbled into Henry when I spilled something on his nicest dinner jacket. He laughed it off and I appreciated dear Henry right off because he didn't make a fuss.

"I came as a guest of the ship's owners," Henry interjected trying to explain why he was here at all.

"So as a dutiful hostess, I offered to have his jacket cleaned and pressed here at the house. I took him upstairs to find something of uncle Charles to wear in the meantime, and that's when it happened."

"What was that?" James queried.

"James came out of Uncle Charles' walk in closet with a small painting in hand that he had found on a dressing table. 'Who is this?' he asked. When I told him it was some local woman named Elizabeth Weller, he almost started shaking. I asked him why the interest? He said the woman was his mother, and the rest as they say is history."

"I thought Henry was raised in an orphanage?" he asked casting a jaundiced eye towards the captain.

"I was old friend. It came as a complete shock to me too," Henry stated flatly. "I still have the letter and locket left at the orphanage by my mother in her own hand when she dropped me on the doorsteps of St. Henri's. She was a woman who was as alone as I was at the time. She couldn't take me home to her parents for the shame of what she had done, and her lover couldn't bring her and his new baby home to meet the wife, if you get my meaning. There was no other way. The letter instructed I was Henry Boles, and the locket found inside my blanket had a picture of my mother painted inside. The Sister's all knew my mother, and the letter stated clearly the picture was of my mother, but because of privacy issues, no one ever told me her name until that fateful night. Even Aunt Mamie couldn't pass it off as a coincidence."

"I've bet you've been the topic of conversation around the Boles' dinner tables ever since," James said shaking his head.

"Probably, but it's not mentioned in polite company, or in my presence; Aunt Mamie saw to that. For those who dared to ask, she merely told them I was the offspring of her late husband. Since she couldn't bear him a child, she insisted he find a suitable stable mate and get on with producing an heir lest the family idiots inherit the estate through probate once they're gone. She felt a sense of duty to all their business associates and employees to keep their end up and functioning, so to speak. There are a lot of people in England who depend on Boles Enterprises and Shipping L.T.D. to make their living."

"So is Aunt Mamie your aunt or your step-mom?"

"That's yet to be determined completely," Henry retorted.

"Regardless, has she made you an heir of her estate?" James asked flabbergasted by the concept of Henry the orphan, as an heir.

"That also has yet to be determined. I mean there's no will to that extent that I know of," he replied with a smirk.

"Oh, I can see it all now on the back cover of a Dickens novel, 'Lowly orphaned cabin boy becomes a man of means by an ironic twist of fate. Will his newfound wealth bring him happiness or will it be a curse? Will he find true love or scorn at the hand of the woman he loves?'" James laughed as he held out his hand like a Shakespearean actor to dramatize the imagined book. It was a lot to comprehend.

Anne laughed too at James' portrayal of poor Henry's unfolding saga because, it did parallel a Dickens novel in so many ways.

Johnny stood motionless in their presence unable to fully comprehend adult humor. Finally he asked his father to be excused.

"Where are you going?" James questioned.

"To dance," he responded shocking his father.

"Can you really dance?" he asked curiously.

"What a silly question," the boy stated.

"Is it now? Alright if you say so, go have fun."

As the three watched, the boy walked confidently into the great hall and promptly gathered up a dance partner a foot taller than himself. They strutted to the main floor following traditional courtesies and joined in like old friends. It appears Aunt Lorna had been busy after all preparing him for his future role as a gentleman.

"I gather you didn't know he could dance," Anne observed.

"I wasn't sure. His aunt will have to take credit for that particular skill set. I'm merely his mathematics teacher and tour guide at present," James replied.

"Did Aunt Lorna teach you how to dance, Mr. Temple?" Anne queried hoping he might take the hint. Dancing is a good way to get to know someone you have an interest in.

"No, and it's been some time since anyone has dared to follow these sea legs as they graced a dance floor. But if you're asking, then my answer is yes," he replied with a gleam in his eye. He didn't come here tonight desiring to meet a lady, but this woman intrigued him. She's wasn't pushy and silly as some females are, giggling over every word he said, but rather she was mature and calculating. As she held out her hand requesting his presence, he took it, slightly squeezing it to show his interest, and she squeezed back to show hers.

Henry stood grinning with genuine delight, since his role as matchmaker appears to have gotten off to a good start. Of course, his intimate knowledge of both participants made the job an undeniable pleasure to put in motion. James has been a very dear friend of many adventures aboard ship and a man to be trusted above all others. He knew his judgment was always sound and without question which makes him a perfect match for his analytical cousin. Anne on the other hand was a dear treasure. Since he stumbled quite literally by accident into the family, she has been his greatest defender against attackers from within and without. He knew everyone saw him as a gold digging fortune hunter and merely assumed he was a fraud. After Anne pulled out all the stops and did her due diligence through help from friends at Scotland Yard, she has never questioned his integrity again. Once she set her cap to be his champion, she tolerated no outside comments or objections from any quarter. A few of the extended family have tested her resolve and received the tongue lashing of their lives in short order. She was also not above a good right cross if a particular person and occasion warranted it. (One need only ask Ross Higgins, a very distant cousin, if it's not true).

 Yes, Henry felt he had scored a direct hit with his first effort, and was quite pleased with his work. Of course Aunt Mamie and unnamed others had issued the real invitation for James to be here, but that was merely incidental to Henry's true mission.

Unknown to James Temple, there were a dozen or more sets of eyes watching every move he made throughout the evening. Without knowing it, he was on trial again, but for an entirely different reason. This trial however, would not place him behind bars, but behind a desk managing the biggest commercial enterprise in Liverpool should the verdict come in favorably. They would linger in the background tonight allowing him to reveal himself in layers to the people he came in contact with. Anne Boles knew nothing of this unofficial trial, but her opinion would certainly carry a certain amount of weight too, should she be asked. She was, after all, a very good judge of character.

As the night wore on, the all seeing eyes of the party put into motion their first test to find out the measure of their man. During one particular time of musical rest, one of the eyes nodded to a large man across the room to begin his staged performance. As James was seeking refreshments for he and Anne, the test began in earnest as the man deliberately bumped into his pigeon spilling James' drinks all over the refreshment table and the hired help standing behind it.

"Bloody Hell Yank!" he screamed at James. "Did you learn your manners in a London bordello?"

"I beg your pardon sir. Since I'm new in town, I don't know London nearly as well as you apparently do. Please accept my apology, and we'll call it even." he bantered, turning his back on the man hoping nothing would come of it. However, the man appeared clearly drunk, and drunks are often unpredictably nasty.

The man spun James around attempting to take a poke at him. James stepped back out of reach causing the drunken man to stagger forward and fall to one knee.

"You're a slippery one, but I'll get a hold of you yet," the man grunted and stood back up. As he made a run towards James again with both arms outstretched, James sidestepped the man blocking his arm with a quick spin. Slipping in behind, he pulled the man's jacket up over his head where he couldn't see, causing much laughter from the crowd of onlookers. Grabbing Anne's hand, he pulled her from the room back out onto the terrace as quick as possible. He was hoping that without a sparring partner the man's pent up energy would dissipate into so much hot air ending the conflict.

"Bravo Mr. Temple. We've made our escape without so much as a single glass being broken. Henry said you were very resourceful," she beamed with delight.

"I'm sorry if I've embarrassed you Miss Boles. Please give my apologies to your aunt. I'll gather my son up and we'll slip out before we make an even bigger scene," James explained trying to avoid any further conflict in this fine house.

"There's absolutely no need for that Mr. Temple. Be warned, I'm not a woman easily embarrassed. I've had a scrap or two in my day, and it can be quite exhilarating if the cause is just. Do you fancy this a just cause?" she asked.

"What kind of a question is that? Fighting with a slobbering drunk isn't a cause," he responded.

"Well, I'm afraid it's one which you're going to have to answer for. It seems your man has followed us out here, and he looks a lot more determined this time. Since there's nothing out here to break, you have my blessing to defend yourself. Just cause or not, I think he intends on doing you harm," she stated matter of fact quickly moving to one side.

James didn't come here to fight, and this poor man was in no real shape to defend himself, or so he thought. All at once, the laughing, jovial, dancing crowd moved out of the way in unison to positions around the terrace to see what and how Mr. Temple would handle himself this time. Even Johnny had taken up position to watch his dad's backside against any treachery.

"What's your name Mister?" James asked with hands on hips trying to talk the man down from his exalted purpose.

"My name is Chaos!" the drunk man roared thumping his chest as he slowly walked in a circle taking the measure of his man.

James started laughing. He couldn't help it. Was the man being melodramatic, or did he really see himself that way. The laughing only infuriated his adversary, and he began taking deep breaths getting up a head of steam for another run.

"Look friend, I apologize if I've offended you. Please don't make this any worse than what it already is. If our actions get out of hand, we both could end up spending the night in the pokey," James spoke softly trying to diffuse the man's anger as they continued to walk in a circle. That's when he saw Henry in the crowd. "I'm sorry Henry. Somehow I've managed to pick up a new dance partner and become part of the evening's entertainment."

"Well, James old friend, entertain us. This fine fellow will soon wish he hadn't charted his course across the path of a hurricane. You're an able teacher, so teach the man the error of his ways," Henry responded.

"Fine friend you are!...Help me stop this before I have to hurt your guest," James declared raising the tempo of his voice a little higher.

"Oh it's okay James, I didn't invite him," he laughed as if that was somehow an adequate answer.

"Some friend you are Henry Boles, but I don't see any reason to hurt the man just because you and your friends are bored." With that said he turned suddenly to leave, nodding to Anne as he walked by. The man saw his quarry getting away and he grabbed Anne roughly by the arm instead, trying to draw him back into the fight any way he could. James heard her cry out as she winced in pain, and he turned to see the drama unfolding behind him.

In quick step, James was upon his troublesome man and slapped him hard across the face. The man stumbled back from the blow releasing Anne in the process. Once he regained his composure, he tried another run at James to no affect as he quickly stepped aside tripping the drunken man and forcing him to land hard on both knees to ill effect.

"I'm sorry Anne," James whispered to her as he placed her out of harm's way.

"There's no need to apologize sailor. Go finish swabbing the deck, and come back to me. You're on my dance card for the next waltz," she answered without any hesitation or cause for alarm. That answer alone put wind in James' sail as he turned to address his immediate problem.

Taking his jacket off and handing it to someone standing nearby, he spoke softly to the man one last time trying to diffuse the situation.

"I've done my best to avoid this, but you have made it impossible. I hope when you come to your senses, you won't have any hard feelings for what I'm about to do. I have a waltz to finish, so I'll be quick."

"You talk big, can you back it up?" the man chided.

James struck him with a hard right hook across the left side of his face, and he stumbled back,...back,...back a little more and fell unconscious into the fish pond hidden beyond the garden flowers. The cold water woke him almost instantly as he went under, and he splashed around in knee deep water trying to gather his breath and wits about him in this disoriented state. Standing slowly in the water, he took both hands and attempted to readjust his jaw back into alignment as he stumbled awkwardly back into the fight soaking wet.

From across the room, the same eyes that originally had set all this in motion signaled for him to end the conflict. The man acknowledged them, glad to bring the conflict to an end.

"You hit plenty hard mister, I quit," the drunken man declared before the house as he turned and staggered off into the darkness beyond the lights, and just like that it was over. The assembled crowd clapped and cheered as he and Anne walked triumphantly back into the great hall as champions to finish their waltz.

"I'm sorry you were drawn into the fight. Is your arm alright?" James asked.

"I'm fine. He just caught me off guard when he grabbed me. Shall we dance Mr. Temple?" she answered without any more comment as the musicians put their waltz into motion.

Across the room, the all-seeing eyes of the party huddled to discuss their findings concerning the first test. After a few moments of discussion, they seemed quite pleased with the results thus far. Next up was a test of a different kind meant to judge his moral character. Seeing his jacket laid aside, one of them placed an expensive gold watch in his pocket with the end of the chain dangling out just so.

After the waltz ended, James went for his jacket having forgotten for the moment he didn't have it on. A gentleman never dances with a lady without his jacket. As he was buttoning his jacket, he discovered the end of the dangling chain. Pulling the chain out further, he found an attached watch worth a sailor's wages for a year stuffed into his pocket. He could have pushed the chain back down and no one would have been the wiser, or so he thought. However, it wasn't in him to steal knowing that it probably belonged to someone here at the party. Pulling the watch and chain from his pocket, he stepped over to Henry and delivered it to his care.

"I don't know where it came from, but it's not mine. Could you please find the rightful owner?"

Henry looked around the room to find Aunt Mamie, who avoided his gaze. He knew the substance of this test, because it had been done to him when he first arrived as a new heir.

"Certainly James, I think I know just the person," he answered knowingly.

"If it's all the same to you, Johnny and I will take our leave and return to town. It's been an interesting evening. Are all your parties this much fun?"

"Up to now, most have been rather dull. You made the evening a splendid success. Say, what do you think about my cousin Anne?" Henry goaded trying to pry a hopeful morsel of information from him.

14

"She is remarkable Henry. Maybe you should court her, and keep all that 'blue blood' in the family business," James stated plainly.

"Well you see, that's just it. I don't know if she's my cousin or my sister. As it stands, Anne's father was also known to dilly-dally around in the shadows some nights," he winked and then laughed at his own gag. "I just know I'm a Boles, by which one I'm not so sure. My poor mother was just a simple tavern girl and apparently was well known to many men in these parts, including the Boles men."

"I see your dilemma. It would appear your family tree is going to be filled with endless possibilities. Please give my regards to your cousin, Mr. Matchmaker."

Henry grinned. He had been caught fair and square, but he was not about to give up without a fight.

"No James, you'll have to do that yourself. It would be very rude of you to leave without saying goodnight to Anne and Aunt Mamie. Auntie was actually your hostesses tonight. Here hold out your hand, I have something for you," he said.

"What for? You going to put a toad in it?" James asked suspiciously. As youths together, they frequently played those games.

"No champ, I'm just splitting the pot with you. I won a dozen pounds off you tonight, and I figure I owe you half at the very least," Henry laughed.

James held out his hand allowing Henry to fill it. It might be only English money, but they were in England after all. Maybe it would help offset some of their expenses while they were ashore.

"Now let's march you over to say goodnight to Aunt Mamie, and of course, that other woman you barely noticed," Henry scoffed.

Motioning to Johnny his intent to leave, he quickly followed on the heels of his father to pay his respects.

"I'm sorry I never got to dance with you young Mr. Temple," Anne apologized. "I've heard nothing but high praise tonight from all your other conquests. If you promise to come back and dance with me sometime, I promise to put your name at the top of my next dance card."

"I would love to, and thank you for a lovely evening. What do you think of my father? Isn't he just the greatest?" Johnny asked as only a child can. James rolled his eyes heavenward feeling the blush of being on the spot yet again. He placed both hands on his son's shoulders smiling, and squeezed a little extra hard. Johnny knew that signal all too well and ceased with the questions.

Anne was very kind in her response and without pretense.

"It would appear that your father really is a great man. Speaking from my own experience, I'm not so sure that I've ever met a man of his caliber before. English men can be so stuffy and boring, but your father certainly isn't. Why do you think that is?"

"That's because he's a Virginia man from America. Bet you never seen one of those before, have you?" Johnny piped up before his father squeezed his shoulders again. He was quite proud of his father and didn't care who knew it.

Anne couldn't help but admire the boy's enthusiasm.

"No young man, I don't believe I've ever met a real Virginia man before, and I must say it has been very enlightening. Now would you two gallant Virginians please have dinner with us here tomorrow evening so we can get to know you better? If you come early, we can go horseback riding."

"Oh boy!" Johnny yelped as he turned and pleaded with his dad. "Can we father? Can we please come tomorrow?"

"Well, we wouldn't want to wear out our welcome on our first visit. Given enough time, it's possible we too might become a tad boring," James replied with a bit of sarcasm.

"You'll need to let us be the judge of that Mr. Temple," she responded without any reservation.

"Alright then, we'll come on one condition. After tonight, you call us by our given names. I'm James and this of course is Johnny, the brightest of the Temple sailors," he replied giving into the pressure.

"Splendid. Come around four o'clock, and that'll give us time to ride some of Aunt Mamie's fine thoroughbreds. She has some of the finest animals in Liverpool, and I feel for certain we can find something that an American from Virginia would find fit to ride," she instructed.

"Thank you too Mrs. Boles for a lovely evening. I hope I haven't embarrassed you too much. It's certainly been interesting," James said to Aunt Mamie. He was not up yet to calling her by her first name until he was instructed to do so.

"Quite the contrary, Mr. Temple. Your presence here has been extremely well received. I look forward to seeing you again tomorrow for dinner promptly at seven. Don't be late," Mamie Boles answered discretely not wishing to over play her hand.

****

All the way back to Liverpool that night, Johnny couldn't stop talking about the people he met. Some were bankers, and lawyers, and a few were schoolteachers. Some were merchants with interests all over the world, even into exotic lands; his head was filled with the wonder of it all.

"Have you ever been to any of those places father?" he asked.

"I've been to a few, but the world is a mighty big place. If we spent a lifetime going to all of them, we still couldn't see it all. As sailor's, we'll see our share of it in time," he answered.

As Johnny talked, James listened as best he could while floating the thought of Anne Boles around in his mind. She was the unexpected highlight of his evening. Though he fussed at Henry about it all, he didn't really mind so much once he let his guard down allowing Anne to enter the ring and land her first blow. He liked her precisely because she wasn't dainty and silly like most women, or his late wife. He looked forward to riding together tomorrow with expectations of whether or not she can ride and jump a horse like a man. The only question remaining was, would she do it sidesaddle like a woman, or in the saddle like a man, breeches and all?

Inside the manor, there was much discussion amongst the individuals who arranged the evening as to what they saw, or didn't see in James Temple. Anne was out of the loop completely unaware of the group's intent having gone to bed early, but Henry sat in on the meeting taking place downstairs. It was sort of his idea at the outset to introduce James to the owners and let them decide for themselves if he was the right man for the job they had in mind. Since Charles Boles had died a few years ago, the company and owners have been adrift and rudderless. Uncle Charles was the visionary, and without him they had lost their way. What they needed now was a man of action who knew how to lead, and Henry knew just the man for the job, if he'd take it.

"What do you think Mamie? Is he our man?" one of the merchants questioned. Her voice and vote would have final say over everything they decided, so it was best to get her thoughts out in the open first.

"Personally, I like him," she began. "He showed good judgment against poor Zack by doing everything possible to talk him out of a fight. That shows he's not a hot head, but a thinking man. The only thing that brought him back into the fight was when Zack took hold of Anne so roughly forcing her to cry out. This man will fight to protect what he holds dear, which is a good quality in a leader."

"I sense he's an honest man," one of the bankers from the Liverpool Union spoke up. "I personally saw him give the watch and chain to Henry after he discovered it in his pocket. A lesser man might have kept it. He certainly has the makings for honest dealings."

"Henry, you know our man better than anyone. Do you think he might be tempted to join us," still another asked.

Henry mulled the question around for a moment before answering.

"I think he might do it, if he has the right incentive," he began.

"We have the right incentive," another stated flatly. "We'll each pay him more in a year than a dozen ship's captains make. What more incentive is needed than that?"

"I hate to be the bearer of bad news, but James Temple is not a man to be sought out and purchased like one of your foreign commodities. He is guided by a different set of principles than you people in the business world are used to," Henry expounded.

"Then what incentive would lure him into a partnership with us Henry?"Aunt Mamie asked bewildered that money wouldn't do it.

"That particular bit of incentive is probably upstairs with a book in her hand by now dear Aunt Mamie," Henry stated. "Don't you get it?"

"What in the world are you talking about? Who's got a book?" she asked stumbling completely over Henry's question.

"Come now Auntie, Anne is the only thing in this house tonight that James showed any real interest in. I don't know if you saw it, but she showed an equal amount of interest in him too. If those two managed to somehow fall in love and marry, he might take the helm if she asked him. Can't you see it?" Henry chided. "It was after all, her idea for dinner tomorrow night."

"By Jove, I think you might be onto something Henry. I've been so long in business I've forgotten what young love looks like. I'm going to defer to your instincts on how to proceed," Aunt Mamie declared. "What do we do next?"

"The seeds have already been planted. All we need do is water them and see how quickly everything grows. If we need any fertilizer, I'll let you know," he answered.

"Do you think he'll consider our other little venture Henry?" one of the merchants wanted to know. He had a strong vested interest in that specific request.

"Come back tomorrow night and ask him yourself."

****

Arriving back at the manor the next day, the Temple men were instructed to dress into riding clothes which had been prepared ahead of their arrival in a room next to the stables. James saw the big man he had fought with from the night before working at the far end of the long stables. He was putting hay into the clean stalls and mostly minding his own business when James approached him.

"How's the jaw friend?" he asked.

The startled man turned to look at James with pitchfork in hand. James couldn't tell if he was angry or simply caught off guard. Then the big man spoke his peace once he realized James wasn't a threat.

"Sorry about last night Mr. Temple. I was just following orders," he said causing James to scratch his head.

"Following orders? Whose orders?" James asked quizzically.

"The owners wanted to know what you were made of. Before you arrived, I was instructed to start a fight with you at a time of their choosing and see it to the final conclusion. I didn't think you would be so tough," the big man explained. "When they saw what they wanted, I was then instructed to quit and leave. It wasn't anything personal Mr. Temple, and the jaw is still plenty sore too."

"Sorry about the jaw. What's your name friend?" James asked. He liked knowing people personally where and when it was allowed.

"Most people just call me Zack; it's short for Zachery," he answered.

"Can you tell me what it's all about Zack?" James questioned again. "If it's some kind of practical joke, I'd like to be in on it."

"I don't know sir. I just take orders and do them as best I can," the big man answered hoping he hadn't let the cat out of the bag. No one had told him he couldn't say anything about last night.

"I wonder if Miss Anne was in on the gag?" he wondered aloud.

The man heard him and responded trying to head off trouble.

"Mr. Temple, Anne is a wonderful lady. She wouldn't have been in on any of last night's shenanigans, because she's not an owner. Miss Anne has always been very nice and treats me just fine since she got here. Please don't say anything about this to her, cause it might upset her, and I wouldn't want that," the man pleaded.

"Don't tell me what?" Anne Boles asked as she stepped around the corner of the stables in her smart looking riding breeches.

The two men looked at one another like children caught smoking behind the outhouse. Quick as a wink, James schemed up something to say and the stableman heartily agreed with every word.

"Why, hello Anne. Zack and I were just discussing last night's activities, and I wanted to see if he was alright. He apologized and asked if I would extend his apologies to you as well for making such a scene. He said he would never do anything to upset you because of his great respect for you. Isn't that about it Zack old friend?" he said whipping up a load of good ole' Irish blarney off the top of his head.

"Yes Miss Anne, that's about it," he responded to James' prompting.

"Well never let it be said that I'm not one to forgive and forget," she smiled and moved on to her next topic. "Where's Johnny? Didn't you bring him with you?"

"He's at the other end of the stables getting dressed. I just saw Zack here working and came over to talk. If you'll excuse me, I'll go change now," James commented, turning to wink at Zack knowingly before leaving.

"Thanks again Mr. Temple for stopping by," Zack responded with a wave of the hand. Then he turned to Anne speaking under his breath. "I like him Miss Anne. That one's got a good head on his shoulders. If you was looking for a good man, I don't think there's a finer one in all of England than that one, even if he is a Yank."

"Oh, he's not just a Yank Zack, he's a Virginia man," she quipped making reference to Johnny's comment from the previous night and snickering just a little. "Find me a horse with some life in it for him. I want to find out if he knows how to handle a spirited animal."

"You best be careful Miss Anne, or he may be handling one spirited woman before the day is over," Zack teased back.

"You best mind your manners mister, or I'll tell Aunt Mamie I caught you smoking again."

"One spirited horse coming right up Miss Anne!"

In a few minutes, the Temple men reappeared dressing in proper English riding gear from head to toe.

"Say, you two look like proper sportsmen. Shall we ride?"

The two thoroughbreds Zack had picked out were the finest animals in Aunt Mamie's stables. The more gentle pony was for Johnny, while the stallion was for James.

"Follow me Virginia men, if you can!" Anne shouted as she mounted her horse and took the lead.

It wasn't an all out horse race to be sure, but things developed at a pretty intense clip for two sailors used to life aboard a ship.

"Are you okay son?" James asked worried that he couldn't keep up. "If you get in trouble sing out. I don't won't you hurt."

"Don't worry about me father, if I get to where I can't keep up I'll drop back. Just don't let that woman win!"

James gave a thumbs up and rode hard to catch up to Anne. This particular course was well known to Anne, but not to him. He would hang back until the last mad dash, then he would show her what a Virginia man looks like from the back side as he raced by. Judging by the energy of his animal, James thought it possible the stallion could swim all the way to Virginia if he runs out of land.

The two experienced riders were having a fine old time of running the gauntlet of challenges laid out on this particular course. In fact, they were laughing like school children on a playground, albeit a dangerous playground at these speeds. Jumping horses at speed is exhilarating but very risky if you're not comfortable with your animal. James may not have taken this course before, but the stallion certainly had as he raced ahead taking the lead.

"There's a resting place up ahead with a watering pond," Anne shouted loudly. "We'll stop and wait for Johnny there."

Like a shot, James' horse took off leaving Anne three or four lengths behind. It was usually her horse that won this particular stretch in the road, but it wasn't going to happen today. She had just been bested by a Yank from Virginia, just as Johnny had predicted. James slowed and dismounted as Anne came riding up. He walked to the left side of her horse and offered her assistance in getting down.

"I can get down by myself. Just because I lost doesn't make me a helpless woman," she chided. She wasn't used to a man beating her and then offering to help her with the dismount.

"In Virginia, a Southern gentleman always offers a lady a hand down, whether he won or lost his race. May I?"

He liked the fact she rode her horse like a man dressed in proper riding breeches. As she threw a leg over the saddle, she began to slide down on his side. He was there to catch her placing strong hands around her firm waist. He caught her in mid flight and slowly lowered her to the ground hesitating for a moment to look deep into her beautiful dark eyes before her feet touched the ground. It was only a brief connection, but he liked what he saw and felt. He could tell she was not some dainty princess too, because she had real muscle where most women went soft. It certainly might have intimidated some men to know she was so strong, but it built a fire under James Temple's bonnet. Had he finally stumbled onto a woman who was his equal?

"You can let go now. I believe my feet are actually touching the ground," she whispered startling him. She would have given a sixpence to know what he was thinking at the moment with his hands still firmly clutching her firm waistline as he looked deep into her eyes.

"Sorry Anne, I guess I forgot myself," he blushed.

"Has it been so long since you were near a woman," she asked brushing up close to him when the horses moved suddenly together.

"Apparently, it's been so long I've forgotten my manners," he answered. Suddenly the horses jostled together as they sometimes do and he placed a hand on her arm to steady her. "My heavens, you're a strong one. How do you manage to stay so fit? I've never met an athletic woman before. Are you in some kind of training?"

"No, I'm not in training, but I like to be active. I ride as much as I can, and I swim when the weather permits. This may sound silly, but I like to run sometimes too just for the fun of it. I've been known to run all the way to the edge of Liverpool and back on plenty of occasions, because the road just called out begging me to do it. Do you find me an odd sort of a duck?" she asked.

"Quite the contrary, I happen to like ducks," he responded.

Anne measured his statement and wondered if maybe she had finally met her match too. James was not some dumb brute like those who roamed the Liverpool docks, but was rather a highly skilled artisan who chose words over violence to persuade. She knew at this moment, he was no mere sailor either, and wondered what Henry was really up to by introducing him into her life.

Soon Johnny came riding up forcing those questions onto the back burner.

"Oh boy Miss Anne, this is some fine riding pony. She stopped to eat some clover, but I didn't mind. I got off and simply laid down in the clover by her as she ate around me," he laughed as only a child can encouraging the two adults to laugh with him.

"Give your horse some water, and we'll ride back to the stables another way. I'll show you where the best trout in all of England are lurking in case you might want to come back and fish sometime," she directed.

"Father can we please come back. I haven't gone fishing in ages," Johnny pleaded in desperation.

"Easy does it son, we don't want to abuse the lady's hospitality."

"Come now gentlemen, I would love for you to come again and try your luck in the brook. No true fisherman would pass up an opportunity to catch and cook trout over an open fire in this kind of weather. If you've never done it, I could teach you how to fly fish," she stated amazing the two Virginians even more. Most women don't like catching fish, but here stood one who does it willfully and with one of those new fangled fly rods. What have they stumbled onto with this angel of the outdoors? Was she really the same elegant lady from the previous night, or was there some other form of trickery afoot?

All they could do was grin and nod their heads in agreement at one another.

"Take your horses and walk with me," she directed. "Tell me about Virginia. Is it a nice place? I think I might like to go to the colonies someday and see for myself."

Johnny laughed out loud as he shook his head.

"What's so funny?" she asked.

"You're still calling us colonies," he laughed again.

"Well excuse me 'mister know it all,'" she laughed as she tickled him forcing out even more contagious laughter. It was good to feel this sort of companionship with real men for a change. Though they had just met the night before, she felt as if she had known them all her life, and knew they were worthy of her attention. She had searched for a man of this quality and character in every nook and cranny of Liverpool, and in one fell swoop of good fortune she had found two quite by accident who were bristling with life and energy the way she was. Heaven had surely laid a blessing on her this early in the day.

Chapter II

Dinner was promptly at seven as was customary. Aunt Mamie was scouring the room to make sure all her guests were there, but didn't see any sign of the Temple men anywhere, nor her niece.

"Gladys dear, would you go upstairs and check on Anne. I'm afraid she must be ill, or she would be here. Horace, will you go find Zachery and find out if our American friends ever made it to out to the stables today. I've not heard a peep out of anyone all day long."

Before the two servants had a chance to leave the room, the trio of misplaced miscreants suddenly appeared at the open doorway laughing at something delightfully funny and known only to them. Suddenly they stopped, coming to attention as they gathered themselves up to meet the assembled guests. For whatever reason, the threesome couldn't hold it together and started laughing all over again.

"Have you been drinking Anne darling?" Aunt Mamie asked perplexed by her behavior.

"Yes Auntie, I've been out drinking the elixir of life with my two new friends. I've learned a lot about American virtues and more specifically those from Virginia," she stammered out with a straight face. "Did you know Auntie that people in some parts of Virginia give hogs as a wedding gift instead of fine China? That is if they can catch them. Did you know it's impossible to rope a hog?"

Suddenly, Anne was laughing again in the presence of the moneyed class without the good taste to restrain herself. Auntie recognized her guests might not have been royalty, but by Jove, they deserved some respect.

"Mr. Temple, please bring yourself and your son down this way and sit next to me," Aunt Mamie instructed trying to break the hold they had on her niece hoping she would come to her senses once she sat down. "Anne darling, sit there by Mr. Whitaker, and maybe he can help calm you down so we can begin eating our evening meal."

Anne took one look at poor, dour faced Mr. Whitaker and broke out laughing again as she made an attempt to sit down by him. Mr. Whitaker was leery of sitting next to her in this heightened state of silliness, thinking maybe she was coming down with something.

She was certainly coming down with something alright, and it was contagious. This great house was not exactly known as a place of laughter as such, being all business, twenty four, seven. Since there had never been any children running through these empty old halls, the grownups who lived here had forgotten how to laugh, and their tickle boxes had dried up years ago. It was not an intentional thing the three of them had brought to the table, but rather a happy accident. Anne merely assumed poor Aunt Mamie needed to limber up, and this was as good a time as any to do it, because she looked ever so dour most of the time herself.

Across from James, Henry sat looking stupefied at his friend trying to regain his composure in the presence of Aunt Mamie's pouty face . Henry was doing his best to hold it all in, but was failing miserably as James was on the verge of a total relapse himself. Suddenly the dam burst and Henry exploded in laughter thereby supporting his friend and beloved cousin in their folly. Man it felt good to laugh again without all those foreboding English restraints!

"What in Heaven's name is wrong with you Henry Boles? Have you taken leave of your senses?" Aunt Mamie blurted out scolding her nephew. The bewildered look on her face made Mr. Whitaker snicker at the other end of the table and that set in motion everything that happened next. The other guests at the table took Mr. Whitaker's cue as approval to join in, and before you can say, 'go catch your pig and make it squeal,' the whole lot of them began to laugh until their sides ached. Even poor Aunt Mamie could hold it back no longer and she began to giggle like a school girl after her first kiss. In time she was bellowing, and blowing wine from her nose onto Henry and James. Oh,...it was all quite vulgar by English standards, as they slowly come to realize they were in the battle of their lives against the Yanks for control of the giggles. But just like before, they were slowly losing the battle with the colonists all over again. Only God in heaven knows how good it felt to laugh in the company of such good friends who had the audacity to keep needling and prodding it on. Occasionally, Mr. Whitaker would squeal like a pig and the whole darn thing would start up all over again.

Poor Gladys and the help from the kitchen were beside themselves not knowing what to do. Having never seen such an outburst of insanity like this before, they disappeared into the kitchen until they could figure out for themselves what to do next. With tears running down all their faces, the laughing marionettes soon began slowing down their rate of descent back into the world of civilized behavior. Once they caught their breath and wiped the last vestige of tears from their eyes, things settled down quite a bit. Gladys reentered and went about trying to reset some of the glasses that had tipped over during the melee. That's when Henry piped up.

"Whew! That was some icebreaker cousin Anne. Thanks for showing us how to begin a proper meal."

Those at the table shouted a hearty, 'Here, Here,' as they lifted their glasses in a toast to Anne, the lovely barbarian.

"I can't take full credit for any of this. Our friends from Virginia were just sharing stories from back home, and all I've done is laugh since we left the stables. So raise your glasses my somber, pouty friends as we salute our Virginia friends. Thanks for blowing a little life back into our stuffy old sails," she toasted. The group of merchants and bankers shouted 'Here, Here,' once again like they really meant it this time. James and Johnny weren't used to being fussed over like this, and it made their cheeks flush.

Aunt Mamie had something more to say.

"Thank you all for coming. After we've eaten, I'd like us all to retire to the library where the rest of our evening will be filled with matters of a more serious nature. You won't mind too much Anne, will you?" she asked.

"Not at all Auntie," Anne replied.

"Now eat up all before our food gets cold. Even happy people like their food at a proper temperature," Aunt Mamie continued while slapping Henry's hand as he tried to steal a fork from her setting. "Behave young man, or I'll have to send you to your room without dessert."

Henry took it all in stride winking down the table at his sweet cousin who was smiling moonbeams. This had been the most fun he'd had since entering the house more than a year ago.

****

Back in port, Mr. Sims the quartermaster was busy loading the ship preparing for another trip. He had been given the Bills of Lading and was doing his best to coordinate everything into a place where space is always at a premium. However, there was something else afoot that he couldn't quite put his finger on. Down the docks a ways, was another ship being fitted out that was black as night, from her top mast down to the water line. Even the sailcloth appeared to be dipped in ink. It was hard to tell, but she appeared to be a fully armed corvette or frigate of some kind, though there were no visible markings as such. So the question remains; who owned her and what was her purpose. He had even wandered off down there on a couple of occasions but to no avail. He had been turned away by armed guards who knew their business. So what was it all about?

✳✳

"Anne darling, would you be so kind and take Johnny to another part of the house while we discuss business with his father in the library?" she asked.

"What's the big mystery Auntie?" Anne questioned.

"I will discuss it with you at the proper time, but not now," she replied. Anne didn't see the sense in pursuing it any further, and did as her aunt requested.

"Follow me young man, and I'll show you Uncle Charles' trophy room. He's got a stuffed lion and an elephant head in there," she directed. She didn't know what was going on, but it must be important.

Once inside the library, the doors were closed and locked. There was plenty of hot coffee and cake prepared, because it appeared they might be awhile. Aunt Mamie started off the topic of their discussion.

"I must swear each of you to an oath not to discuss anything that will be heard in this room tonight. Will you do so now?"

In unison they all swore with the exception of James Temple. He didn't like the cloak and dagger secrecy nearly as much as the others. He couldn't have foreseen what was coming next as Aunt Mamie directed all her energy now at him.

"For a long time Mr. Temple, all of us have been dealing with a most unpleasant situation. In certain waters off the Barbary Coast our ships have been seized and held for ransom by pirates operating out of Tripoli, Tunis and Algiers. Apparently, it's easier to steal than to work in that part of the world. Some time ago, your American president Thomas Jefferson set about waging war against these marauding pirates who operated on behalf of those countries and succeeded. Since then, your country has prevailed through a tough policy of retaliation for acts of piracy and violence. Unfortunately for us, our English politicians like to talk a problem to death before ever deciding to act on it. As such, we have never officially declared war or even acknowledged there was a need for one in that region of the world. Thus with their hands off approach, they have allowed ransom and extortion to continue unabated as pirating is still practiced at the most inopportune times against English ships."

Mr. Whitaker butted in about this time to offer a little clarification of his own.

"Understand sir, they don't take every ship, just the occasional one, and everyone of us have lost plenty to them. The politicians are happy to look the other way, because they see it as a form of poaching in a forest full of game. The truth is, our nation is war weary Mr. Temple and as such, our government will offer no official protest or threats against any nation over there for fear of starting another bloody war. Although the governments of those countries have declared they don't officially sanction pirating any longer, you can rest assured they get their cut off the top for looking the other way. Both sides wink and nod their heads in protest when the pirates take a ship now and then, because that's how the game has always been played. We have valuable trading partners in that region of the world, but quite frankly, it's almost impossible to do business with any of them because we're afraid to go to sea."

"What has any of this to do with me? Quite frankly, I shouldn't even be in this meeting as an American citizen," he protested. "May I be excused?"

Aunt Mamie raised her hand and continued.

"Please hear us out Mr. Temple. For some time now, we have been looking for a man of your caliber to help us in an experiment to help put an end to our problem. We also have the undeclared blessing of Parliament and the Royal Navy to do what I'm about to ask of you."

James began to squirm a little in his big overstuffed chair.

"We're looking for a man to pilot a companion ship sailing just behind our merchant vessels that will protect them from pirates should the need arises. We have outfitted a decommissioned frigate of forty guns to oppose them when necessary, and more guns are being loaded aboard our merchant ships as we speak. Though the government has no official policy of confrontation, they have given us permission to do as we will against them with our own private funds. Should our venture prove successful, then more privately owned frigates will begin showing up outfitted in the same manner and our merchant marines will handle the problem outside the bounds of diplomacy," she winked.

"First off, I can't captain a ship anymore. If you've done your homework, you would have known that," he stated emphatically.

"We have done our homework Mr. Temple, and it appears you can't pilot any American ships anymore. It's just because of your unique situation that we can do this at all," Mr. Whitaker declared joining in the discussion once again. "In one sense, you don't exist because you're completely off the books."

"Oh, I get it now," James responded candidly. "If something goes terribly wrong, there's no one to officially blame, because I and the ship don't really exist. Is that about the sum of it?"

All heads in the room nodded in agreement.

"That's about what I figured," he said standing to leave. "I hate to spoil your evening, but you'll have to find yourself another chump."

As he stepped to the door, Aunt Mamie played her trump card.

"If this goes as planned, there could be a commission in the Royal Navy as a captain on a ship of the line. Would that sweeten the pot any Mr. Temple? You're still a young man, think what a career in the British Navy would mean to your standing in the world. People would cheer once again as you go down the street, and of course, there's your son to consider. He could go to the finest academies in the world because of a father of your standing, and get a real education. America may have discarded you over their devilish slave politics, but we need you desperately. Henry says you're the only man capable of doing this job."

James hesitated facing the door. Never in his lifetime did he foresee such an opportunity to once again be the captain of a sailing vessel. Mrs. Boles was right, he wasn't anything but the victim of devilish American politics, and his heart was leaping at the chance to make things right. America's loss might be England's gain after all. As he turned and leaned back gently against the door, he spoke.

"You play dirty Mrs. Boles."

"I'm sorry Mr. Temple, but we are desperate people."

"Well, you have my interest. Where do we go from here?"

"Everything is ready for your inspection. When would you like to see our handiwork?" she asked.

"How about tomorrow morning? I'd like to see your frigate and judge for myself if she's a worthy competitor against the Muslim pirates. With all the wealth they've stolen from the English and others over the years, they should have some mighty fine vessels at their disposal by now. The bigger question before us now is where can I get a crew of experienced sailors who know naval tactics and gunnery?"

"The Royal Navy has agreed to provide us with the experienced men we need,...from their brig. They are all able bodied seamen and very willing," Mr. Whitaker replied.

"You mean to man a ship using the dregs from a naval prison?" he asked.

"Yes, but not just any prison. These are the experienced dregs Mr. Temple from our 'best' naval prison," Mr. Whitaker replied. "These are battle hardened men who have no war to fight at the moment. In a time of peace, they don't cope as well as others so they get into trouble looking for ways to vent their pent up frustrations. Every man has been scrutinized and declared himself willing to volunteer his services to get back into the fight, so to speak."

"No doubt, they will be officially drummed out of the Navy too, so there will be no record of them on the books," James mused aloud.

"But of course," Mr. Whitaker replied unapologetically. "They will be handpicked by you and approved by the Navy brass."

"After you say yes, I will make arrangements for you to meet with some of the Navy hierarchy who helped us put this little adventure together. If we're successful, there will be much to discuss in the next meeting of parliament," Aunt Mamie added.

"How will you handle our papers, and what flag will she fly under?" James asked testing the waters. "How could a ship like that sail anywhere without proper papers?"

"Good question Mr. Temple, but don't worry, those things will be handled at the appropriate time," Mr. Whitaker replied

"Alright, I'd like to see your ship tomorrow. If it passes muster, I'll consider your offer. Does Anne know about any of this?" James asked.

"No," Aunt Mamie declared quickly, "and for the moment, I'd like to keep her out of it and in good standing with plausible deniability Mr. Temple. She's a strong willed woman, as I'm sure you noticed, but this is not her fight. If something does go wrong and I lose, she will have to take over the family business. If we fail, I and all those in this room might go to prison on some trumped up charge the government will levy against us in order to save face. Sound familiar, Mr. Temple? You see, we're pretty hard headed too, but willing to fight for what we believe is a just cause. I believe I heard you say the other night that you only fight for just causes."

"You don't miss a thing, do you?" James bantered back remembering the night at the dance.

"I can't afford to. We have a parliament filled with cockle doodle do roosters, and all they know how to do is lay eggs. I'm tired of being robbed and cheated of my wealth on the high seas without a whimper from those blathering idiots. In the meantime, you'll stay here tonight and leave for the docks at first light. Anne will take care of Johnny tomorrow. Are we agreed?" Aunt Mamie asked.

"Agreed," James answered. It had been a long time since butterflies danced in his stomach, but they were certainly dancing now. "Henry, please show Mr. Temple to one of the guests rooms. We have a big day tomorrow," Auntie declared relieved to be underway at last. If James Temple doesn't accept, they're sunk. Outfitting a ship like this is expensive for the Navy, let alone private citizens. This has to work or else all is lost.

****

Inside their room, Johnny asked about the mysterious meeting, and James deflected as much as he could. When he explained about going to the docks tomorrow, Johnny wanted to go too. He had seen one of those steam powered ships coming in and really wanted to see it up close.

"We'll have to go another day son. Tomorrow's strictly business. Anne will be your guide if that's okay," James said.

"That'll be fine father. I really do like her," Johnny replied eagerly. "She hasn't actually said it in so many words, but I think she likes you too. She's always asking me lots of questions about you, if you get my meaning. What do you think of her?"

"Alright cupid, enough with the arrows," James answered trying to deflect Johnny's questions before he got too far afield.

"Come on father, you have to give me something."

"I'll say this and that'll be the end of it. I find Miss Anne a very intriguing woman," James muttered out.

"That's it?" Johnny grumbled back. "If I was old enough, I'd marry her myself. Did you know she once hunted a tiger in India that ate people? She killed it and had it made into a rug with its big head and teeth showing. I saw it laying there on the floor of the library. She even let me handle the big Purdy double gun that she killed it with."

"Well, since you got such a fancy for her, maybe she'll wait on you to grow up," James teased trying to get his son to cease and desist.

"No father, you need to marry her so we can keep her in the family before someone else makes off with her," Johnny pleaded shocking his dad. "I don't want her to lose her. She's not soft and silly like most women,...she's like us."

James raised an eyebrow remembering Aunt Lorna and Lena, his late wife. The only way a person could tell them apart was one had brown hair and the other had blonde. They were also very soft women, not used to the stresses of hard living. In fact, athleticism was frowned upon as unladylike when they were growing up in their father's house. Their father was a businessman who had spoiled them rotten in their youth. Sometimes James enjoyed the long sea voyages just so he could have time to himself to think. When he was at home, the women always had some drama going on like bees in a hive, and it almost drove him crazy. The only good thing to come from his marriage to Lena was a son just like him in temperament and discipline, and for that he was extremely thankful.

"John Temple you need to call it a night before I have to bind and gag you. I just met the lady yesterday and one doesn't hardly propose marriage after such a cursory introduction. I don't even know if she has a middle name," James stated trying to strengthen his argument.

"Anne is her middle name, Elizabeth her first. Anything else you want to know, just ask me," Johnny piped up obliging his father with the official stats.

James laughed at the boy as he threw a pillow at him. They tussled for a moment and finally James tickled him till he begged for mercy.

Of course all the noise drew the attention of the lady down the hall, and soon there was a knock on the door.

"Everything all right in there you two?" Anne asked curiously.

"My dad's tickling me, please make him stop!" Johnny yelled out.

Opening the door further revealed the two sailors tussling their hearts out for dominance. Anne grabbed a pillow and went to swinging it at James' head giving him a good pounding. He turned and looked up at her with mischief in his eyes. Grabbing her by the arm, he pulled her down onto the bed where they both could tickle her. She hadn't been tickled like this since she was a little girl by her brothers, and she began screaming in heightened ecstasy. Soon there was another presence at the door observing the chaos.

"Don't forget you have a big day tomorrow Mr. Temple. Please try and conserve a little of your strength for that," Aunt Mamie instructed before turning to leave with a smile across her lips. She too had once been young.

Finally the three of them lay across the bed exhausted from the melee. Anne was first to speak.

"Is this how you sailors go to sleep aboard ship?"

"No way Miss Anne. Mostly we sleep in hammocks or on feed sacks. It's really wherever you can lay down without bothering someone else," Johnny reported matter of fact. He reckoned she didn't know much about sleeping aboard a packet ship.

"Well, I don't mind roughing it some nights, but I still like a bed," she answered. "That's not too sissified for you is it?"

"No way ma'am, you're our kind of lady," Johnny beamed as he rolled up on his elbows looking her in the eyes. "Isn't that right father?"

"Time to call it a night young man. Go down the hall to the facilities and change into your night clothes, and brush your teeth while you're there," James commanded trying to turn the conversation into less of a head wind. As Johnny gathered up his things and marched off, James began a feeble attempt at an apology.

"There's no need for that James. I believe we're well beyond that. The truth is, I feel myself being irresistibly drawn to you. I hope I'm not overstepping, but I find your presence here very stimulating. I'd like to take a chance on strengthening our friendship if you're willing," she said.

"I admire a woman who speaks her mind. The thing is, I haven't had any desire for womanly attachments since my wife passed, and I didn't come here seeking any now. I must say in all honesty, I am intrigued by the offer. I've never met a woman of your particular persuasion before and it's thrown me off balance. Even with sea legs that can ride a twenty foot swell, I'm still playing catch up since I met you. Do you have that effect on all the men in your circle of influence?"

"There are no men like you in my circle of influence Mr. Temple, so I wouldn't know. In the circles I travel in, I'm merely known as a spinster or the old maid who's too old to marry and too young to die. Please accept my apologies if I've presumed too much upon you," she stated matter of fact as she slid off the bed and stood to leave. James stood quickly blocking her path of escape.

"Anne, please don't be offended. I merely assumed you probably had plenty of suitors trying to win your hand."

She laughed out loud.

"There are no men vying for my affections, because I've scared them all away. Ask anyone who knows me, they'll tell you straight out. To them, I'm a frigid thirty year old virgin because I'm either too strong, or too smart, or in some cases too tall for the whole damn lot of them!" she spoke in frustrated anger. "Most men who come courting want a gentle, defenseless woman they can train and boss around like the family dog, but I'm no sheep dog mister. Do you understand? Are you scared yet Mr. Temple? Am I too strong for you too?"

"No, I say you're just about right," he answered as he pulled her in close and kissed her firmly on upturned lips. She offered no resistance feeling the same kindred tug of the lonely heart. Here were two powerful personalities being drawn together like strong earth magnets. There was no way it could have gone any other way. As he released her, she bobbled her head shaking the stardust from her eyes before speaking.

"Whew! Didn't see that coming."

"Do I scare you Anne? Am I too strong for you," he asked rhetorically speaking back her own words for dramatic effect.

"No sir, I think you're just about right," she answered as she leaned back against him wrapping both arms around his neck this time, kissing him with fire and great passion. As waves of desire and longing coursed through their lonely souls, they knew at this moment they were meant for each other.

In the heat of the moment, they had forgotten about Johnny or anyone else for that matter, but Johnny hadn't forgotten about them as he reentered the room and got an eyeful.

"Mama Mia!...Does this mean we can keep her father?" he blurted out forcing James and Anne to release each other's impassioned embrace. Anne blushed and quickly stepped from the room disappearing without a word being said, leaving poor James to defend himself.

"Don't get excited, she just kissed me goodnight. English women do that sort of thing around here, so I'm told. It was nothing more than that," James shrugged trying to downplay what happened. Inwardly, he knew Johnny wasn't buying it.

"Ha! Then why didn't Auntie Boles kiss you like that when she stopped by?" Johnny laughed as he crawled into bed.

"Boy!," James said deepening his voice, "that'll be quite enough."

"Is she a good kisser?" Johnny asked more giggly now than ever.

"John Henry Temple, I said that'll be enough! A gentleman doesn't discuss such things about a lady behind her back. Now get in bed," James said laying down the law as Johnny giggled off to sleep in delight.

It was a restless night for both sailors as each dreamed of Anne in very different ways. Johnny dreamed of the possibility of a real mother for himself, while James dreamed of her as first a lover, and then a wife, but gnawing at him was the real possibility she might end up a widow before she was ever a bride. The mission Aunt Mamie and others had put together was very risky and fraught with unimaginable danger. He knew the sea stories of sailors being beheaded by the uncivilized Barbary pirates should they happen to win a sea battle. He just had to make sure they didn't. Anne's affections merely added another layer of concern why this enterprise had to work successfully. He greatly desired to come back and see their journey together through to its logical conclusions. As Johnny might have said, 'Then we can keep her.'

Chapter III

The early morning brought with it fog and plenty of it as is customary in an English seacoast town. Aunt Mamie had arranged for Zack to take James to the docks and wait for him, however long it took. There would be others there waiting to meet him as well.

As they rode by the posted guards, Zack waved to them. They knew him well enough that no questions would be asked even if the stranger he was bringing through was unknown to them. James could barely see the menacing black hulk in this pea soup fog, but he could sense she was a purpose built ship with only one mission in mind. Stepping up to the gangplank, he could see Albert Whittaker at the top standing by another older gentleman dressed in dark clothing.

"Ahoy!" James called out. "Permission to come aboard."

"Permission granted. Come ahead Captain."

As he climbed the steep gangplank, he couldn't help but wonder what he was getting himself into. Would this be the beginning of the end for him, or a real chance at a new beginning? Placing his feet firmly on deck had a wonderful familiarity about it. It was a feeling only a captain gets when taking command of a new ship.

"Good morning Mr. Whittaker," James said as they shook hands.

"Top of the morning to you too," the gentleman replied. He then turned to the other man with him and spoke. "For security and political reasons, this gentleman will have to remain unknown to you as we make our inspection. He is here to answer any questions you may have and make notes of anything you still may need. Where would you like to start?"

"How old is she?" James asked first breaking the ice.

"She's been at sea fifteen years, and was dry docked six months ago to check her hull. The hull is twenty inches thick and made of good, hard, layered English oak and plated with a quarter inch copper sheeting. Sound familiar?" the man asked.

"Of course, 'Old Ironsides.' However, her hull was twenty four inches thick as I remember it," James responded.

"Very true, but our ship is still a worthy vessel and possibly some faster than the American vessel without all the extra weight."

"Tell me her draft and tonnage," James inquired.

"She drafts twenty feet at approximately fifteen hundred tons. Her hull is one hundred ninety feet long with a hundred sixty foot main mast. The sailcloth is new and has been dipped in India ink in order to work our covert operation," the unknown gentleman answered. "She has four decks and a crew compliment of two hundred sixty men and fifteen boys."

"There'll be no boys on this trip, so make that two hundred seventy five men," James instructed. "Tell me her gun strength."

"Ship's compliment of guns run twenty each, twenty-four pounders, and twenty each, thirty-two pounders. There are also four, nine pound bow chasers forward," the men recounted.

"I want two nine pound carronades mounted aft as well. The last thing I want is pirates crawling up my backside without any way to tell them no," he stated matter of fact.

"I'll see that it's done today," the man submitted.

"How are the bilge pumps?"

"They are new and well tested. Would you like to see them for yourself. There are lanterns below," the mystery man offered.

"We might as well get to it," James declared. He wasn't about to go to sea without a thorough inspection. "We've got a long day ahead.

Has she been to sea yet in this configuration?"

"No sir, we've just been waiting for the right captain, and I've been told sir, you're that man," the unknown gentleman stated.

"That's yet to be determined. How do you know so much about the U.S.S. Constitution? Have you ever seen her up close?" James asked.

"No sir, but I have family who has. He was a young midshipman aboard the H.M.S. Guerriere in 1812 when Captain Dacres declared to his crew that capturing such a prize would make his career and theirs. Unfortunately for our side, Captain Hull from the American ship had other ideas on the matter. When cannonballs bounced off the sides of the American ship, 'Old Ironsides' stepped into the history books as a real legend. They knew then they didn't stand a chance, and finally surrendered after the captain was wounded," the man declared flatly. "Wars are such a waste, don't you think Mr. Temple?"

"Yes, but sometimes they are necessary when dealing with mindless evil," he bluntly stated reminding the elder gentleman as to why that particular war was undertaken.

"Of course," the old man admitted not wanting to reopen old wounds. As he lit off a lantern, James followed him down the stairs.

Over the next few hours, they poked about into every nook and cranny looking for any sign of disrepair and not finding any. The anchors fore and aft were looked at and approved, and lastly of course the bilge pumps were approved. The flag box was inspected, but no colors as yet, or marking for the ship had been found anywhere on board. James felt compelled to ask about them.

"What colors are we flying under?" James asked.

"That's yet to be determined," the older man declared shocking James with such an indecisive answer.

"Are we supposed to hoist the 'Jolly Roger' when going into battle against these pirates?" he asked.

"You know, that's not a bad idea," he laughed. "Don't worry, all will sorted out in due time. What do you think of the ship thus far Captain Temple?"

Captain Temple? James hadn't been called by that designation in some time and it felt kind of strange to hear it again.

"It's a fine ship," he answered, "and for the time being it's still just Mr. Temple."

"Of course," the man acknowledged.

"When do I meet the crew?" James queried.

"Tomorrow afternoon Mr. Temple. They are being transported as we speak into that warehouse yonder. I'll have papers on every sailor in your hands by two o'clock today. In the meantime, we've made arrangements for you to stay in town tonight so you'll have privacy with your thoughts."

Hearing church bells ringing twelve o'clock. James made a declaration.

"I'm hungry gentlemen. Where does a sailor go to eat around here?"

"We'll have to go back into town to eat Mr. Temple, because I don't want any suspicious characters seeing you here. In fact, when you take command, I would prefer you go aboard during the night. You're our secret weapon, and we don't want any of our Muslim merchants to see you and wonder what we're up to. Their pirate friends back home always seem to know when we're coming. It's happened before, but with any luck it won't happen this time," Mr. Whittaker explained.

"How is the harbormaster taking to this idea. Is he on board with us sneaking around on an unmarked ship?" James inquired.

"Yes, and he's been informed that he knows all he needs to know for now," the older gentleman scoffed. "There is a lot more afoot than you can know Mr. Temple. So for the moment, please relax and ask fewer questions about the details. Your task will be to destroy pirates, bandits and cutthroats in all sizes and shape with zeal, and our job will be to sweat the details. Now, let's find a suitable diner the three of us can enjoy without any scrutiny."

****

"Hold onto him Miss Anne and I'll get the net. Oh boy, he's a whopper!"Johnny yelled at her as he stomped out of the creek to get the net. "I bet he's a five pounder, if he's an ounce."

"He's not going anywhere, just don't slip and fall on the rocks," she warned as he staggered towards shore.

As Johnny grabbed the net and reentered the stream, he came slipping and sloshing back towards her falling almost at her feet. Though totally submerged under water, he never let go of the net placing it under her big trout for the catch.

"Are you alright?" she asked as he slowly emerged.

"Yes ma'am, why wouldn't I be?"he asked puzzled by the question while standing victoriously with fish in hand.

"Well, for one, you're all wet."

"I'm a sailor Miss Anne, I get wet a lot," he retorted with the glee of a ten year old' s view of the world.

Anne chuckled with delight as she watched him string the trout with the other four they had caught previously. Hers was the biggest thus far allowing her some bragging rights and an opportunity for a little ribbing.

"Have you ever caught a trout as big as that one before?" she asked boastfully.

"No, but I did help catch a whale once that was almost big as our ship. Does that count?" he asked.

Her eyes went wild at the thought of a ten year old boy throwing his first harpoon at a thrashing sperm whale, while a proud father stood by giving instructions on how to do it. In her mind's eye, these were without a doubt the kind of men who could do such a thing as they laughed in the face of danger. Johnny did laugh, but only at the startled look on her face.

"I'm just kidding Miss Anne. I didn't really catch a whale, but we did see one being chopped up for its blubber on the way over," he laughed and laughed. "I wish you could have seen the look on your face when you thought I had caught a real whale."

Anne laughed too at being caught flatfooted, allowing her imagination to run away with her. She made a mighty sweep with her hand splashing water on the boy, but this time it was Johnny who got the last laugh. He began kicking water with his feet and hands, soaking her through and through from stem to stern. She fell backwards in the knee deep water trying to avoid his onslaught, and got the soaking of her life. As her head popped up from under the water, she formed her mouth into a fountain head and squirted water high into the air.

"Do I look like a whale?"

"Yeah, a real skinny whale," he laughed. "They'd probably throw you back cause you got no blubber on you."

"I can live with that," she giggled as she sat there in the stream. "I say it's high time we cook up our fish and eat. What do you say sailor?"

"I say, yes ma'am!" he answered as he offered her a helping hand.

Grabbing the hand that was offered, she pulled him down into the water and began tickling him. He had a real funny bone.

"Okay, I give up!" he screamed above the giggles, "You got to let me go, I'm starving!"

"Last one to the fire's a rotten egg and has to clean all the fish," she cried out as she got her footing and a head start.

Johnny lost the race, but he didn't mind so much. In no time at all he had the five fish cleaned and ready for the fire. In the meantime, Anne had wrapped a blanket around herself and waited for Johnny to join her by the fire. As he wrapped himself in a blanket too and settled in beside her, Anne began asking questions trying to learn what she could about these remarkable Temple men.

"Did you ever know your mum?"

"I know her name was Lena, but she died before I was a year old. I lived off and on with my Aunt Lorna most of the time after that. People told me they looked exactly alike because they were twins."

"Did you see much of your father growing up?" she asked again.

"Not really, he came and went a lot trying to find work. A lot of bad people tried to hurt my father when he was in the Navy, but he beat' em back. Did you know my father was in the Navy?"

"No I didn't," she answered shocked by this revelation. Had he done something of a criminal nature to be removed, she wondered?

"He was a captain," Johnny continued proudly.

"Would you tell me about it? I would like to know what happened," she requested reserving judgment till she heard the whole story.

So for the next half hour, Johnny retold his father's story just as he remembered it. He also told how his father took a whipping aboard ship for him, and how he found the older scars. That's when he learned the truth about his past.

Anne listened intently, but grew profoundly angry at Henry for not stopping it. Johnny tried to explain how life was aboard a ship.

"Captain Boles didn't really have a choice, because the quartermaster and I set all that in motion. He had to follow through as a matter of ship morale. If the Captain showed favoritism or weakness to one, then he has to do it for all. A ship runs by a different set of rules than people are used to on land. Please don't say anything about this to father. I think he would be very angry with me if he knew I told you. Please Miss Anne, please," he pleaded.

"Don't worry sailor, your secret is safe with me," Anne finally conceded placing a cold hand on his for a moment.

"Thank you Miss Anne, that means a lot to me. My father is a great man and I wouldn't do anything to hurt him." he said.

"I understand Johnny. I happen to think your father is a great man too."

"You like him, don't you?" the boy asked catching her off guard with his bluntness.

She didn't want to say too much for fear things might not work out. He was a sailor after all, and could take off over the horizon tomorrow and never be seen again. However, the boy needed an answer.

"Yes Johnny, I suppose I do, but don't read too much into what you saw last night. We've just barely gotten to know each other, and these things take time. Please don't pressure him to make more of it than that. I have a feeling he has a lot more on his mind right now than courtship."

Anne wasn't for sure, but she suspected something was going on behind her back that she didn't fully comprehend. Something that involved her aunt and Henry, and perhaps some of her business associates for sure. Come to think about it, there has been an inordinate amount of activity in the house lately, with comings and goings by a host of unknown actors. Then she recollected that Aunt Mamie seemed to know a lot about James Temple before he ever set foot in the house. It never occurred to her until just now that something very mysterious was already underway. She planned on asking some questions when she got back to the estate.

✳✳

By two thirty that afternoon, James Temple was sitting comfortably in the same room they had rented their first night in Liverpool. As sunlight came in over his left shoulder, a list of every sailor who wanted in on their little adventure was in his hand. There was half a dozen warrant officers in the mix filling out his need for officers. There were a dozen sailing masters, pursers, surgeons, and one preacher which seemed rather odd in the mix. Also available was a dozen petty officers, three scores of able seamen and landsmen by the hundreds. It looked as though most of the fighting would be done by the most unskilled and uneducated of the bunch, and that just wouldn't do. If he could somehow determine who would go and who would stay, the serious training could begin immediately. He had been given one month to prepare his ship and crew for sail, but what he needed was six. The one thing he had in his favor was they were willing to fight and with the right kind of training, it might be enough. By six o'clock that evening, a knock came unexpectedly on the door.

"Hello Mr. Whitaker, please come in," James said standing to one side allowing him entrance.

"Have you made a list of the crew yet?" the man asked.

"I'm sorry to disappoint you, but the answer is no. From the look of these resumes, I can give you a quick laundry list of cutthroats, burglars, card sharks, and rapists that should be hanged. You're not seriously thinking of chasing this pipe dream with men like these are you?"

"It was our understanding you could get them into shape in a month," the bewildered man answered.

"With an experienced crew, a month's training would be enough to make a real difference in a serious fight. What am I supposed to do with barflies like these in a sea action?"

"Come now Mr. Temple, it can't be as bad as all that. All these men have gone to sea and most have served in the Navy. Surely you can pull it together and salvage a crew of fighting men to accomplish our goal."

"Give me six months and maybe I have a fighting chance. This is no leisurely sailboat ride on a calm sea we're talking about sailing into. We're going to war against a battle tested enemy with a proven record of conquest. We'll be lucky if any of us come back with our head," James scowled. His role as captain had just been downgraded to nothing more important than one of the galley help. For the first time, he sensed the hopelessness of it, and it soured his stomach. Did these people really think such an endeavor could be pulled from a magic hat with no more to work with than that? Confound the lot of them!

"Would you at least meet the men before throwing all our hard work and expense out the window? They have a lot riding on this too, you know. Some of them were under a life sentence," Mr. Whitaker remarked as if that would somehow elevate their status.

James fumbled around with the papers before giving an answer.

"Alright, I'll meet them tomorrow."

"Tomorrow is fine, but you'll have to wear a disguise of some kind. I'll have someone come round in the morning to help you with it," the man stated matter of fact as he prepared to leave.

"I don't want a disguise," James rebuffed.

"It has to be this way Mr. Temple. There are spies everywhere," Mr. Whitaker commented.

"Before I take off on this fool's errand, you have to answer a question for me of some importance," James demanded.

"But of course sir, what is it?"

"Was I chosen because I'm an expendable commodity?" James asked boldly. He thought he was beginning to understand his real role in all this. "Here's how it looks to me. Even if I fail, it would send a powerful message to the pirates that you're willing to fight for the right to sail in open waters. As far as the Barbary coast knows, you might have a fleet of ships like these lurking in the wings willing to take up the fight."

"Dear Mr. Temple, let me put your mind at ease. You were chosen because you were exactly the right man for the job at hand, and you have a very particular skill set this venture desperately needs. You are well known to us on the committee as a highly educated sailing captain, but what this mission really needed from the beginning was a man with a strong moral compass. We have found over time that men with high moral standards make good business partners and great fighting men. No Mr. Temple, you are not expendable, as you are the face of things to come and the most important fellow among us," Mr. Whitaker said hoping to put his mind at ease.

"What's with all the moral compass references? Think I might steal your ship and become a pirate myself?"

"The thought had occurred to us," the old fox snickered.

"I figured as much," James laughed. "I'll be ready in the morning."

****

Late into the evening, word came that James Temple would not be returning as expected to the Boles estate. Johnny was used to hearing such news having lived with unexpected delays most of his life, but Anne was not. For a woman who didn't wish to make too much of their first kiss, she was chomping at the bits to understand why he wasn't coming in as expected.

"Why do you think he's not coming in tonight Aunt Mamie? And who is he with? I thought he was a stranger in Liverpool," Anne commenced with her inquiry.

"Oh, he might have met a sailor friend or some other person and decided to stay the night. Don't fret your head over things that don't concern you child," her aunt chided as she went outside with some friends to see the moon. "Men will be men, whether we like it or not."

That was not the thing to say to Anne Boles. If she was going to throw herself at a man, she wanted to be certain he wasn't throwing his affections around somewhere else. But, where was she to look for her mystery sailor? Then she had an idea. Racing up to Johnny's room, she entered after knocking catching Johnny napping. Rolling his eyes around to see her, he asked what she wanted.

"Johnny, where did you and your dad stay in Liverpool your first night ashore?"

"Captain Boles arranged our accommodations in a nice hotel off James Street. I don't remember the name, but it had a big fancy glass door at the front. Why are you asking?" he questioned.

"No reason, just curious. Now roll over and go back to sleep," she ordered.

Anne knew the hotel well. She quickly changed into some riding clothes and made for the stables stumbling into Aunt Mamie outside as she was coming back indoors with her friends.

"Anne dear, where do you think you're going this time of night. Do you realize the hour?" she asked.

"I won't be long, I have an errand to run. Goodnight Aunt Mamie," she declared as she walked quickly by.

"That's not like you to be so secretive. Where are you going really?" Aunt Mamie asked roughly stopping Anne in her tracks.

"I'll tell you what Auntie, you tell me all your secrets and I'll tell you all mine. How's that strike you?" Anne snapped back.

In all the time Anne had lived with her, she had never spoken to her in such an abrupt tone. Mamie suspected whatever burr was under her saddle must have really set her off.

"I have no secrets from you Anne that you need to worry yourself with. Why are you so gruff with me?" Auntie asked confused and embarrassed by her tone.

"No secrets! I live in a house full of them," she all but screamed.

"You know, as your aunt, I'm not required to tell you everything that takes place in my own house. What's come over you? Where are you going in such a huff?" Mamie demanded.

"Where is James Temple Aunt Mamie?"Anne fired back.

"That's none of your concern."

"Well, I'm making it my concern. I'm going into Liverpool tonight to find him, so don't wait up for me," she stated flatly as she turned and walked hurriedly away.

"Anne, you come back here this instant. It's too late to travel alone with robbers prowling the roads at night looking for silly women just like you to prey upon," Aunt Mamie called out after her.

"Don't worry, I've got my gun!"

Aunt Mamie placed her hand over her mouth in dread as she watched Anne disappear into the darkness of the stables. What has she discovered that's got her bonnet turned upside down? There's nothing more she could do now except go into the house and wait for her return,...if she returns.

Anne quickly saddled her favorite horse and disappeared into the moonlit shadows of a country lane hoping her animal could see better than she. Twenty minutes into her ride, she noticed movement on the road ahead that caught her attention. It was a small cart deliberately turned over to catch a wandering fly in its snare. As she pulled up trying to see a way around it, voices came from the side of the road.

"Hey Clem, I think we got something in our little trap. Step out and stop his retreat before he makes a run for it," the robber shouted to his comrade across the road.

"Don't worry Dudley, I got him boxed in with my shotgun,...he ain't going nowhere. Light your lantern so we can collect our bounty," the bandit called out as he waited patiently for his friend to appear. Anne was also waiting for the man to come out into the light as she held tightly onto her nervous steed with one hand, and her gun with the other.

"I can't quite see his face, but he rides a good horse. Get down from there rich country gentleman and empty your pockets, or else I'll have to shoot you. Come on, you won't miss a few quid, " the man demanded as he stumbled casually out into the moonlight.

Anne turned to the shotgun wielding bandit behind her holding his lantern and shot him first with her pepperbox causing him to wince in pain and drop his lantern and gun. Suddenly, she was upon the other scoundrel in a flash and fired two rounds into his chest dropping him to his knees in deathly silence. As his lantern crashed to the ground, she drove her steed over him making her getaway.

Though wounded in the hand, Dudley called out to his friend in the dark.

"Clem, you okay? I heard two shots."

"I think she's done killed me Dudley. If I don't make it, take my body down to the sea and throw it in before my missus finds out. I would rather the fish chew on my backside than her. She's a mean one Dudley, promise you'll do as I ask," he pleaded with his friend.

Dudley fumbled to get his lantern relit and went to have a closer look at his friend Clem. Kneeling down beside him he could tell he was hurt bad. Without any warning, he pulled off his hat and began praying just like his momma had taught him to do in a time of crisis when he was a little boy.

"Lord forgive this awful sinner of his thieving ways before he dies. He's been a good friend of mine for some time now, even though he's a bit addled in the head. If you was to look around up there, maybe you could find a place for him among all them saints where he could be of some use. He's pretty good with shoeing horses and chickens whether they was stole or not, and could be right handy when it comes time to clean out the heavenly stalls. Thanks for listening,...amen."

"I didn't know you was a praying man Dudley. That was plum pretty the way you put it," Clem grinned in the dim light grateful his friend was on such good terms with the man upstairs.

Thus the vigil began as Dudley held onto Clem's hand waiting for him to die. After some time passes, Clem is still among the living.

"For a man about to die, you sure take a long time in doing it," his friend grumbled. "Can't you hurry it along some, I'm getting cold."

"I'm going as fast as I can, don't rush me Dudley," Clem responded. He was doing the best he could under the circumstances, and he was cold too. "Hold me Dudley, I'm scared. All of a sudden it's getting really dark."

"Hush up you dimwit, it's getting dark cause the lantern went out again. It looks as though the man's bullet punched a hole in my lantern and all the oil's done leaked out. Here, let me have yours," Dudley chided. "Come on, let's get you into the wagon and see you home. I don't think you're gonna die tonight."

"What makes you say that?" Clem said as he stood to his feet with help from his friend.

"For one thing, you talk too much for a dying man, that's why," Dudley declared. "You're more worried about Ruby fussing at you than you are of kicking the bucket. You ain't gonna die tonight."

"What am I gonna tell her? You know she'll beat me with the hoop duster again if I don't have a good excuse this time," Clem worried aloud.

"Don't worry, I'll think of something," Dudley mused putting his dull brain to work. As the gears turned slowly, it suddenly came to him. "How about this, we tell her we got mugged on the way home and the bandit made off with all our money. With three bullets wounds between us, she's bound to buy it."

"It's bloody brilliant," Clem cheered.

"I'm glad you think so, now Ruby can dig the bullets out on her time," his friend declared freeing himself of any guilt for his well being. Whether he lived or died would be Ruby's responsibility from here on out. "Brrrrr! It's time to get you home old chum. It's colder than a well diggers bum out here."

"Thanks Dudley, you're the best friend I ever had," the wounded man cried as Clem laid him down gently in the wagon for the ride home.

"As far as I know, I'm the only friend you've ever had, but who's counting," Dudley answered as he began pulling the little wagon by hand to Clem's abode.

"No matter, you're still the best friend ever Dudley."

✳✳

On and on Anne pushed her steed until she saw the first outcroppings of the city laid out before her. The street lanterns were still lit and she could finally see clearly where she was going. She was probably ten minutes from the hotel when it occurred to her how silly this might look to James when she knocked on his door at midnight. Was she just acting like a foolish schoolgirl caught up in her first crush, or was there something more that would justify her actions. She had never been in love before, but had heard plenty of stories from others how it makes one do crazy things. Whatever happened next didn't matter so much, she just needed to see him to verify he was okay and find out what Aunt Mamie's hold over him was.

Ringing the bell inside the hotel brought forth a little widget of a man with hair parted in the middle, glasses, and a pencil thin mustache.

"Yes dear lady, may I help you?"

"I'm looking for James Temple. What room is he in?" she asked.

"I can't tell you that, it wouldn't be proper. We're not that kind of hotel, just so you know," he answered roughly.

Anne appeared stumped, then she had an idea.

"I have to see him, I'm his wife," she beamed confusing the hotel manager even further.

"Where's your wedding ring? It seems an odd thing that a married woman doesn't have on a wedding ring," the little man piped up thinking he had her trapped.

Anne slapped her riding crop on the counter making a fine noise startling the manager.

"Look here little man, I've had just about enough out of you. Our boy Johnny is laying sick at my Aunt's house and I need to fetch his father. Now tell me the room number, or I'm going to take you over my knee and beat you with this whip," she barked out her demand.

The little man's eyes lit up excitedly with the possibility of being physically roughhoused by this energetic beauty, and it brought back a few fond perverted memories from his past.

"Ooohh, you're a feisty one! Alright, I'll tell you his number,...if you promise to strike me with your whip a few times before you go," he purred as his eyebrows moved up and down with anticipation. "It would mean a lot to me."

Anne was startled by his request, and at once she realized how sheltered she had been her entire life. She didn't want to strike him now for fear the little twit would like it, and then begin telling all his friends about his new mistress. She wouldn't be able to walk down the streets without suspicions that everyone was talking behind her back, so she chose another course of action. Pulling her pepperbox from inside her coat, she cocked it and laid it on the counter hoping his eyes wouldn't light up with delight at the sight of her gun. If he asked to be shot, she was surely sunk.

"Your offer to use the whip intrigues me little man, but I'm in a hurry," she said softly. "The number please, or you'll be the third person tonight I've had to shoot."

"Room number twelve, Mrs. Temple," he answered quickly as he backed up against the wall with his hands in the air.

"Put your hands down you silly toad, I'm not robbing you. If you're a good boy, I might come back later and lay down a few lashes just because you've been so cooperative," she quipped snapping the riding crop against her high top boots as she turned quickly to head up the stairs. She wouldn't actually do such a thing, but she knew it would keep his mind racing all night long with the endless possibilities.

At the top of the stairs, it dawned on her that the man had called her Mrs. Temple. Anne Temple,…Mrs. Anne Temple. It had a good ring to it she thought as she tapped on door number twelve.

James opened the door bewildered that Anne was standing there. His first thoughts were ones concerning Johnny's well being, but when he couldn't sense any urgency in her voice, his fears vanished.

"Aren't you going to invite me in, or do I have to stand out here and talk in the hall," she chided.

"Of course, please come in," he answered moving to one side.

Once inside, she waited for him to close the door. As he turned and leaned back against it, he spoke.

"I must say, you're the last person I expected to see tonight."

"Does it bother you that I'm here?" she asked.

"No, quite the contrary. I think it's having a very positive effect on my mood," he bantered back. "Come closer."

Upon his command, she came closer pressing her strong supple body against his, slipping her arms around him once more.

"Isn't that better?" he asked as he looked deep into her eyes.

"Yes, I believe it is," she answered kissing him firmly with lips filled with passion and dripping like honey. This time there would be no interruptions, or she would shoot someone with the last round in her pepperbox. After a moment, she pulled back laying her head on his shoulder.

"What are you doing here?" James asked after a time of reflection.

"I'm afraid something's going on and I've been deliberately left out of the loop. Normally, that wouldn't bother me because it happens all the time," she began.

"Then why are you so troubled now Anne?"

"Because, I know somehow all this revolves around you. If it involves you, then eventually it's going to involve me. Can you deny it?" she pressed him.

"If I do, then what?"

"Don't give me that kind of answer! How are we supposed to have a life together if you're always dodging the questions I ask while trying to keep things from me. Remember what I said, I'm no sheep dog," she bantered back.

"That's some comfort," he said kissing her intently once again. When they finished, he asked her to repeat that line about their life together. "What did you mean by that?"

"I told the desk manager downstairs I was your wife; he wasn't going to give me your room number otherwise. So on the way up here, I asked myself what it would be like to really be Mrs. James Temple. Has a nice ring to it, don't you think?" she asked.

"Don't you think it's a little early for us to get that serious Anne. We barely know each other," James responded, "and besides, I'm a man of very little means. If something did come of our friendship, I couldn't provide for you in the lifestyle you're probably used to living."

" Oh I see it all now, it's the wealth I live in that scares you. I didn't think I could scare you away, but you're starting to sound like all the others with their flimsy excuses."

"Anne, it's too soon, don't you see? I'm vulnerable, and so are you. Our emotions are running on high alert since last night's kiss, and if you stay much longer I'm not sure I can hold my desire for you in check."

"Then bed me James Temple, and hold nothing back."

James fumbled for words at the boldness of her statement.

"I'm not taking you to my bed without a proper marriage Anne Boles. I'm just old fashioned that way," James answered more frustrated now than ever at his own words. His mind meant it, but his body was on fire screaming with desire for her.

Sensing a stalemate was in the making from this honorable man, she moved in a very unexpected direction.

"Is Henry in the hotel here?" she asked.

"Yes, across the hall. Why do you ask?"

"I have an idea, follow me."

Across the hall they went, hand in hand waking Henry in the process. As he opened the door in his nightshirt, he looked completely dumbfounded and confused at the two of them standing there.

"Well hi Cousin. Fancy meeting you here this time of night. Can I help you?" he asked curiously, groggy from his sleep being interrupted in the middle of the night.

"As the captain of a ship, you can marry people right?"

"Yes, but technically we have to be on water in a boat or ship when I do it," he answered. "Wait a minute, you two are not seriously wanting to get married at this hour of the night, are you?"

"Of course, why do you think we woke you," Anne snipped.

"Holy smokes Anne, Aunt Mamie will have a conniption fit if she finds out. She wants the big wedding and everything. You know how much hot water I'll be in if she finds out I married you two?"

"Then you best keep it to yourself. I'm pretty sure you're good at keeping secrets judging by all the practice you've had lately," her eyes glistened with menace as she spoke, warning Henry that she was onto him and all his secrets.

"James, you're not seriously contemplating going through with this, are you? I know cousin Anne has lost her senses, but I thought you were a more practical man. Why don't you two just go on back to bed and get this out of your system, and I won't tell a soul. As you said, I'm pretty good at keeping secrets," Henry quipped.

"I'm not sleeping with her outside of marriage, cause I want her committed to the cause. You got to help us Henry. Since you set all this in motion, you're practically responsible," James insinuated.

"I can't believe I'm letting you talk me into this. Oh alright, let me get dressed, and then we'll make a run to the docks and find our ship."

Anne had already considered another possibility.

"Grab your pants and come with me Henry, I have an idea."

Taking the two men by the hand, she led them into the bathroom at the end of the hall. As Henry dressed, she posed a question.

"If we filled this tub with some water, could you technically marry us if we all stood in it? I believe the tub could float like a small boat if called upon."

Henry shook his head knowing he was licked. So without further fanfare he rolled up his breeches and crawled in barefoot. James and Anne followed suit after pulling off their boots and stockings. James turned on the water from the overhead storage tank and filled the tub up to their ankles in cold water.

"I always knew you two were meant for each other, because you're the same kind of people. However, I didn't know at the time how mentally daft you both were. Since it appears all the right stars are in alignment, I say let's get on with it."

As the threesome stood in ankle deep water, Henry performed the most beautiful wedding ceremony of his life just as if he was aboard a real ship. When he asked for the ring, the two prospects for marriage never considered needing one when the inspiration first hit. Henry was not unsettled by their dilemma as he reached inside his nightshirt and pulled out a small chain with a wedding ring attached to it. Pulling the ring off the chain, he handed it to James.

"It was my mother's. Would you mind too much using this until you get your own?" Anne kissed the side of his cheek and they continued on to the best part. "And now you may kiss your bride."

James kissed Anne with the blessing and approval of God as Henry looked on proudly admiring his work as a matchmaker. Henry hoped that God would also watch over him after Aunt Mamie found out.

"Thank you Henry," James said as they abandoned ship and dripped down the hallway back to their room. "Not a word of this to Mrs. Boles. She might have me drawn and quartered at this stage of the game, if she found out."

Anne knew from the inflection in his voice that something truly was going on after all. She thought James would surely have to let her in on it now, since they were officially husband and wife.

At the bedroom door, James halted scooping Anne up before they crossed the threshold.

"I hope you don't mind. I'm a little old fashioned that way too."

"I'd be disappointed if you hadn't," she answered sweetly.

From his bedroom door, Henry saw them enter and lock the door completely enraptured with one another. He just hoped that in the morning, they would still talk to him.

"I'm a little rusty at this Anne," James began as he set her back down. "We could wait until tomorrow when you have all your things about you and a decent nightgown."

"What I have in mind sailor doesn't require much in the way of clothes," she said seductively. "Come closer and I'll show you what I mean."

And thus began the honeymoon of James and Anne Temple.

****

At four o'clock in the morning, Henry heard a loud pounding on his door. Rolling out of bed this time of night with this much fanfare usually meant something big, like fire in the building. He turned up the dimly lit lamp to see where he had lain his pants and boots and hobbled to the door with sleepy eyes. He was stunned to see who was at the door when he opened it.

"Anne darling, what are you doing here this time of night wrapped in a bed sheet. Come on in out of the draft," he offered. Cousin or not, he couldn't help but admire her raw and sensual beauty as she marched angrily into the room with fire blowing from each nostril. "If you've come for a refund don't worry, I haven't had time to record any of the required paperwork yet. So, at the moment you can be officially not married, if that's what you're here after."

Anne was furious as she stomped around the room half naked wrapped in her loose fitting bed sheet. She was mad as a wet hen, but not at Henry.

"If you're not going to talk cousin, I'd like to go back to bed. Ordinarily at this stage of the game, I'd offer you half the comfort of my bed to lay on, but you can't seriously expect to come in here dressed like that and just hop in. I'm afraid even I'm not above that

55

sort of temptation. So for the time being, I think you had better sleep over there on the couch, alone, till morning."

Anne kept mumbling under her breath as she paced the floor not hearing a thing poor Henry said. He did his best to interpret her meanderings, but was getting nowhere. Finally he came out and asked her to explain herself.

"Are you wanting me to go next door and take a poke at him? If you are, you certainly came to the wrong room."

"He told me I couldn't know what he was working on," she fumed. "I'm his wife! He can't hold secrets like that from me."

"So this whole marriage thing was just a ruse to get at the secrets James held in his head. That's devious cousin, even for you." Henry scolded her. Then came a soft rap on the door. "Come in."

"Morning Henry. Sorry to barge in like this, but I'm looking for my newly wedded wife," James stated matter of fact looking across the room at her as she fumed. "She's about this tall with long, dark hair and a body to die for, last seen wrapped in a bed sheet. I was hoping since you're her nearest kin, you might have seen her in passing."

"Oh, she's here old friend, won't you come on in," Henry said coyly as he glanced over at Anne pouting in a darkened corner of the room. "Since this room is starting to get a little crowded, I think I'll go across the hall to your room and try again to get some sleep. You two jaybirds certainly need to work this out, cause I have a lot of time and energy invested in bringing you together."

As the door closed behind Henry, James spoke softly to Anne.

"Anne, please come sit by me."

She came and sat down next to him on the overstuffed couch still wrapped very loosely in her sheet. He tried once more to tell her what he could, but he didn't want her or Johnny in harm's way if this adventure of his went sideways.

"Can't you just trust that I have your best interest at heart?"

"Can't you just trust me," she answered. "I'm certainly no child."

"That's right, and you're no sheep dog either," he laughed trying to diffuse the sour mood between them.

She snickered at the reference, encouraging him to continue.

"You want to call the whole thing off?" James asked her bluntly. This was her 'out' if she wanted it. He knew human nature well enough to know that people sometimes confuse lust for love a lot more often than they're willing to admit. Henry would never on his honor repeat a single word of their escapades, so their secret was very safe with him. This night would be their only reminder of mistaken infatuation, and he could live with that. If he and Johnny moved from the house tomorrow, maybe she could learn to live with what she's done too.

"You're not getting out of this that easy James Temple, if that's what you're wanting. I'm your lawful wife now and you're stuck with me till death do us part."

James smiled, very pleased with her answer.

"I didn't say I wanted out. I thought perhaps you did," he said. "At the moment, I'm a very happily married man, and a very contented one at that. Would you be willing to call a truce and come back to bed. I'm not quite through plundering the bounty of my newest acquisition."

"Oh James darling, I love it when you talk merger and acquisitions like that," she said in her sexiest, sultry voice as her playful side began to return to what it was an hour ago. She stood slowly allowing the sheet to drop gently at her feet, teasing his hungry eyes to feast with passionate desire once again upon her beautiful form in the dimly lit room.

His heart danced too with joy because they had survived their first official fight, and now it was time to repair the rigging after the storm. Now she was finally his, and she was all the woman he imagined she could be. For James, her keen intellect was as sensual and stimulating as her body was desirable, and he knew she was expecting a goodly return on her investment tonight as well. So he saw no reason, they shouldn't continue to enjoy the dividends of their very real marital partnership.

While holding out her hand to him, she blew a seductive kiss as only a new bride can, enticing him to return to the lover's bed for one more round of unrestrained ecstasy. As James took her outstretched hand to follow, she turned her back to him allowing him a moment to drink in her delicious nakedness with each deliberate step she took. Her stride was powerful and supple as the gait of a thoroughbred horse unleashing a visual torrent of pleasure to his longing eyes. Closing the gap between them, he embraced her from behind holding her so very close to his aching, lusting body. As he gently kissed the sides of her neck, she pushed back firmly against him, begging him to trace every line, sinew and female attribute of her glorious form with loving hands in unadulterated pleasure. It was here at this point, his mind played the dirtiest trick of all, flashing back to the honeymoon night of his late wife, Lena Johnson. It almost spoiled the mood.

The sensation of holding a strong sensuous woman like Anne in his arms was a very different experience than what Johnny's mother offered on their wedding night. His late wife was a sheep dog among sheep dogs, to use a common phrase. She was soft and compliant as a dish towel, and never challenged his body or mind in any way. Sex to her was a duty she had to perform once a month when he was in port, and never a thing of beauty or pleasure to be indulged in on a whim. She never sought it out, or seemed to enjoy it when he pushed her to make love. Every time they finished, he felt as though he needed to ask forgiveness for violating her sacred chamber and that infuriated him beyond words.

His arranged marriage to Lena turned out to be the biggest mistake of his life, but one he thought important at the time. Her father had a great deal of influence with those who ran the Navy, and he offered to help him move up the ladder quickly to become a captain. His gamble paid off when he became a young relief captain shortly after their marriage. After the Navy's mistreatment of him, he landed in hot water at home with a wife who showed no love or pity towards him, and offered no support or comfort in his greatest hour of need. She became an albatross of misery about his neck nagging constantly on his failures, forcing him into a very dark season of despair. Months later, she caught pneumonia and died an untimely, miserable death. At the funeral, he didn't have it in him to cry, because it was all he could do to keep from laughing. The death of this particular albatross set him free, and he vowed never again to marry another woman of Lena Johnson's temperament, preferring to go through life alone rather than chance another like her. As he grew, Johnny made up for some of her shortcomings as the brightest spot in his darkened world. Lena exists only in his mind now as an object of pity and the palest of memories from another time.

Maybe he needed this unpleasant flashback to compare and contrast the two women, forcing memories of Lena forever from his mind. Heaven has seen fit to grant him another chance at true love and fulfillment the way it was intended, and he was going to enjoy this moment with every ounce of strength and desire his body could muster. With his last breath, he would love and adore this woman above all others as their life together began tonight in earnest.

Chapter IV

As the morning sun danced it's pleasant flickering light on Anne Temple's brow through the curtains in her room, she smiled gently as if nature itself was trying to rouse her from her dreamlike state. Was last night a dream, or was it real? The only thing left to do was roll over and verify if James Temple was truly in her bed. With outstretched arm, she rolled over expecting his strong muscular presence to still be there, but there was no one. She jumped instantly from the bed confused, wondering where she was. And where were her clothes?

Sitting down on the couch, she began to recount the events of last night over in her head. That's when she remembered starting out in another room across the hall. Then it dawned on her,...this is Henry's room! Wrapping the sheet tightly around herself, she opened the door slowly and peeked outside to see if anyone was lingering there. Quickly she marched across the hall only to discover that door closed and locked. Knocking upon it brought no response, and she darted back to Henry's room to ponder her next move. Once back inside behind closed doors, she began pillaging Henry's things trying to find something to wear. That's when she saw the note prominently displayed on the dresser addressed to 'Mrs. James Temple,' and it pleased her. Opening the letter she began reading.

Anne darling,

I had to leave early, so forgive me for not being there when you woke. Please go home and I'll see you this evening. Not a word to anyone for now. It's best this way.

Your loving husband,

James

Anne held the letter to her bosom holding back tears, glad she hadn't dreamed it after all. He had accepted her ridiculous arrangement from last night in full faith, and she was, 'until death do they part', Mrs. James Temple. Putting the letter aside, she dressed in some of Henry's clothes and went home to check on Johnny and poor Aunt Mamie as instructed.

At the docks, James and Henry met Mr. Whitaker, and the unknown gentleman from the previous day. It was a nice day with good light, so looking over a bunch of men should be easier to do.

"Good morning Mr. Temple," Mr. Whitaker said casually. "Did you get any rest at all last night? You did appear anxious when I left."

James looked at Henry. Had he spilled the beans, or was it merely coincidental conversation?

"I had a wonderful night sir, and thanks for asking. Shall we have a look at our crew," James responded.

"Yes indeed, follow me."

Inside the warehouse, three hundred and eighty five men gathered and were milling around awaiting a chance to meet the future captain of this mysterious adventure. There were plenty of armed Navy guards at each exit in case some in the group decided on a different strategy for leaving.

There had been some large shipping containers placed together and Mr. Whitaker and James stepped up on them to see the men and speak to them. The other gentleman and Henry stood to one side out of the way.

"Gentlemen, may I have your attention," Mr. Whitaker said loudly holding up his hands to draw their attention. "Come around as close as you can so you can hear us clearly. We have a lot to discuss and a short time to work out the details. Please reserve any questions till the end of our opening remarks."

Having their attention, he turned the meeting over to James.

"Men, you don't know me, but my name is James Temple," he began but was cut off short in mid stream.

"Are you the Yank who lost his commission and was drummed out of the American Navy?" one of the men asked loudly.

"I'm your man sailor. You want to see the scars where I got thirty-nine lashes as a parting gift on the way out?"

"Well I for one don't want to go to sea with no has-been captain who's been washed out of the American Navy. If they didn't think you was good enough, I don't want on any ship with a man like that?"

James fired backed with a little banter of his own.

"If you don't want to go to sea with me, then go stand over there and the guards will take you back to your nice comfortable cell. After looking over your records last night, I suggested to the big wigs they should build gallows in here and hang the lot of you. All I see is a flock of misfits, criminals, and Navy rejects. You don't know me, and yet you've made a judgment call deeming me an unworthy captain. Well, I got the true goods on the lot of you, and I still think you need hanging."

The men broke out laughing cause he had them dead to rights. If there was anything a sailor liked and appreciated, it was blunt honesty.

"If any of you big strong sailors are afraid to chance the open seas with an unknown captain like me, then go stand over there against the far wall and we'll make sure you get back to your nice safe prison where you can serve out the rest of your days in peace and quiet. Now go on, git!"

The men grumbled in low moans amongst themselves until one of them finally spoke up.

"I'll go with you Captain Temple. I don't have any desire to go back to that rat infested prison as long as I got a fighting chance to go to sea. Where do I put my mark?"

That was the kind of remark James was hoping for. Sometimes it only takes one man.

"Alright men, that's more like it."

"What's our mission Captain?" another in the crowd bellowed.

"Did any of the captains you served under ever tell you before leaving port what your mission was?" James responded.

The man scratched his head before answering.

"I can't say that they did. Sorry Captain Temple."

"That is the right answer sailor, and I can use a man like you."

The sailor beamed as he turned around to show his fellow inmates that he and the Captain were on good terms.

"What I can tell you men is the mission we're undertaking is a very important one, and we need men who are not afraid of a good fight should the need arise. I see where plenty of you have had time at sea under combat conditions, but many of you haven't. I'll need veterans to steady the others when the time arises and keep them focused. Today I need two hundred and seventy five men spoiling for a fight to sign up for the fight of their lives. There will be men sitting over there on your right to sign you up. After you've made your mark, go to the tables on the far left and sign your will. If any don't make it back, your families will be looked after financially. Any questions?"

A little man in the middle of the crowd raised a hand.

"How much does my family get if I die?"

Mr. Whitaker took the question knowing the financials better.

"A hundred pounds," he answered.

"What if I just get wounded? Say I lose an arm or leg or some such thing," the little man asked.

"Twenty pounds per each body part," Mr. Whitaker answered again.

"Take me back to prison then, I don't want my old lady to get rich off me. If I die, she'll just marry the miller's son and raise his fat kids off my arse getting shot off," he bantered heading to the back wall for transport back to prison.

"I'm glad to see there is at least one honest man among you after all, and there he goes," James laughed. "Any more takers?"

There were quite a few more once an honest man showed the way. The ones who decided to leave were too old, or damaged, or sickly to contemplate the journey any way, but there were no hard feelings against the Captain for dangling fruit they would never be able to taste. In fact, one young man came forward to ask for guidance in making his decision. In his own way, he already trusted the Captain.

"Captain Temple sir, may I have a word?"

"Yes sailor. what is it?"

"I only have six months left on my sentence and I get to go home. I have a wife and a little one waiting there. What should I do?"

James felt pity for the young man as he saw him grappling with a difficult decision.

"Well, when you get out in six months, you will still be known where ever you go as an ex-convict, isn't that true?"

"Yes Captain, it's true."

"Sign up today and you're a pardoned man once you set foot aboard ship, wiping the slate clean. You'll get paid fair wages while at sea and the money you earn can be sent home to your wife and kids. Getting work once you're back would be a lot easier too because you're no longer a convict with a record. It's your call."

The young man stood contemplating his options.

"I'll sign up, but I fear I might not come back. Are you certain that my missus and children will be taken care of?"

Before James could answer, another man behind him answered for the captain as he slapped the man smartly on the back.

"Don't worry lad, I heard tell the miller's son is still looking for a good wife," he said slapping him on the back again. The gathered crowd began to laugh embarrassing the young man. He turned to the man mocking him and spoke harshly.

"As long as it's not you or any of your filthy kin, you pig."

"The miller's son's a distant cousin, just so you know," the man jostled back in fun, but the young man wasn't having any of his foolishness and slapped him hard across the left ear knocking him unconscious and down onto the floor.

"Anyone else got a distant cousin?" the young man exploded.

James looked down at the fallen man, and then at the triumphant face of the young father and was quite please by his actions.

"Quick, someone sign this man up. What's your name son?"

"Keely Potts, sir," the young man answered without hesitation. He didn't know it yet, but he had just become the poster boy for all the sailor's in James Temple's great adventure.

"Now that's the kind of man I'm looking for. If you don't have something in your life worth fighting for, then you won't make it back. Have no fear young man, you and I are coming back. Now you men make lines behind these tables and sign your name where they tell you. You're going on the greatest adventure of your lifetime, and when you come back, you'll get a chance at a new life with honest money in your pockets."

As the men made long lines behind the four tables, James called for one of the men to come forward and speak with him privately.

"Is there one among you by the name of Wallis Keye?"

At the far end of the last line, a hand went up.

"Come here sir, I need a word with you," James instructed.

Wallis Keye stepped out of the line and made his way around the others to see what the captain wanted.

"You wanted to see me Captain?"

"Yes I do," James stated. "I understand you're some kind of preacher. Is that true?"

"It's true Captain, but I'd be hard pressed to prove it. Prison does things to a man," Mr. Keye said flatly.

"If you don't mind me asking Mr. Keye, how did a preacher like yourself wind up in prison?" he asked.

"Well, I wasn't always a preacher Captain. I was once a sailor and the biggest sinner in my village. I always drank too much whenever I came into port, because I was constantly trying to forget what I had done in the name of king and country," Mr. Keye reflected. "One night in a drunken brawl, I accidentally hurt someone who got mixed up in our fight. There were a dozen men just like me fighting in a tavern, and the fight spilled out onto the street outside. This little snippet of a girl who was just passing by got her head cracked open by one of us. I don't remember doing it, but I got the blame anyway because my accusers were all the other men who claimed to be fighting against me. They all hated my guts so much, they thought it a good opportunity to rid the village of the likes of me. I wasn't a very nice man in those days."

"So you went to jail based on circumstantial evidence and false testimony?"

"That's about the sum of it Captain. Truth is, I might have done it, I just don't remember."

"So you made a jailhouse conversion after you saw the error of your ways."

"Something like that Captain. I know it sounds like so much corned beef, but that's how it really happened," Wallis answered respectfully. "A woman came by the jail one day to pass out literature and teacakes to the men in the local clink. She was some kind of a missionary I guess, but she told me that Jesus loved me. Since I couldn't see her and she couldn't see me, I told her she must have the wrong cell. I told her no one in the world ever loved me and I had the scars to prove it. Then she said the craziest thing Captain, she said, 'Jesus had scars on his body too to prove how much he loved me, and then she told me how he got them. Later when I went to prison, I asked permission from the Savior to come aboard his ship, and I've been a sailor under his watchful care ever since. Like I said Captain, it's a load of corned beef to most people."

"Not to me Mr. Keye. I respect your story because it parallels some of my own experience," James stated plainly. "What happened to the girl Mr. Keye?"

Wallis hung his head in shame. "She died Captain, three months after I went to prison. That's when the conversion really happened, and I hurt to this day for the loss of that little girl's life. I went in for one year, and once she died, the court gave me ten more. I still have five years left to go."

"How old are you Mr. Keye?"

"I'm forty nine sir, but I think I can still pull my own weight. I was a pretty good gunner in my day," he replied.

"Do you think you can teach these men how to shoot a cannon?"

"I'll make fine gunners of them all, if you give me half a chance sir," Wallis said proudly, "and the ones who don't cut it, I'll personally throw 'em overboard myself."

"I don't want you to throw anyone overboard Mr. Keye, I'll just move them somewhere more useful if they can't cut it. Okay?" James said startled by the man's training techniques. "Are you sure you're a real preacher?"

"For the record, I'm a jailhouse preacher, not a trained one. Sorry Captain, I just slipped back into old habits, but it won't happen again, I promise," Wallis Keye said with a straight face.

"Can you read Mr. Keye? And do you have a Bible?" James asked.

"Reading the prison Bible made me a good reader over these last six years, but no sir I don't have one of my own. I read the prison Bible whenever I could," he answered.

"Remind me when you come aboard, and I'll have one just for you. I have a feeling you're going to be needed in the coming months. I want you to help the men spiritually, and once underway we'll have services every Sunday at dawn, weather permitting. Would you speak to them if called upon Mr. Keye?"

"These men know me already. Some think I'm nothing but a crackpot, but if you were to ask me, it would lend credibility to my claim, and I would consider it a great honor sir," Wallis answered as he snapped to. "Might even consider getting ordained once we get back."

"Do you really think one of the English churches would ordain you knowing your story?" James asked.

"No sir, but I plan on moving into the Baptist circles once I'm back in circulation. They're a small group, but made of sturdy stuff. I admire their doctrines and their lack of ritual. The Jesus I read about didn't care much for all that other fluff either. I think the Baptists would ordain a salty old sea dog like me without too much hesitation, and besides, the little girl that died was from a Baptist family. I can't think of any better way to honor her than that," Wallis said. "Anything else Captain?"

"No, that will be all. You'd better get back in line."

"Aye Captain," Mr. Keye saluted and went back to his spot in line.

James was pleased at his acquisition of a minister, even if he did have a questionable past. He could sense the man's genuine sincerity, and just hoped he was as good a gunner as he was a convert.

The anxious men wanted to know when they would be allowed to board the ship. Waiting till all those who wished to return to prison had left, he stood once again on his makeshift platform to answer their questions and explain what happens next.

"Men, you will spend the night here in this warehouse getting ready to go aboard tomorrow. Soon, you will eat and then you will bathe in the next building over. You will change into new clothes after being checked to make sure you are lice and tick free. Ship's doctor will examine all of you for anything else and determine your fitness for duty. We wouldn't want anything to leave port with us that can't be washed off at sea, now would we?"

The men laughed heartily.

"So mingle around till the dinner bell rings, and contemplate seriously your decision to come along. There is still time to change your mind if you wish, but once aboard ship, there is no turning back."

The men seemed to take the news just fine, that is all but one. The unconscious man Keely Potts had flattened earlier finally came round and wanted satisfaction from the man who knocked him out. As he began looking for his mark, James saw him and stepped in.

"Sailor, do you have a problem?"

"I want a piece of that no account wharf rat who got the jump on me Captain. He had no right to hit me like that," the man demanded.

"You were struck down sailor because you have a big mouth, and said a lot of stupid things about the man's wife. If you had said those things about my wife, I would have killed you. Now, why don't you go find the man, apologize to him and consider yourself lucky to be alive."

"I beg the Captain's pardon. Since I'm not officially in your little Navy yet, and judging by the fact my man over there ain't either, I would like to have another go at him to kind 'a square things up. Are you going to deny me satisfaction?" the man demanded.

"I'm going out on a limb trying to help you sailor."

"I'm not interested Captain. I want my shot at his head."

James knew there was no use arguing with him. When men bring those kinds of charges to you as Captain, there's really only one thing you can do, let it happen in a fair fight. So he climbed back up on the crates to announce the coming fight.

"This man demands satisfaction from you Mr. Potts. Are you up for another go at it?" James asked the young man.

"Yes Captain, but this time I won't be so nice. If I hurt him where he is unable to continue, will I be in any trouble? Now that I've made my decision to go to sea, I do not wish to go back to prison for another crime of passion," the man needed to know.

"Whatever happens to either one of you here will be upon your own heads, with these men as witnesses," James stated matter of fact.

"Then I am more than happy to grant his request Captain."

After bringing the two men to the center of the building, he made everyone back up to give them room.

"Gentlemen, here are my simple rules. In this fight there will be no eye gouging, biting or resting periods, and let it be known, that whoever loses will not bring this matter up again. If there is by chance a reoccurrence of this once we're at sea, I'll have one of you thrown in the brig for the duration. Do we understand each other?"

Nodding their heads in agreement they backed up and commenced to fighting. The trash talking began in earnest from the agitator as he began to slow march in a circle around Keely Potts.

"I'm going to bust you up bad and break your back when I get my hands on you. You ain't going home to your little woman either cause I got my eye on her," the instigator started jabbering by throwing the first official slurs of the fight along with his pathetic left jabs.

"You talk too much," young Mr. Potts said as he threw a hard right punch across the man's jaw. Down the man went crumpled in a big heap on the warehouse floor. James went to check his condition and discovered he was dead, much to his surprise.

"Fights over, Mr. Potts wins," he declared raising the young man's hand in the air. "Go get back in line young man. I'll call for you later."

"Am I in trouble Captain?"

"Not at all, now go do as I say," James instructed not wanting him to know what happened. If the dead man had any friends, the young man's life could still be in grave danger.

"Henry come here," James called out.

"Some punch huh?" Henry commented as he made his way casually over.

"Yeah, some punch indeed, the man's dead. Take a few of the guards and move his body onto the ship. When we leave port tomorrow, we'll bury him at sea. Slap him around some and talk to him while you're moving him to make it appear he's still alive, or we might have a mutiny in the building. Get at it quickly," James stated trying to keep a lid on things.

"Hey, where are you moving him?" one of the man's friend called out to him. "He's going to miss dinner."

"Oh, he probably won't wake up for some time now. We're taking him out to the ship where he can recuperate and think about the error of his ways. Don't worry, he won't miss eating tonight, I assure you," and that seemed to settle down any potential controversy for the time being.

In time, everyone ate good as promised. It was steak and chops for everyone and plenty of them. They rationed out rum too, but not nearly as much as everyone would have liked. The last thing they needed tonight was a prison riot inside these walls. Like it or not, discipline began now.

After dinner everyone took bathes which lasted up into the night, and were issued a uniform of sorts. Everyone wore black pants, but the shirts were marked according to what they did aboard ship. Warrant officers wore solid blue shirts with their black pants, midshipmen wore blue shirts with white stripes on the sleeves, while petty officers wore blue with black striped sleeves. On this ship, blue was the color of authority. All crewmen shirts would be black to match their pants with other colors of red, green, yellow and white on sleeves or collars to identify their status aboard ship. It would take a few days, but soon everyone would know the colors making it a very different kind of ship and work environment than they were used to.

Everyone with lice got a shaved head and a dosing of mercuric oxide known also as 'red percipity' for its coloration, and any itching was rectified with sulphur and lard. About half of the men had shaved heads by the end of the night, but no lice would go aboard ship. The many crates that James had stood on earlier contained bedrolls, blankets and hammocks for the men to be carried aboard ship and used as needed.

Since much of the mundane work of feeding and bedding had been left to the care of others, James and Henry left for the Boles estate to rest. By now, James was one very weary man having spent most of his night in the honeymoon suite embracing the bodily concept of marriage to its fullest.

In the meantime, Bob Kitchens, the dead man had been carried aboard ship and thrown off the opposite side of the ship to make it look like he fell into the water and drowned. The official story was he awoke, stumbled and fell disoriented to his death. He would be mourned at sea as is customary for sailors.

****

As Henry and James came into the rear entrance of the house, Aunt Mamie met them with an odd look on her face.

"It's about time you two came home. I've been worried sick," she lamented.

"What's the matter Auntie?" her worried nephew inquired.

"It's Anne. She came home after being out all night and went straight to bed. I thought she might have a fever, and when I went to check on her, she locked the door and wouldn't let me in. What do you think could be wrong with her?" she asked.

"Is she still in bed?" Henry asked again.

"No, she got up some time ago and took off with Johnny on another fishing excursion, but they haven't got back yet. For heaven's sake, I hope nothing's wrong with her," she moaned.

"Dear Auntie, I think Anne is giving you a little taste of your own medicine," Henry chided, "and it's a little hard to swallow."

"Whatever do you mean Henry Boles?"

"Secrets Auntie. How does it feel to be left out of things for a change. Cousin Anne is a smart girl, don't you think it's high time we brought her up to speed on everything that's going on. She has a vested interest too as you know," Henry stated plainly, and she did too in more ways than Aunt Mamie could possibly know.

"How much should I tell her. I've been trying to keep her safe with plausible deniability for her own good."

"She needs to know about James' mission first and foremost," Henry stated flatly. "You've kind of got ole' James between a rock and a hard place by swearing him to secrecy. Release him from his oath, so he can tell her, or I will."

James stood by waiting for the other shoe to fall, so to speak. He had a feeling before this night was over, a lot more secrets would be revealed.

In the background noise beyond the house, laughter could be heard in the distance as Anne and Johnny approached the rear of the great house just like James and Henry had done moments before. As the backdoor opened into the vestibule, they placed their fishing tackle against the wall. From there, the two happy fishermen entered into the kitchen with their catch as all eyes shifted onto them.

"Whoops! Did we accidentally break into another one of your secret meetings?" Anne asked putting her hand to her mouth. "Come on Johnny, we'll go out to the barn and clean our fish."

Aunt Mamie was looking more frumphed now than usual at Anne, while James' face showed only delight at seeing his wife again. Henry was merely watching their faces and enjoying the moment.

"Don't go cousin, we were just talking about you. Please come in and set a spell. Auntie and I wish to talk with you. James, would you and Johnny give us a few moments alone?"

"Come on son, let's go clean your fish and you can tell me all about your day," James said to Johnny as they turned about and went to the spot reserved for cleaning fish behind the barn.

"Father, is Miss Anne in trouble?" Johnny asked reluctant to leave the room.

"No son, she's a big girl and quite capable of taking care of herself. I think this is a family matter meant for her ears only."

"I'll be just right outside if you need me Miss Anne cleaning our fish," Johnny piped up showing his growing concern for her well being. His desire to protect someone he loved looked very similar to his father's.

"Thanks sailor, and don't forget to tell your father who caught the biggest fish," Anne smiled as they disappeared from sight.

Once out of earshot, their meeting began in earnest.

"Come Anne and sit with us. Against my better judgment, Henry thinks we should talk. Would you like some tea first before we begin?" Auntie asked being ever the gracious host.

"Yes, I believe I would Aunt Mamie," she answered kissing her troubled Aunt on the forehead. After a moment to satisfy the sugar and cream needs of good English tea, they began.

So from the very beginning, Aunt Mamie began to unravel the whole adventure, and it seemed to get bigger and bigger with the telling. If scheming a Naval vessel from the Admiralty on this crazy quest wasn't farfetched enough, securing an ex-Navy captain to execute their plan was over the top. Did they really think they could succeed with such a hair brained scheme? Needless to say, Anne was fuming. Not only about the money spent, but rather how they were about to involve her husband on this ridiculous suicide mission.

"Henry, I'm disappointed with you most of all. I understand Aunt Mamie's desire to always get what she wants, but you're James' closest friend. Do you care so little for the man that you would send him off to his death so casually?" she pleaded.

"Anne darling, you're blowing this way out of proportion and diminishing James contribution to the effort. First off, James chose to go on this mission of his own free will before you came along, and he did so because he had something left to prove to himself. He is a man of the sea and a veteran combat fighter of the first order, and I pity any pirate who crosses his path. Furthermore, there will be five other ships going along and they will be armed as well, and just so you know, I'll be going along too. James is our ace in the hole, don't you see," Henry explained as best he could.

Aunt Mamie decided to add a caveat where she probably shouldn't have.

"Anne dear, you've only known the man for four days. I think by now it's obvious to us you're attracted to him, and in time, he may even take an interest in you once he gets back. However, at the moment, he is of far greater importance to a lot more people than he is to you and your silly schoolgirl crush."

Anne stood defiantly, and Henry caught her before she did anything stupid.

"Just so you know Aunt Mamie, I have a lot more interest in this particular venture than you know. I married James Temple last night! We spent our honeymoon across the hall from Henry, and I have to tell you, it was quite a night!"

Aunt Mamie's eyes bugged out as she gasped and passed out, falling from her chair. Henry sprinkled water on her face and patted her hand till she revived. Looking glassy eyed, she tried to talk again.

"Anne, what have you done? You barely know the man."

"Auntie, I've been looking for this kind of man my entire life. I know you've drained the swamp in Liverpool looking for someone with any sense to sweep me off my feet, but Cousin Henry brought me one all the way from Virginia that suits me just fine. He's handsome to a fault like many of the others you brought in, but unlike those court jesters, this one's got a backbone of iron. I won't be able to run over him and neither will you."

"You've always been a strong willed child, some might even say willfully difficult, but I never thought you would go behind my back to this degree without at least giving me a heads up of your intentions," Aunt Mamie stewed.

"You're a fine one to talk about going behind someone's back. I've lived in this house filled with your jaded secrets for three years, and you didn't offer once to give me a heads up about anything, even when it involved me. It wasn't until I suspected you'd involved James somehow that I cared two shillings about what you did, but things are very different now," Anne chided.

"Well be that as it may, you can't stop what has begun Anne, I won't allow it. We have too much at stake to step aside, and far too many fortunes at risk to consider pulling the plug on this enterprise. Go ask your new husband if he's willing to throw it all away at this late date, and see what he says. I have a feeling his backbone of iron works both ways Anne darling," Aunt Mamie finished her speaking as she stood up at the table. It was about here that the back door opened again and two weary sailors from the sea reentered the fray.

Anne went to James grabbing him by the hand.

"We need to talk," she said leading him outside away from everyone. Johnny stood with fish in hand looking confused.

"Come Johnny, let's see if the cook will fry up your fish for dinner tonight while Anne and your father talk," Henry urged trying to get the boy from the room before Aunt Mamie blurted out something unforgettable. James and Anne needed this time to themselves.

"Alright, but something mighty queer is going on around here, I can tell," he responded looking around as he scratched his head.

Aunt Mamie eventually left the room to consider her options hoping nothing changed for the sake of all who have invested so heavily in this expedition. It could potentially ruin her and those within her circle of influence if he changed his mind.

Away from the house under a lean-to shed, Anne and James found their place to talk. She began first.

"Hello lover," she said leaning in to kiss him.

"Hello Mrs. Temple. It's still Mrs. Temple isn't it?" he asked.

"Till death do us part," she answered, "and that's what I need to talk with you about. Aunt Mamie told me what she's conned you and

Henry into doing. I don't want you to do it James. Let's leave here and start over somewhere else. We don't need any Boles money for that."

"I can't Anne, don't you see. Everywhere we go, I'll always be an outcast sailor and you'll be married to one. If this comes off like I plan, then Johnny could have a real advantage when it comes to his schooling too. I've always had you and Johnny in mind from the very beginning when negotiations began in earnest the first night we discussed any of this. I just didn't know things would move along as fast as they did when it came to you," he said.

"Are you disappointed that I rushed that part of your plan ahead of schedule," she asked while walking her fingers up and down his chest. He kissed them tenderly to show he wasn't.

"I'm tired of living with the shame the American Navy branded me with, and the idea of walking down Main Street again with my head held high appeals to me. I might even get a captain's commission in the Royal Navy before this is all over, and believe it or not, that stills means something to me," he said openly hoping she would understand.

Anne stood very quiet with her head pressed against his shoulder. There were some tears, but nothing she couldn't cope with. She would not rob her husband of his opportunity at reconciliation, or shame him into submission. Her love for him was such that she would willingly submit to his greater need. She had just found the man, how in the world could she live without him if something went wrong?

"Alright James, as you wish. Can we tell Johnny about us?"

"Thank you Anne, that means a lot. Yes, we can tell him,...tomorrow. Tonight, I need rest and lots of it thanks to you and your late night antics. I haven't slept in two days and I'm bone weary, so you'll have to stay on your side of the hall tonight my love."

"Aye, aye, Captain," she smiled as she kissed him again and again.

Inside the house later, they feasted on fresh cooked trout with all the trimmings, and Henry got word to Aunt Mamie of the good news of James' decision to continue with the plan as formulated. She was delighted of course for the information, but more importantly, she was pleased to have harmony in the house once again between she and her beloved niece and nephew. They were for all practical purposes like her own children, and that's why she was leaving everything she owned and the company to their care once she was gone. She knew they both had good, sound judgment because they each had chosen James Temple for different reasons to be in their lives. Though he may not comprehend it yet, Mr. Temple was the last piece of whole cloth necessary to be woven into the magnificent tapestry of her life as well.

****

The next morning after a good night's rest and breakfast, James and Anne took Johnny for a walk. The boy thought nothing of it, because it was a beautiful day for it. Finding a log to sit on, they set Johnny between them and began to tell him the news of their marriage.

"Johnny, do you remember in the Bible where it says it wasn't good for man to be alone?" he asked.

"Yes father, Genesis, chapter two as I remember," Johnny answered quickly. "But you're not alone, you have me."

"Yes I know son, and I'm a very lucky man for the privilege, but God was talking about a man taking a wife. There are some things a man needs that only a wife can give him...," and he was cut off in midstream.

"You mean like sex," the boy blurted out catching his father flat footed and embarrassing the boots off of Anne.

"Well, that's part of it," James stammered out. "A man needs and wants companionship of the female persuasion in his life, but it doesn't diminish his desire for male friendship or time with his son in any way."

"Before we left Virginia, I kissed a girl in my school," Johnny stated matter of fact.

"What?" his startled father asked. "Why would you want to do that?"

"I'm not real sure, but I liked it. When we get back, I may have to look her up and do it again," he said.

"As you get older, you'll find yourself wanting to do that a lot," his father snickered. "God made men and women differently so we would be attracted to one another. You follow me so far?"

"If you're going to tell me you're attracted to Miss Anne, don't bother. A blind man could see that," he giggled.

"Well, it's more than that,...we got married yesterday."

Johnny's eyes bugged out with a look of surprise and excitement as he turned to Anne and grinned.

"You mean we really do get to keep her?" he asked as he hugged her sweetly.

"Aye, aye sailor. From this day on, I could be your mum if you'd like," she said.

Johnny seemed a little perplexed by the possibility of a new mother at this stage of his life. Even though he hadn't known his real biological mother, he wasn't sure he was ready to abandon her just yet. So formulating an answer, he came up with a different approach than what she was expecting.

"Would it be okay if I still just called you Miss Anne for now?"

"I think Miss Anne would be just fine," she grinned. "Maybe later, we'll come up with something better."

From here on out it got a bit more difficult as James tried to explain how he had to go on a special voyage without him.

"Why can't I go father? Wasn't I a good sailor on the way over?"

"Yes Johnny, but this is not a merchant vessel I'm going on. There will be no children aboard this ship," he explained.

Johnny looked puzzled and for good reason. As far as he knew, his father couldn't go aboard a Navy vessel and perform his duties anymore, so how could he go on such a dangerous mission.

"This is a very special ship built for a very special mission. I'll be back in a few months and tell you all about it. In the meantime, it'll be your job to teach Miss Anne all about Virginia."

"Alright father, I'll do as you ask."

"There is one more favor I need to ask of you son," James proposed. "I'll be moving into Anne's room down the hall tonight, and you'll finally have your own room. Will you be okay with that?"

"A sailor's life is a hard one, but I'll manage," he said as he took Anne's hand and placed it in his father's hand. "We're going to have a lot of fun together, I just know it."

****

James and Henry left the next morning before anyone woke, because each hated saying goodbyes. Arriving at the docks under cover of darkness, they boarded their mysterious black ship in disguise awaiting the arrival of their crew. Within the hour, the first of the men started coming up the gangplank single file reporting for duty. The prisoners had not seen the black vessel before that day, and it spooked some of them into thinking this was some kind of a death ship. Two hours later, all two hundred and seventy five men were on board and stored away. At ten o'clock in the morning two small steam driven vessels began towing the huge, black frigate out into deeper waters where she could make sail and get underway.

Upon the captain's commands, the able seamen went about their duties getting the sails a billowing while the less skilled sailors learned as they went along. In a few days, they would know their roles more readily allowing for rotation of the watch to begin. So for the next few hours, men explored the ship as it sailed along, storing their belongings in the lower gun deck and, generally trying to understand their roles aboard her. By two o'clock, James called a meeting from the main deck next to the mizzenmast. As the men gathered in close, he spoke to them as he leaned forward against the taffrail.

"Men, we're going out on a shakedown cruise for a few days to see how this tub and her crew perform. In one week, we'll rendezvous with a supply ship to take on supplies for our cannons, where we will begin target practice on an old hulk. Once I'm satisfied with our progress, the first leg of our journey begins. Once underway, there will be training in hand to hand combat and swordplay on the main deck every day until we reach our destination. Rifle training will take place on the aft deck, and I'm looking for any volunteer sharpshooters who can shoot from the high masts."

"Can you tell us where we're bound yet Captain?"

"No, but once we're finally underway, I'll tell you everything you need to know. For now I want every man concentrating on his training. Helmsman, keep a heading of south by southwest for now. Our new cooks have assured me that dinner will be served at eighteen hundred hours, so in the meantime try to satisfy any hunger pains you may have with beef jerky and hardtack from the galley."

Henry met with the navigators aboard ship and found half a dozen anxious to work with him. It would be of monumental importance to have more than one aboard in the event of an unnatural death. So for the next few days, the black ship and her crew were put through their paces allowing the men the opportunity to get their sea legs back under them. It had been a long time for many of them, and the roll of the sea felt good beneath their feet.

At the end of the week, the black ship rendezvoused on schedule with their supply ship. They dropped sea anchors and all sail within a hundred yards of the old ship that had been towed out to sea for their use. After loading gunpowder and cannonballs aboard for target practice, the supply ship disappeared from sight. Within the hour, cannon practice began in earnest with Wallis Keye as master instructor.

"How many of you ever fired a cannon before?" he asked as hands went up all around him. "How many of you ever fired a cannon in battle?" Only a few hands went down. "Good, now we can begin."

Taking the more seasoned gunners from among them, he broke them up into groups of four. Forty cannon needed one hundred sixty men to fire them and each group should have at least one experienced gunner in the midst to see that things are done right. Mr. Keye continued.

"We're going to fire one of these beast in a minute so everyone can experience the roar she makes. Before the day is over, we'll be doing broadsides in volley's making some real noise. Each one of you will take pieces of waxed cotton and pack it deep into your ears to help deaden the sound. Once I'm done with you, a crew should be able to load and fire a cannon every ninety seconds. Now let's fire off one of those twenty four pounders and begin today's lesson," instructed Mr. Keye. James could tell he was the real deal, by his training experience and how confident he was around the cannon and men.

As the experienced men gathered round, they began loading the cannon as the others watched. Though it had been a while for most of the men, they snapped to like it had only been yesterday since firing their last volley.

"FIRE IN THE HOLD!" screamed Mr. Keye as he fired off the twenty four pounder for the first time forcing the cannon to roar to life belching fire and smoke across the water. The cannon ball hit the old ship square in the middle six feet above the water line for a direct hit. Amid the cheering, Mr. Keye lined the top deck with four man crews on each remaining gun and began teaching them the finer points of how to fire and care for their angry beasts of battle.

All day long the cannon roared to life again and again, and by the end of the day every man aboard ship had tasted the fury of the guns. There were only a few minor injuries as toes got rolled over by recoiling cannons or hands got burnt on hot barrels, but men learned even from those things. As James stood on the deck grinning, he ordered a mug of rum all around for such a fine day of training. Looking down on the black faces of the men sooted from the gunpowder, he made an observation.

"We will shoot our cannons again tomorrow, but this time it will be at night. So throughout the day tomorrow, you will spend time in mock training in an attempt to get our loading time down to Mr. Keye's ninety second mark. Our lives may well depend on the speed of our guns to reengage in battle, so practice like you mean it. Any complaints thus far?" James asked.

From way in the back, a hand went up.

"Yes, what is it sailor?"

"I came on board to be a cook. Do I have to be a gunner too?"

"Everybody on this tub will be required to be a gunner before this is over. Do you really think you'll have time to make a mulligan stew once combat begins? If you don't want to be a gunner, I'll have Mr. Keye throw you over board. I'm pretty sure I can find a replacement for you once we're back in port," James teased unnerving the man. He knew Mr. Keye would do it too had he been asked.

"Oh I'm quite happy to be a gunner if that's what you be needing Captain, forget I ever mentioned it," the man replied looking around nervously for where ever Mr. Keye was.

"I'm glad you see it my way. Now why don't you get cleaned up and help get supper for the men."

"Aye, aye Captain," the man said scurrying off to his duty in the galley.

From high up on the top mast, a voice calls down to the captain.

"Ship ahoy off the starboard bow!"

James grabbed his glass and ran forward for a better view. Of all the rotten luck, they have been discovered by a U.S. merchant vessel coming into the English coast for repairs to a broken mast.

"What are we going to do Captain," Henry asked. "We're not flying any official colors as such. As far as they are concerned, we could be pirates, and they'll tell the local authorities."

"I have an idea Henry," James responded as he left and went below. In a few minutes, he reappeared with a black flag that symbolized they carried the black plague.

"Run this up and see if there is any response."

In no time at all, the merchant vessel was giving wide berth to the shadowy black ship flying the black flag of death.

"I think when we meet our pirate friends, we may use this same flag as our official colors. What do you think?"

"I for one like it James," Henry laughed. "It does seem to send the right message."

****

All throughout the night, the mood of the men seemed very relaxed as they began settling into their roles as sailors again. It sure beat the drum roll of prison life. There was some music on board as the Irish played their flutes and little drums. Occasionally, a Scotsman or two might attempt to dance a highland jig amid the jeers and laughter of his peers. However, there were plenty who were just sitting around daydreaming about what it would be like to be truly free once again, and thankful to be breathing the clean salt air of the sea. Many were having discussions on what they would do once they were released back into private life.

"I'm thinking about going to America. I heard tell, they're looking for people to help settle the wilderness, and build railroads," says one.

"The only thing you know about railroads is how to rob the poor souls who ride them," another snapped back. "Don't you remember, that's kind 'a how come you came to prison in the first place."

"That was the last time, but not this time," he scoffed. "I'm a changed man now and done with that life, I tell ya. I'm going straight and Wallis Keye is going to teach me how to do it while we're on board this ship."

"I heard tell the Captain expects to give us some schooling too while we're aboard, with a real teacher," says one of the older hands.

"I for one would appreciate some learning on how to write a proper letter home to me mum, and tell her I'm alright. She don't know I've been in prison these past five years, and I'm not about to tell her now. If I learn to write and send a letter from some foreign port, maybe she'll think I've been at sea all this time."

And thus the talk went around the ship far into the night.

James lay in his bunk and dreamed too, but of far different things. He longed for the day when he would be able to hold his head up in public without shame, especially here in England. He hadn't planned on living here, but it's as good a place as any he reckoned, and Johnny could get a first class education. Who knows, maybe one day he'd get his shot at the brass ring too. And then of course there was Anne, his angel of mercy who had favored him with her love. All in all, he had very good reasons to dream.

****

The next morning, the captain sent for Keely Potts.

"You wished to see me Captain?" Potts asked standing at attention.

"At ease sailor," James began. "Tell me why you went to prison. You don't seem like the type to end up at the short end of a rope."

Mr. Potts didn't want to tell him, but James insisted.

"Alright Captain, I'll tell you," he began. "I was working on a merchant ship as a carpenter's mate, when I got into an argument with the quartermaster. I struck him and he hit his head on the center mast when he fell backwards, knocking him unconscious for the day."

"Why were you two arguing?"

"He was mistreating one of the crew."

"In what way, Mr. Potts?"

"He said my friend was stealing from the storeroom and threatened to whip him. He was going to the captain with charges when I stopped him," Mr. Potts continued.

"Was it true?" James queried.

"No Captain, it was about cards. The quartermaster owed my shipmate money from playing cards, but wouldn't pay up. He abused his authority by trying to intimidate the man through use of his whip. My friend was a small man of stature who worked the tight places on our ship, and the quartermaster was a bully. It didn't seem like a square deal to me, so I intervened," Mr. Potts stated plainly. "Captain, I hope you don't think I'm a troublesome man who rebels at authority whenever I get the opportunity."

"Well, it just so happens that you and I have a lot in common Mr. Potts," James stated.

"What do you mean Captain?"

"We've both had our share of troubles at the hands of quartermasters, and we both don't like double dealing. I was kicked out of the Navy by double dealers, and that's why I believe you Mr. Potts," James mused. "Now let's get down to why I called you in here. You see, I have need of your talents."

"You need something built Captain?" Mr. Potts asked unsure of his meaning.

"No, I need a man who knows how to fight. I need a trainer for those men who don't know how. Would you be interested in the job?"

"I'm a carpenter Captain, nothing more," Keely Potts implied, but James knew he was holding back because he had seen him work.

"Come now Mr. Potts, I've seen you move. You're an artist in a room full of mashers. Who taught you how to move and fight like that?"

Keely Potts bowed his head reluctant to talk.

"Come now Mr. Potts. I need you to step up. We're heading into dangerous waters to meet an enemy of indefinable evil, and I wish to give these men as much of an edge as possible in case we are engaged in hand to hand combat. I don't want an enemy to ever board us, but if he does, I want him to pay dearly for the privilege. Can I count on you?"

"I promised my wife I would not fight again after the quartermaster had me charged and jailed. She threatened to leave me if I did," the troubled young man answered.

"I assure you sir, she will never find out from me. What you will be able to impart to these men could mean the difference between life and death for many of them. Lessons begin after breakfast tomorrow, are you in?" James pressed.

"Aye Captain, I'll do as you ask."

"Good, now here's what I'd like for you to begin teaching tomorrow," the happy Captain said as he moved to one side showing Mr. Potts his training regimen. "Can you read?"

"Yes Captain, I can read," he said while looking over James' drawings and recommendations.

"Good, you teach them fisticuffs and how to move, and I'll have someone else teach the proper use of the boarding pikes and cutlass. I want them able and willing to repel men coming up the side or over the top as fast as they can. Fisticuffs will be a last resort when a man has exhausted every other weapon at his disposal. My personal philosophy is when a man can move like you, then he can go toe to toe with anyone. Your job will be to teach them to move, and move quickly. I know you understand what I'm trying to say."

"Yes Captain, my parish priest had the same philosophy when he taught me," he grinned.

"I suspected as much, but I'm shocked to find a man of the cloth behind your training," James laughed.

"He wasn't always a priest," Keely Potts beamed remembering when the priest was merely a local boxing champion trying to teach young misfit boys in Liverpool how to avoid trouble.

****

Tomorrow morning everyone was looking for something to do as the ship was anchored in position near the old hulk. With all hands on deck, James broke them up into three groups and began their training in earnest after cannon drills. From up high on the rigging, he shouted down orders for the day's activities.

"Rifle practice with our new Enfield muskets will begin on the aft deck in ten minutes. We have set up targets in the water and on the ghost ship for you to shoot at. Best shooter of the day will receive an extra ration of rum at supper, so use steady hands. Mr. Keye will supervise your drills with the musket, with everyman getting five shots each. In the middle of the ship, Mr. Potts will be teaching the manly art of fisticuffs. Every man will find a partner to work with, and any man who sluffs off will become shark bait. If you're quick enough, you might make it back up the sides with both legs intact. And last but not least, I want eighty men on the forward deck for sword practice and proper use of boarding pikes. We will practice the proper techniques for repelling and killing an enemy with whatever is available. Quickly men, before we lose the day!"

As the sounds of rifle fire began in earnest off the aft deck, Mr. Potts began pairing his men into twos and commenced with teaching basic blocks and jabs. While most fighting men knew some moves, there were always a few others who were very noncommittal to the training. After a few moments toleration with the slackers, Mr. Potts took matters into his own hands by throwing two of the laziest combatants off the ship into the frigid cold waters below. It had the desired effect prompting the two men to indulge in more robust activity once they climbed back aboard. One of the biggest men took offense at his actions demanding a real fight with Mr. Potts over what he'd done.

"Hey Potts, why did the Captain give you this job? You two got something going on in his quarters?" he laughed prompting the other men around him to snicker with their vulgar laughter too. It did seem suspicious that their instructor had been elevated so quickly.

"I did not ask for the job," Potts replied.

"Good, then I challenge you here and now for the right to teach the men," the big fellow glared down at him. He was a good six inches taller than Potts, but size alone isn't always enough against skill and speed that's utilized correctly.

"One moment please," Potts said as he yelled to the Captain on the fore deck. "Captain, a word please if you will."

"If you ain't the biggest willie I've ever seen," yelled the big man. "Go on bring the captain over here, but I'm telling you straight up, ain't no man on this ship big enough to throw me overboard if this turns into a free for all."

James entered the picture and visited with Mr. Potts in full view of the men.

"Yes Mr. Potts."

"This man has challenged my authority and by association yours too. He has hereby challenged me to a fight for the rights to teach the men. I will do as you command," he said.

"Can you take him Mr. Potts?" he asked in full view of the men.

"Yes Captain, but not without your permission. I do not wish to hurt him, since I have nothing to prove here," Potts answered.

"Alright men, here's how it stands. Mr. Potts will engage Mr. Luggs in the art of fisticuffs, and I will oversee the bout. Whoever the winner is, will be the instructor. Are we agreed gentleman?"

"What are your rules this time Captain?" Mr. Luggs asked.

"No rules Mr. Luggs. As far as I'm concerned you're an enemy combatant who has just crawled over the side, and is here to take my head," James instructed. "It's Mr. Potts job to make sure you don't."

The two men squared off as everyone backed up to give them room. Luggs was a big strong man, so he felt obligated to make the first move by lunging at Mr. Potts, but it was all to no avail. Mr. Potts was slippery as an eel and almost as quick. As Luggs slipped by him, Mr. Potts spun away slapping him hard behind the head forcing him hard to the deck. Luggs rolled over onto his back and kicked out at his man while trying to regain his footing. Once the big man was standing again, Potts came in quick and gave him two short left jabs on the end of his nose setting him up for a blast to the gut which brought him down onto one knee. He wasn't so big then. Luggs clenched his stomach, but not before lunging once again to grab his opponent's leg in an effort to pull him down onto the deck. Mr. Potts went to work on the shoulders of the big man by driving his fists into his neck muscles on both sides almost paralyzing his arms. Luggs let go as he tried once again to stand up on wobbly legs. How could be happening? He was the bigger, stronger man, but here he was in big trouble just the same. He was breathing hard now with blood dripping from his battered nose and hurting plenty. However, he wasn't about to give up without at least one more Herculean effort to rip his opponents head from his shoulder. All he needed was one lucky punch.

"You're a slippery one Potts, I'll give you that, but you ain't won yet," he growled throwing a wild haymaker at the instructor's head. Potts slipped easily under it and went to work on the man's gut once more with four swift blows in a row. Then he spun around and kicked the man's legs out from under him, dropping him onto his back with a loud thud. Luggs was unable to move and cried out yielding his attack just as Mr. Potts was about to put his boot across his mouth.

The men on deck stood bewildered as they watched their finest representative take it on the chin and succumb to the onslaught of this lesser man in what seemed like mere seconds. How was this possible? James stepped up with final instructions.

"Men, you have seen for yourselves how a smaller man can take a big man down. When you're in a fight with someone, don't plant your feet like a tree, rather move like a cat on the prowl, alert and reacting to any movement or sound. Mr. Potts, are you ready to resume your duties?"

"Aye Captain, I'm ready if the men are," he answered.

"Men, I know you've been cooped up in prison without any real exercise and your bodies are not combat ready yet for a fight that requires any endurance. I'm trying to give you every advantage to prepare for a fight with a brutal enemy we expect to meet in six weeks, who will show you no quarter or mercy. If you train hard, we win. If you chose not to train, then we die. After our night time firing exercises tonight with the cannons, I expect every man on board to make twenty laps around the deck every morning in an effort to get your wind up. Any man who won't run, gets no rum ration. Any questions?" James asked eyeing each man over thoroughly. "As you were then Mr. Potts."

"Come Mr. Luggs, your courage is unquestioned, now we practice on your skills a little," Mr. Potts offered helping the boastful combatant to his feet.

"Thanks Mr. Potts, I guess I really did need the lesson after all," said a humbled Mr. Luggs.

"The men look up to you Mr. Luggs. Work hard for their sakes and all is forgotten," Mr. Potts instructed and Mr. Luggs acknowledged the wisdom of his remarks.

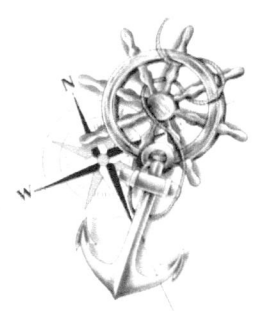

Chapter V

All throughout the day, the men continued working hard as they rotated in and out of each stage of their training. Gone was the reluctance and whimsy some had earlier succumbed to, and in its place came genuine desire for conditioning of the mind and body. That night cannon practice began in earnest as men practiced loading in the darkened recesses of the night without benefit of lanterns for fear of a fire. Range was approximately one hundred yards on the old wreck, but tomorrow they would move out to five hundred yards and practice. It was Mr. Keye's idea, and it turned out to be a good one.

"I've always wondered how far out a cannon could be effective. With Captain's permission, I've devised a little sight of my own design that I'd like to try out. If it works, it could give us an edge."

All the men gathered around on the upper deck that next morning and some up on the rigging to see the big gun work.

KA-BOOM!!!, the cannon roared to life belching smoke and terrible fire from its nostril like a Chinese dragon on the fourth of July. The ball fell short by a hundred feet and hit the water. Mr. Keye made an adjustment to his makeshift sight while his men reloaded the gun.

KA-BOOM!!!, the monster roared to life again, and this time the ball scored a direct hit on the main deck evoking cheers all around as the men applauded Mr. Keye's handiwork.

"Can you do it again Mr. Keye?" James asked. "I want to see if it can be duplicated."

"I believe so Captain," he returned.

"Then get to it," James commanded.

Mr. Keye's crew loaded the gun and set off another round striking the hull right at the water line where it's most effective.

"Mr. Keye, I do believe you have given us a real advantage with your little sight. How soon do you think all the guns could be outfitted," James asked speculatively.

"The first one took most of a day to build, so maybe three or four a day once we get going," he answered.

"Well, try to fit them in where you can, and well done Mr. Keye."

✱✱✱

The ten day shakedown cruise was coming to an end and things were coming together very well. James could sense the strong feeling of camaraderie and confidence building among his sailors as they came together in their quest to feel like men again. It didn't matter where they were going or who they were going to fight, it only mattered that they were free men once again. James Temple had done that for them, and they were beholding. As the black ship eased into a harbor on the far side of Liverpool and dropped anchor, there were ships awaiting to unload provisions for their trip into the Mediterranean.

"Why don't you go ashore James," Henry suggested knowingly. "I'll take care of things here."

"You wouldn't mind?"

"Not at all. Go be with her and give Auntie an update on our progress. I'll hold things together till you get back," Henry declared. "See if you can smuggle some of those French cream-filled éclairs back on board when you return. Of all the things I miss at sea, those soft little pastries are the one thing I most crave. I know that's not what you're longing for, so go on and git. Visit with Mr. Whitaker too and verify where and when we rendezvous with the other merchant ships."

"Will do Henry, and thanks," James exclaimed as he gathered up his coat and went topside. As the captain of the merchant ship came aboard with his bill of lading, James met him with a request.

"Good day Captain. I'm glad to see you are prompt. Is there any way possible to borrow the services of your skiff for a quick trip to land? I have business ashore."

The Captain grinned knowingly having made a few trips to shore himself when the opportunity presented itself.

"But of course Captain Temple. I am at your command," he said as he signaled to the men in the skiff to take him ashore.

"I'll be back in three days to get underway. In the meantime, Captain Boles will aid you in resupplying our ship. Thanks."

Over the side he went and settled down in the skiff for a swift ride to shore. Though he had sailed on some of the finest ships in the seven seas, he still loved the feel of a small sailboat and a single sail. That was true sailing.

By midday, James had arrived at the Boles estate unannounced with intention of surprising everyone. The only problem was, no one was home except Johnny.

"Father, father, I've missed you oh such much," Johnny cried as he jumped into his father's arms. "Please tell me I can go with you when you go back to sea."

"I'm sorry sailor, not this time. I only have a couple of days to be here, so where is Anne and Mrs. Boles?"

"Oh, they went over to Mr. Whitaker's house last night. His son and daughter-in-law came for a visit yesterday and they had a new baby boy right there in the house. You know how women are about such things," Johnny stated squinting up his face to show his disgust.

"One day when you're a father, you won't find it so disgusting," James teased. "Say, how about something to eat?"

"The cook went too, but I'm pretty sure I can fetch you something from the pantry to hold you over till they get back," Johnny perked up pulling his father by the hand into the kitchen.

Inside the kitchen, Johnny found fresh baked bread and jam, plus some leftover sausages and cheese from breakfast. That would have to do until help arrived.

"How's the fishing?" James asked his son.

"Fishing's fine, but we don't go every day," he answered. "Yesterday Mrs. Anne took me grouse hunting, and even let me shoot her shotgun. She's a good shot father, better than most men I reckon."

"Do you still like her son?" James asked unexpectedly.

"Yes father, and more every day," Johnny answered as he poured fresh chilled milk into a glass. "Do you still like her father? You've been gone for a long time."

"Yes son, I still like her too and more every day," he grinned at Johnny as his son grinned back at him. Both of these sailors knew they had made an amazing catch, and were quite pleased that she seemed very content to be caught up in their simple net.

As they finished catching up, they heard noises in the outer vestibule of the kitchen. It was the cook who came in first, and it shocked her somewhat to see James sitting and eating in her kitchen.

"For heaven's sake Mr. Temple, you could have given an old woman a little warning," she gasped clutching her chest as she turned around from hanging up her wrap.

"Where's the fun in that Mrs. Hilda," Johnny giggled as James laughed along with him. "Where's Mrs. Boles and Anne?"

"They're right behind me," she answered stepping to one side so the others could see him sitting there like a king in his robe and slippers as they entered.

James watched the two of them enter the vestibule laughing like schoolgirls at something Mr. Whitaker had said earlier. He only caught part of the conversation when they spotted him. Anne dropped everything and ran to him plastering his face with loving kisses while Auntie Boles looked on pleased by what she saw. She had hoped that their impetuous marriage wasn't just a fluke, and from all appearances it didn't appear it was.

"Well, Mr. Temple, I hope you have something to report after your ten day vacation on the high seas," Mrs. Boles stated slyly.

James looked over Anne's shoulder with a huge grin and answered.

"I'm happy to report, we're still afloat. We have met the enemy and he is us," he jested as he continued kissing Anne in her little game.

"Anne darling, if you could pull yourself together for just a few moments, I'd like to have a word with your new husband, if it's not too much to ask," Mrs. Boles teased, happy to see her niece so consumed.

"Yes Auntie," she said pulling herself away where he could see and talk without interruption, but she never let go of his arm.

"Johnny, could you give us a few minutes alone with your father? It's very important," Auntie Boles asked.

"Yes ma'am. I'll go upstairs to my room and read the new book Mrs. Anne gave me, but don't be too long," he answered politely.

"Good boy," she said as he left the room. "Well sir, your news?"

James cleared his throat and asked if he could have some hot tea brought in to wash down the snack he had just consumed, and hot tea came almost instantly since Hilda was listening at the door.

James waited till Hilda left before continuing.

"It's a fine crew Mrs. Boles. I anticipated some problems, because of where they came from, but I've been pleasantly surprised. Some are

91

raw and inexperienced, but they are a willing group of men who have invested themselves heavily to perform to our standard. They don't want to go back to prison for any reason, so by the time we reach our destination, they should be a first rate crew."

"That is good news Mr. Temple. I'll get word to Albert about your progress too. Now tell me how Henry is,...I do miss him so."

"Henry is at the top of his game. He sends his love and wonders if there were any way you could help him stock up on French cream-filled éclairs before leaving port."

"That young man certainly has a sweet tooth," she laughed. "I will see to it personally. Now if you will excuse me, I wish to go lay down for a while. I'm exhausted after helping deliver Mr. Whitaker's new grandson. Anne darling, I relinquish control of the good Captain back to your capable hands."

As Auntie Boles waddled out of the kitchen in her usual fashion, Mr. and Mrs. Temple merely laughed at her unusual antics. Once the door closed behind her, they picked up right where they'd left off.

✳✳

Galen Sims had taken a night for himself to visit some of the old pubs in Liverpool to see if he could dredge up a few old friends. Years ago, the quartermaster was not an easy man to like because of his slaving ways and combustible attitude. Some even dared say he smelled like the dead once the drink began flowing through his veins. Galen's darker side had been tamed somewhat since then, and he hoped to make amends. He soon found that most were willing to overlook his faults as long as he was buying. On this particularly noisy evening though, Galen accidentally overheard some things he probably shouldn't have between two foreigners as they sat crowded around a small table close to his. He listened intently to what they had to say.

"They have moved the black ship out of port as you predicted. However, I do not yet know where it is bound or to what purpose it was intended, but I will find out and report back as soon as I can. One thing is for sure, it was well guarded while docked," the little rat faced informer explained.

"You have done well Hakeem. I have suspected for some time now that something was afoot among the English merchants, but to what end? Since I have just arrived, I will have to meet with the others to get the bigger picture. Perhaps when I have enough information, I will send word back to Tripoli and Tunisia to prepare a special welcome should they decide to come through the Mediterranean again without paying their tribute," the fat man stated while stroking his long chin hair.

"I have one more thing for you," the little man whispered. "They have hired an American captain of questionable character to pilot their black ship. It sounds as though they may be planning for an expendable crew should something go wrong."

"Do you know who the captain is, or where I might find him?"

"No my lord, not at this time. I only know he was once a blacklisted Naval officer from America," the little man confided.

"Yes, I see it all now. One of my sources inside the Navy tells me they are preparing for a conflict. You have provided me with valuable insight and for that you will be well paid," the fat man declared sliding a small bag of gold coins towards his man. "I will contact you in the usual fashion when I need your services again."

"Yes my lord, and Allah be praised."

Galen watched the little man leave, marking well his appearance, because there would come a day of reckoning for him. He understood enough of the conversation to know that James Temple was up to something extraordinarily dangerous, and he wanted in on it.

Cautiously, the fat Turk stood and left the pub with Galen hot on his heels to see where he went. The foreigner meandered all over the city as if someone was following him. Galen wondered if the man saw him, or was he just the suspicious type? As he turned a darkened corner, a hand reached out from a doorway placing a knife to his throat and drawing blood. He had certainly been seen!

Galen was an old hand at this kind of attack and knew best how to counter it as the struggle for life and death began in earnest.

"You're not about to run Galen Sims through, and that's the plain truth of it!" Galen shouted as he grabbed the man's hand and spun around to strike the fat man, pulling his own knife in the process.

The fat man stumbled backwards at this unexpected resistance and fell against the wall. Then he lunged again at Galen and they both fell out into the darkened street. Over and over they rolled on the cobblestone street with each man making stabbing and slicing efforts at the other's head in an effort to end the conflict. In a moment, they rolled up against a lamppost and Galen plunged his big knife deep into the fat underbelly of his adversary and pulled up with all his might ripping his insides to shreds. The fat man made one last desperate swipe at the quartermaster cutting the side of his neck near the jugular. Grabbing the side of his neck, Galen knew he had to act fast or he would pass out from blood loss. Standing wobbly to his feet, he moved back into the lighted area of the street and called out for help from a passing cab, leaving the fat man mortally wounded.

"I've been stabbed, help me to a hospital before I die!"

The passing cabbie didn't want to stop at first, but decided to help once the person inside the cab insisted he do so. That someone was Albert Whitaker.

"Let's get this man to the hospital as quick as possible. His wound is very grave," he said as he placed pressure and a handkerchief on his bleeding neck. "Tell me sir, how did this happen?"

"My name's Galen Simms, and I'm a quartermaster aboard the merchant ship 'Argyle'. My Cap 'n is Henry Boles. Find him and get him to me as quick as you can. I have information for him that's a matter of life and death."

Mr. Whitaker's eyes went wide. Whatever could this man be involved in that could drag Henry Boles into his problems?

"Sir, I own half of the 'Argyle'. Can you tell me what this is all about since Captain Boles also works for me?" he asked.

"It's about the black ship," Galen whispered softly as he got weaker and weaker. "I think they know James Temple is going to be her new Cap 'n, and they're preparing a welcome committee for him where ever he is going."

"Who are they?"

"Foreigners from Tripoli and...," his voice trailed off as he slipped into unconsciousness from blood loss.

"Hurry man!" Mr. Whitaker yelled to the cabbie.

In a few more twists and turns down the narrow streets, the cab arrived at the Royal Southern hospital on Greenland Street. In a matter of minutes, Galen Simms was deposited into the hands of the best doctors in Liverpool as they set about helping him fight the greatest battle of his life.

Mr. Whitaker ran back to the cabbie with instructions.

"I need you sir to ride quickly to the Boles Estate and find Captain Temple, and hurry back here with him as soon as you can. I'll double your normal fees if you're back within the hour."

With the crack of the whip, the man was off like a shot on his hurried mission. He didn't know the reason behind the hurry, but it must have been mighty important for this man to pay double the usual cab fare. He was soon at the front door knocking loudly.

"I beg your pardon sir, I know it's a late hour," the cabbie began as he stood at the front door "but I'm looking for Captain Temple. It's a matter of life and death, and I'll be needing a word with him on behalf of Mr. Albert Whitaker."

The butler went quickly and found James Temple in the library. He responded in short order after hearing Mr. Whitaker's name invoked.

"Tell Mrs. Boles where I've gone and of course my son and Anne," he instructed the butler and left with the cabbie.

Within the hour, the cabbie returned with his man and Mr. Whitaker paid him the double rate as agreed upon. In the meantime, James had located Galen's room and went in. Stepping inside, he could sense things weren't going so well for his friend.

"Galen, it's James. Can you hear me?"

"Yes Cap 'n, I can hear you," he whispered softly.

"I'm not a captain anymore, remember? I'm just a sailor."

"I heard the man say you were the Cap 'n of the black ship. Did he lie?" the quartermaster asked. He would have hated to die without knowing the truth of it. "Tell me true Cap 'n."

Reluctantly he answered. "Alright Galen, it's true. Now what's it all about, can you tell me what's going on?"

"I always knew you'd make it back," he grinned.

Galen took a deep breath and told his story. The only thing he didn't know was whether or not the man he fought with still lived. If he did, then he may have conveyed his message to someone just as he too had done, and all this pain and bloodshed would have been for naught.

"Galen, you've done something extraordinary above and beyond the call of duty, and I thank you for it," James said clutching his friend's hand.

"It was purely an accident the way it happened Cap 'n," Galen said taking no real credit for anything. "The fat man was an Arab or a Turk judging by his language. Can you tell me anything about it?"

"I can tell you this Galen, you are right now in the center of the first action. When I get back, I'll tell you everything and we'll compare notes. Now lay back and get some rest."

"I am kind of tired. Bleeding like that sure takes a lot out of a fellow for some reason. Know this, by the time you get back, I will have found my little ferret faced informer and I'll save him for you," Galen said plainly. "He might be the key to an underground pack of them little snitches."

"If you find him, don't kill him,...Captain's orders," James grinned gripping his hand in friendship. "They'll see that you're well tended till I return. If you find your man, let Mr. Whitaker here take care of him, because he carries a lot of weight around here."

"Yes sir," Galen grinned as he closed his eyes to sleep. "Fair winds to you Cap 'n Temple, and dry sheets all the way."

Outside in the hall, Mr. Whitaker and James talked about this new twist in the plot.

"What do you make of it Captain Temple? Is this going to jeopardize our mission?"

"I like it better this way," James said unexpectedly after studying on it. "This way we're not going into it blind, and if they're waiting for us, we'll be more than ready for them when they appear. All the formality will be out of the way, and we can just go in with guns a blazing."

Mr. Whitaker liked James' can do attitude. He never felt more confident in the mission than right now knowing they had found the right man for the job.

When James arrived back at the estate, he brought Mrs. Boles and Anne up to speed on what had transpired. Johnny had already gone to bed.

"What do we do now Captain Temple?" Auntie Boles asked of him expecting some sort of game plan. What she got was the unexpected.

"Well, I for one am going to bed with my new wife Mrs. Boles.

96

We'll do our best to keep the noise under control, but I can make no promises," he laughed.

"In that case, I suggest you and Anne use the carriage house tonight. You couldn't wake the dead from out there, and it's fully stocked with food and fresh linens. Sometimes when Charles and I were much younger, we were prone to making noises while in the throes of young love. We scared the servants sometimes with our antics, and thus the carriage house became our best kept secret," she smiled and blushed with fond remembrances of those carefree days.

"Come along sailor," Anne snickered under her breath. "I wouldn't want you to get lost in the dark tonight."

"Sailors don't get lost, just so you know. They just scoop up their treasure and go somewhere else to play with it," he laughed picking her up and exiting through the back door. As James held Anne in his arms, she closed the door behind them. Through the glass door, she saw Aunt Mamie smiling with arms folded staring wistfully after them, and she blew a kiss to her. Mamie Boles made like she caught it and pressed it near her heart, happy that Anne was so well loved. James Temple was their future, and right now it never looked brighter.

****

The next morning Johnny was the first to rise. He meandered through the kitchen hungry for some of Hilda's sour dough biscuits, but found none.

"Something fishy is going on around here," he muttered under his breath as he ransacked the pie safe. "Where is everyone?"

"Good morning Johnny, " Hilda chirped as she entered the kitchen and grabbed her apron. "I could use some help, if you're available."

"What do you want me to do?"

"Check the back door to see if there are any eggs in the basket."

Johnny opened the back door to collect the eggs when he saw his father and Anne coming up to the house hand in hand. He ran to his father and grabbed him holding him close.

"Well good morning sailor. What gives?"

"Are you leaving today to go captain your black ship?" the boy asked.

James looked up at Anne with a little angst in his eyes.

"Does everyone in England know about the 'secret' black ship?"

Anne merely shrugged her shoulders not knowing how to answer. She knew she had not told him.

"I heard you last night talking about it when I came down for some milk and cookies. I listened at the door, but was afraid to come in. Can I please go with you this time?" Johnny begged.

"I can think of nothing better than sailing around the world with you son, but this is not the time for it. There will be other times for us, but right now I need you to stay here and take care of Anne and Mrs. Boles for me while Henry and I are gone. Okay?"

"Yes father, but I don't have to like it," the boy answered. "Can you at least tell me what you're doing, and where you're going?"

"No can do sailor, but when I come back, I'll tell you everything," James answered, but not to Johnny's satisfaction. "Don't be upset or angry with me. There may come a time one day when you have to make the same call. It's called Captain's privilege, you understand?"

"Yes father, but I still don't have to like it," he said storming off under protest.

"I have to go Anne. Will you please help smooth his ruffled feathers till I get back. This is the first time we've been apart in more than two years. I tramped around so often from one place to another looking for work that I didn't have much time with him. When I finally got a job teaching school, he came to live with me instead of his aunt. When I accidentally bumped into Henry after so many years, he offered me a job aboard his ship. I decided to take Johnny along, and it's been wonderful between us ever since," James said as he watched the boy disappear from sight.

"Don't worry James, he's just scared," Anne assured him. "And just so you know, I'm a little scared too."

"Stop fretting your pretty little head. You're married to a sailor who knows how to find his way home," he said as he took her in his arms and kissed her lovingly. "I'll be back before you know it."

And just like that, James left for his black ship to sail into hostile waters with a questionable crew to fight an enemy of immense evil and unknown strength. He didn't want Anne to be afraid, so he left her sounding confident that his mission was altogether a simple one.

However, it was far from simple.

On the way to the ship he made a stop at the hospital to check on Galen Sims recovery. To his dismay, Galen was not in bed as expected. He was gone, pants and all. Coming out of the room, he asked a nurse by the name of Dickens where he was, hoping he hadn't died.

"If he's not in his room, then I don't know where the drunken lout is. All I have to say is good riddance to him and his eight octopus hands. That was the rudest, stubbornest man I've ever had the unpleasant honor of knowing," Nurse Dickens fumed. "Were any of his things left in the room?"

"No, I don't think so," James answered.

"Good,...then it's my hope the heathen sailor won't be coming back anytime soon." And just like that she disappeared into another room ending their conversation. James followed her once more into the room because he needed more information.

"So he didn't die?" he asked.

"I couldn't be so lucky," she snapped back.

James smiled knowing she had a strong case against a very unruly

man. Where ever he was, James hoped he was taking care of himself and going easy on the drink.

Arriving at the dock, Captain Temple realized he didn't have a skiff to ride out in and there were none available. Having passed the Argyle on his way in, he returned to it hoping to find a ride out to his ship.

"Ahoy, anyone aboard?" he called out as he stood at the head of the gangplank. From the aft end of the ship, a head bobbed up.

"Come aboard Skipper, what's your pleasure?" Galen Sims called out gruffly looking more like an Egyptian mummy than a sailor wrapped in all his bandages. James couldn't help laughing at his friend.

"And here I was thinking that only cats had nine lives, you old sea dog. Since you got a reprieve on one of your nine lives, you need to spend some time working on your manners. You left one of those nurses in a real fit of anger when I stopped to check on you. What in the world did you do to her?"

"I reckon she didn't like the way I squeezed her buttocks Cap 'n. I am ashamed of myself for doing it, but she had the nicest bum," Galen grinned. "Where we off to today sir?"

"Do you feel well enough to make this trip Mr. Sims? After all, you've had a rough night of it, even by your standards," James queried.

"I'll be well enough by the time we get to where ever it is we're going, I reckon. Please don't leave me here Cap 'n, I'm going stark raving mad walking the deck of this ship."

James could use a man of Galen Sims qualifications on this trip. He wasn't the mean son-of-a-biscuit he once was when they first met, because he had sorted out many of his ways, but he was still a strong fighting man and loyal to a fault. On many levels, Galen Sims had moved up the ladder of civilized living to become a very good man since his days aboard the slave ships. However, he could still use a little righteous tweaking in how not to appreciate a lady's bum.

"Very well Mr. Sims, get your gear. We're going to need a skiff."

"Got one ready on the starboard side, and my gear's already stowed away," Galen snickered.

"Were you planning on running away Mr. Sims?"

"In a manner of speaking I figured on running off with you. I knew you'd be along sooner or later," Galen snickered.

"Alright then, let's get to it. When we get under way, you sit forward and let me sail her on in. I don't want you to open any wounds and draw the attention of the sharks," James teased.

"Aye, aye Cap 'n, as you wish."

As the sailors set sail, the small skiff hugged the coastline to avoid detection, but it took much longer than expected to sail around the far end of the bay to where the black ship sat brooding alone on the water.

As they approached, James could tell something was off, because he didn't see any lanterns lit or men on watch. The moment his skiff bumped the sides of the black hulk, two men in Royal Naval uniforms and muskets appeared over the side declaring they were under arrest. Galen woke from his nap and looked over at James.

"What's it all about?"

"Let's go aboard and find out, shall we?"

Up the side they went till they got almost to the top. Galen grabbed one of the young sailor's forearm's and yanked him over the side. As the other tried to fire on the quartermaster, James pushed his musket aside forcing him to miss his target. James held onto the rifle and the young man backed up, drawing his sword to defend himself.

As they eased over the side, James spoke to the young officer before it went any further.

"Son, I'm Captain James Temple. I don't want to hurt you, but I need some answers. Where is my crew and Captain Boles who was in command of this vessel?"

"They have been arrested and taken ashore by order of Captain Longfellow. You are under arrest too Captain Temple," the young officer commanded as he waved his sword around.

"By whose authority have you done this? The Queen herself knows of this ship and its mission."

"Begging your pardon sir, but we have just come upon her after a six month tour of duty. When we saw your ship flying no colors and anchored in this most unusual place, she was for all intents and purposes under maritime law considered a pirate vessel. She will be seized and sold for a hefty bounty and divided among the crew when she reenters port," the man continued.

"What do you want me to do with him Skipper?" Galen asked.

"Leave him be for the moment, he's not going to hurt anyone," James mulled. Turning to the young officer he gave a command. "Put your sword away young man before you poke one of us in the eye, and go see about your friend before he drowns."

As instructed, the young naval officer replaced his sword and ran to help his friend. Once both men were back on deck, they were confused as to what to do next. Pulling their swords once again, they decided to retake the ship, and that's when the captain decided to act decisively.

"You men put those swords away once and for all, or so help me I'll take and spank you with them. Now sit down over there and be quiet so I can think. Galen, go below and see if you can rustle up something for us to eat. These poor fella's look like they half starved," he said, and they shook their heads in the affirmative.

In a little while, Galen reappeared with bread, cheese and the remnants of a lamb shank along with a little rum to wash it down.

The two sailors drank and ate like they were truly on the edge of starvation.

"A tough tour huh?" Galen asked as he watched the two men devour their food like hungry Vikings.

"We haven't eaten much for the last two weeks. Some of our food stores got wet, and we had to throw it overboard because of the maggots. Thank you for sharing your bounty Captain Temple. This will go well on your report at trial," the young officer said still trying to act as if he was still in control of things. James merely shook his head acknowledging his youthful vigor.

"Where's the glass?" James asked speaking of the telescopic sight.

"It's there by the ship's wheel Captain," the petty officer nodded as he continued eating.

Gazing out upon the landscape and open waters, James couldn't see anything moving and it disturbed him. That's when he decided to go below into his quarters. There on the door was a handwritten note from Henry.

"Captain Temple,

We have been boarded by one of the Royal Navy's finest and taken into custody. Have no fear for we shall return in a day or two as soon as this is straightened out. Don't leave without us.

Henry"

Henry's dry witted letter took some of the pressure off him. The only thing left to do was wait and see if they really came back. In the meantime, they would have to continue to entertain their two petty officers as any good host would.

"How's the wound Galen?" James inquired noticing blood oozing around the bandages on his neck.

"I think I've got a leaker," he answered while trying to stop the flow of blood with pressure. One of the petty officers offered to help.

"My mother is a nurse sir, and she's taught me a few things about dressing wounds. Perhaps I can be of help."

After a few moments of skillful care, Galen Sims neck wound was redressed better than new.

"What's your sainted mother's name?" Galen asked innocently enough after he'd finished.

The petty officer was all too proud to tell him her name, because she was indeed a saint to him.

"Her name is Carol Dickens and she works at the Royal Southern Hospital on Greenland Street. If you went to that hospital with your wounds, you might have seen her."

Galen closed his eyes and smiled as he remembered the boy's mother and her fantastic bum.

"I remember her well son. She was a good nurse gifted with many attributes well beyond those of ordinary women and was most certainly a saint just as you said. Please convey to her Galen Sims fondest regards when next you see her. I would probably have died, had it not been for her skilled hands and tender spirit to guide me in my recovery," he smiled as he looked over at James and winked.

"I'll give her your regards, and thank you for the kind sentiment," the petty officer replied. He didn't know it yet, but Petty Officer Dickens would need to batten down the hatches once he delivered Galen Sims message to his mother's ears. Unbeknownst to the petty officer, a gale force wind of contempt would blow through their house peeling paint as she remembered the quartermaster and his roaming hands.

All throughout the night and into the morning, James kept a careful eye on the horizon hoping at any minute for a resolution to the crisis at hand. The worst part of any sailor's life is the fear of the unknown, and James was working overtime to keep those fears at bay. On the morning of the second day, a ship was sighted way off the port bow heading their way. Unsure of who it was, James decided to run up the black plague flag to warn anyone off. If Henry was aboard, he would know the meaning of the flag and come alongside anyway.

In a moment, the big ship turned to leeward and departed over the horizon. James assumed they too were hoping for a bounty. In less than two hours, another ship appeared on the starboard side and came straight on, black flag and all. It was Henry for sure.

The frigate came in close to the black ship and dropped anchor. The men aboard threw ropes and began the process of pulling the two ships together so a board plank runway could be placed between them.

"Hello Captain Temple," Henry shouted over the din of noise as he ran along on the first stable planks. "Did you miss me?"

"Henry, you're a sight for sore eyes. Did you have much trouble?" James queried extremely happy to see his friend.

"When Aunt Mamie was summoned, she laid into them good and proper, and they arrested her too," he said taking a deep breath. "Lord a' mercy, the Queen's own man finally had to come and intercede on our behalf. It wasn't long after that they sent us on our way."

"Who's the Queen's man?" James asked wondering if they'd met.

"You met him the first day on your tour with Mr. Whitaker. He didn't give a name, but he was her emissary all the same. I still don't know who he is myself," Henry stated plainly.

"How are the men? Did we lose any?"

"Not a man, but it appears we have gained at least one," he said recognizing Galen from a distance. "Are you sure you want him along?"

"Just so you know Henry, our quartermaster might have saved all our lives. Come below where we can talk, and I'll tell you all about it."

"Before we go, I want you to meet the Captain of our abduction. He's a nice enough chap, just doing his duty and all that,"

Henry stated matter of fact. Waving to the captain, he called him over.

"You must be Captain Temple," the Naval Commander declared as he crossed over and extended his hand. "I'm Alexander Longfellow, and no I'm not kin to any famous poets who live in America."

James smiled at his wit, and he could see why Henry liked him.

"It's a pleasure to meet you Captain, and thanks for the use of your two teenage petty officers to guard my ship."

"They are quite the pair aren't they? They are eager to please and prove themselves," Captain Longfellow declared. "I hope they weren't too much trouble."

"Not at all, but they were awful hungry. If you can keep 'em fed, they should grow into something resembling real sailors in a few more years," James laughed as he watched the two of them salute as they went aboard their ship.

"How much do you know about our little enterprise Captain?" James continued. The way things were going, half of England would know about them before the week was out.

"Captain Temple, I just finished a long, hard six month tour of duty. I don't know anything about anything, and even less about your mysterious black ship. I mistakenly mistook it for a pirate vessel, and I'm sorry for any inconvenience," the Naval captain apologized. "Right now I'm tired and cranky and merely want to go home to my wife and kids. Whatever your enterprise is, I don't want to know about it and hope I never see your ship again."

As the last of the men and supplies came aboard, Captain Longfellow saluted the two captains desiring to cross back over to his own ship.

"Hold up one minute Captain. I have a small bounty for you to remember us by," Henry called out, as he took a small package from one of the last crates. Laying the package in his hand, Captain Longfellow opened it and smiled graciously as he saw a dozen cream-filled éclairs resting in his hand.

"Thank you Captain Boles for your generous gesture of friendship. Perhaps one day I can return the favor," he said to Henry as he turned and walked the board plank back to his ship.

"Well Captain Boles, is there anything else hindering us from leaving?" James asked.

"Not a thing Captain Temple," Henry offered back.

"Then I say let's make sail before someone else tries to board us," James declared.

"Hoist the anchor Mr. Sims and prepare to make sail!" James yelled to his quartermaster.

"Aye, aye Cap 'n," Galen answered. Though the sailors didn't exactly know who Mr. Sims was, they sensed enough from his booming voiced to heed his call when he called to hoist anchor and make sail. Over the course of the next few weeks, they would certainly come to know him all too well.

As the black sails unfurled once again, the wind filled the sheets giving the ship a mighty tug as the men cheered to be under way.

"What's our heading Skipper," Galen asked.

"South by southeast Mr. Sims," James answered.

"Aye, Sir,...south by southeast it is," the new quartermaster directed the helmsman, and their course was laid in.

James called Henry below to discuss plans concerning their

rendezvous with the other ships.

"We will rejoin our little band of merchant ships in six days before entering Gibraltar Harbor. Governor Gardiner has been informed of our coming so there should be no cause for alarm from the garrison there when we arrive," Henry stated matter of fact.

"Do you think you'll have enough éclairs to last the journey?" James snickered under his breath.

"Seriously James, at a time like this you have to ask a question like that? Just so you know, I am well stocked. Now tell me, what shall our flag of choice be when we meet our adversaries."

"I think I'm going to stay with the black plague flag. It seems very appropriate to our mission, don't you think?"

"Excellent choice old man. I say, would you like an éclair to go with your tea?" Henry asked as he poured refreshments.

"I say right 'o old man, I believe I would," James answered in that proper old English accent with his right pinky stuck up in the air as he held his teacup. This little act was one they performed often in their youth while trying to dispel the misery they shared as poor orphans. Neither could have ever suspected then that they would one day become commanders of a frigate bound on a mission of such great importance. As they sat reminiscing about the old days, James remembered something important.

"I almost forgot that tomorrow is Sunday. I wonder if Mr. Keye would do us the honor of directing our service?"

"Finish your éclair and we'll go ask him," Henry declared as he took the last bite of his sweet treat and drank down his tea. "Last one topside is a rotten egg."

Up the steps the two men ran like children onto the main deck and burst out the door at the same time startling some of the men milling around on deck. As they stood laughing at themselves, the men around them began laughing too. In short order, they soon found Mr. Keye.

"Mr. Keye, would you mind conducting our Sunday Services tomorrow morning?" James asked of him.

"Not at all Captain. In fact I have the makings for a real stem winder if you know what I mean," Mr. Keye suggested.

"Do as you feel led Mr. Keye, and I'm sure we'll all benefit from your wisdom and preparation," James replied. "As of today, you are my Chief Warrant Officer in charge of all weapons and training aboard ship, and the ship's official Chaplain. So go below and change your blouse to reflect your rank as soon as you can."

"Thank you Captain Temple. I'll do my best not to disappoint you," he said snapping to for a salute.

"As you were. Have the men made their laps today Chief?" James asked.

"They will run laps today before supper, or they won't get any," he stated matter of fact.

"That will be fine. Just see that it's done," James said as he turned on his heels and went back downstairs to study his charts leaving Henry up on deck.

"He's going to be a fine Captain, that one," Wallace Keye stated to Henry as he watched him disappear below. "I've seen them come and go, and the good one's always seemed to know how to motivate the men without fear. He's got the loyalty of every man aboard this tub for sure, because he gave them back their self respect."

Henry piped in to offer his two cents worth.

"Don't think for one second he can't be tough when he has to, because I've seen him. He chooses to lead by example, not by bullying his men into submission."

"Well sir, we'll do our best not to offend him then. If you'll excuse me Captain Boles, I have go below and change my shirt. We have a twenty lap run and some drills to run before supper."

"Hop to it Chief and welcome to the upper ranks," Henry bantered back.

****

In six days of good sailing as predicted, James' frigate met up with the convoy of five armed merchant vessels anchored off the straits leading into the Mediterranean, and all captains were invited aboard the black ship for a final briefing once they anchored. As they sat listening, James began setting the last details in place, and regaling them of Galen Sims' encounter with the Turk.

"As you know gentlemen, we will be in enemy water's within the next week, and we have no way of knowing if they are ready for us or not. I must know before we go in, if anyone has had a change of heart."

One of the captains spoke up meekly.

"Captain Temple, I have never been in a sea battle before. Do you really think we stand a chance against our adversary?"

"Did you receive cannons on board your ship Captain?"

"Yes, we have twelve new cannons, but what are they against a real enemy?" the reluctant Captain answered.

"Have you fired your cannons since they've been placed on board," James queried. "Are your men competent to handle them?"

"I am captain of a merchant vessel, not a warship. We have tried firing two of the large cannon in volleys, but the cannons are so loud we quit before our heads exploded. I am sorry Captain Temple if we do not measure up for you," the troubled man declared.

James was flabbergasted as he began fearing the worst for the other ships.

"Has any other captain here fired their cannons as you were instructed?"

Three of the ships had regular cannon practice after leaving port and practice drills every day since. However, the last remaining captain had not fired a single shot from any of his cannons.

"Alright gentlemen, this is how it will go. The three ships with the greatest degree of skills will go forward in a 'vee' formation through the straits with the two remaining ships following close behind in formation. Our purpose is to assist you in any battle taking most of the work upon ourselves, but we were not meant to be the only means of defense. I will send men aboard your vessels who will instruct you in the proper use of your cannons. We will remain anchored here for a few more days until you two Captains have fired every cannon on board your ship, and your men understand their duties, are we clear?"

"Captain Temple, I must protest," Captain Edgerton declared. "I understood you were sent here to protect us in these waters. I will not take this ship into harm's way if you now say we may have to fight as well. It's unseemly for merchant sailors to fight at this level. Don't you agree Captain Darcy?" Captain Darcy was the captain who had only reluctantly fired two rounds through his cannons.

Captain Darcy stood brooding on this sudden turn of events. He mostly agreed with Captain Edgerton, but he was fearful of standing against this unknown captain from the black ship. Finally he spoke.

"I will go along with you Captain Temple, but I don't like it."

"Do you have room for one more man aboard your ship?" James asked.

"I do, why do you ask?"

"Captain Edgerton has just been relieved of duty and his ship will be turned over to Captain Boles. You determine if he is of any service to you. If not, you have my permission to throw him overboard or put him in chains for all I care," James stated matter of fact. "In meeting with the owners of these vessels before this mission began, it was determined that I would have absolute control at all times. I exert that authority now. Any questions gentlemen?"

Captain Edgerton huffed and puffed his protest, but nothing came of it.

"Take him aboard your ship now Captain Darcy, or I'll have him thrown overboard myself relieving you of the trouble of his care. I also want cannon fire coming from your ship in one hour, or I'll relieve you of your duties as well. I'm sending two men to your ship to make sure you and your men are applying themselves."

"As you wish Captain," Captain Darcy complied.

"Gentlemen, I do not wish to seem harsh in my dealings, but I don't have the luxury of holding your hand throughout this operation. We are five ships of moderate strength, and one heavily armed frigate, but we are nothing unless we work together. My aim is to destroy the enemy should they attack, and I certainly hope yours is the same," he commanded. "Captain Boles, you will take command of Captain Edgerton's ship immediately. I want his men prepared for combat, so take Galen Sims along with you to see it through. Take two men from our gunnery crews to help in their training, and make sure Captain Darcy gets two men as well. We'll meet back aboard this ship in two days. You're dismissed."

The three captains who had seriously prepared themselves were almost jubilant at the prospect of a little payback for the many times they had been mistreated in these waters, but the other two captains not so much as they talked secretly among themselves.

"I have men on board my ship who are loyal to me. When they find out what's happened there'll be a mutiny," Captain Edgerton fumed as he and Captain Darcy eased down the sides of the vessel into the skiff.

"You better hope not. I believe that particular Captain would have you cut up for chum if you dare force his hand. It might be best to go along for now," Darcy replied trying to calm the raging tide inside his friend's angry head. "Admit it, you knew what you were signing up for."

"I signed on for the bonus, plain and simple, and I expect to be paid whether I'm captain or not," he spewed fire with each breath. "Besides, the Turk and I came to an arrangement that night before he died. If I delivered, so would he through his surrogates."

"You made a deal with the devil you fool. I told you not to trust that fat sweaty tub of lard after he double crossed you the last time. Now close your trap before you get me in trouble too. I want no part of this," Captain Darcy stated simply.

Captain Edgerton slid down into the bottom of the skiff with his bruised ego on display, still scheming and brooding for his chance at payback. He had no desire to sail back to England broke with his tail tucked between his legs only to have his title stripped from him by this unknown Captain Temple. He had too much at stake for all that.

In one hour, cannons began roaring off the side of both ships as had been commanded. It was going to be a crash course for sure, but they would eventually get it. In an hour's time, the cannons ceased firing from both ships as the gunners felt they had done their job. Some of the sailors had fired cannons before in combat, but not under these two milk toast captains. Galen Sims had gleaned that most of the men aboard ship had no respect for Captain Edgerton and some even warned him about the men who were still loyal to him.

"Tell Captain Boles to watch his backside and sleep with one eye open, because these are treacherous vermin," one of the men whispered to Galen at a most opportune moment. "There's only a handful of them, but they run the ship. Be warned."

"Would you stand with us if needed?" Galen asked.

"Aye Quartermaster, there's plenty of us at your disposal. There's much that goes on aboard this ship that turns our stomach, and we want no part of it. Tell us when you're ready what we should do."

That night, Galen, Captain Boles and half a dozen armed men set a trap of their own just in case the dethroned captain was feeling frisky.

In the wee hours of the morning as predicted, Captain Edgerton and some of his men crept quietly down the stairs desiring to overtake and kill Captain Boles in his sleep. Slipping the creaky door open raised no alarms as they approached the bed where he slept. They fired their pistols into the form sleeping there causing little white puffs of flour to rise up through the covering, it didn't take brains bigger than a cockroach to realize that wasn't Captain Boles.

As lights flickered to life around the room, the battle for command of the ship began in earnest as Captain Edgerton knew the jig was up for he and his men. He turned attempting to fire his last round at the real Captain Boles, but Galen Sims was having none of it as he jumped in between the two combatants taking the bullet and blast straight on. Down he went to the floor with folded arms as Henry lunged at Captain Edgerton with his cutlass causing him to stumble backwards towards the door. Captain Edgerton deflected his blade in the chaos and made a run for it up the stairs onto the main deck.

As the fighting continued in the captain's quarters, Edgerton's men began dropping like flies as cutlass and pistols came forth to play. It was a desperate scene as, scurrilous, sweaty men continued to fight hard for control of their ship again, but to no avail. Amid the groans of pain and death, Henry dropped to his knees to help Galen Sims.

"What in the world were you thinking Mr. Sims, by trying to bounce a ball off that hard head of yours?" Henry teased as he checked his wounds. They were critical, but not terminal. Pulling his friend away from the fight, he gave stern instructions to Galen. "You stay put."

Up on the main deck, a small crowd had gathered with boarding pikes hemming the renegade captain in until Henry arrived.

"Come on men, help me retake this ship so we can get out of here. You don't won't to lose your head to those Barbary pirates do you?" the captain bellowed as he pleaded with his men. This was his only shot at surviving the night, but it didn't appear to be working as the crew spurned him with their eyes in the dimly lit darkness.

"Turn and face me Captain Edgerton, or I'll run you through from the back like the coward you are," Henry roared.

Captain Edgerton turned with spittle dripping from his lips after fomenting a last desperate plea to his former crew. Sweat beads quickly formed on his forehead as he knew judgment day was about to overtake him. His plan to retake his ship had failed, but if he killed this pretender, perhaps he still had a chance.

"Ah,...Captain Boles, my last stumbling block back to being a full Captain. It'll be good to see you die upon my sword. You had no right to challenge my authority," he said lunging forward at Henry unexpectedly with his blade.

Henry easily parried the blow while pivoting to one side. He then slapped him on the buttocks and the crew broke laughing.

"It's too bad Captain Temple couldn't be here to see this. I think he would have enjoyed watching you come apart at the seams. He always said men reveal what they're made of under pressure. What are you made of Captain Edgerton?"

The angry captain lunged again striking wildly at Henry's head and hit the mizzenmast with his effort. Around and around they went about the mast as Henry teased and toyed with his catch. Captain Edgerton was quickly losing confidence seeing how easily Henry handled him. His hands began to tremble and shake as he saw his imminent death approaching knowing that Henry Boles could easily take him at any minute. He wished at that moment he had practiced his sword craft a little more intensely. Suddenly, he threw his sword down and raised his hands in a last desperate plea for mercy.

"I surrender Captain Boles," he declared.

"Come now Captain Courageous, we're not going to have any of that," he said as he slipped the fallen sword by the handle over his blade and flung it at the captain. "You started this little game and now you're going to play it out to the finish."

Captain Edgerton was frantic with fear. Holding his sword in the front guard, he positioned himself for battle. Leaping forward he lashed out with a series of lunges, striking out at Henry again and again in desperation, spinning and striking this way and that to no avail. Henry blocked and parried all his strikes, save one. He was struck on the arm by the flat of Captain Edgerton's blade with one of his wild flailing blows. There was no blood, but it was sure to leave a whelp tomorrow.

"Ouch! That one stung Captain. You see, with practice you're already improving," Henry acknowledged. "Come now, that's more like the spirit of the contest I was hoping for."

"You're all going to lose your heads if you follow this madman past Tripoli. They're waiting for you, don't you get it! Help me retake the ship men, and I'll see that you're rewarded with a king's ransom," he pleaded one last time, but there were no takers.

"Well, this is where we part company Captain. The only person here who's going to lose their head is you," and with those last words Henry gave a powerful slashing stroke alongside the angry Captain's neck with his highly sharpened blade.

The Captain's eyes went wide in surprise as his head slid eerily from his shoulder to the rolling deck, with the body following a few seconds later. Henry stuck his blade in the bloody stump of the sweaty skull as it blinked one last time and threw it overboard.

"Get this bloody corpse off my deck before it ruins the paint."

And just like that, Captain Edgerton was no longer in charge of anything, as his headless body was heaved into the dark waters below to feed the hungry sharks.

Henry was disgusted as he went below. Killing always seemed such a poor substitute for negotiation. It was obvious to Henry that the good captain certainly had something to hide, otherwise he might not have been so desperate in his struggle to retake the ship. Somewhere, someone had surely gotten to him, sweetening the pot on his particular kind of greed. There were so many veiled references about things he didn't fully understand, he just hoped maybe James could help decipher them when next they spoke. In the meantime, Captain Edgerton got less of everything he bargained for on this particular journey to the Mediterranean, including time to live.

Chapter VI

The following morning, Wallace Keye stepped forward to make a few remarks to the crew with his new Bible, he thumbed to the book of John, chapter three, verse sixteen and began his reading.

"For God so loved the world that he gave his only begotten son, that whosoever believeth in him should not perish, but have everlasting life," he began. "Men, we are about to go into battle and I feel it imperative upon my soul to ask you if you're ready to meet your maker. Some time ago, God went to a lot of trouble so we all can have everlasting life. I'm hoping this morning you'll take him up on his kind offer of love and grace if you haven't already. The state has granted us a pardon for the transgressions we have perpetrated upon our fellow travelers here on earth, but only God can grant us a pardon for the dark sins of our rotten souls. Why not make it a package deal and become completely whole in body and soul, because there may never be another time like today to make it all right."

Wallace Keye continued on for a few more minutes before taking a break to sing the song 'Amazing Grace' as his invitation to the men.

"Kneel right where you are men and ask him into your heart. You'll find the peace you've been seeking after a lifetime of sinning that's festered to an angry pus inside your soul. Give it a go men,...I can tell you from personal experience that you won't ever be sorry for your decision, cause I'm living proof it really works."

As James looked on, many chose to pray and knelt with Wallace to pray the sinner's prayer of repentance. Those who didn't may not have been ready yet for such a dramatic departure from what they were used to, but Wallace didn't shame them. He once walked in their shoes too, and knew they had not yet reached the tipping point of decision. He would continue praying as always for their redemption.

After they finished, Henry came aboard to tell James all that had happened in the night aboard Captain Edgerton's ship.

"How many did we lose?"

"We lost seven counting the Captain, and all of them his people," Henry answered. "I'll need to move a few men into their positions, but we should be alright."

"Very well, do as you see fit. I'm sure glad you made it through the night Henry. This adventure wouldn't have been nearly as much fun without you," James teased.

"It's nice to see you're all choked up about it," Henry jousted back.

"How's Galen, will he make it?"

"He's hurt pretty bad, but the Doc said he'll probably make it if he doesn't get any kind of infection. I'd like to borrow Mr. Keye for a while if you can spare him, cause I believe Galen and some of the others could use a little dose of spiritual comfort at the moment," Henry suggested.

"You're doing a fine thing Henry," James replied. "I'll send Mr. Keye right over when you're ready. While you're at it, send word to the other ships that we leave at dawn tomorrow. Make sure they understand we go through the straits single file allowing the eastern currents to take us in and we'll reform as soon as they're pass the worst of it. They don't call the Straits of Gibraltar a 'ditch' without just cause."

"We have three captains who have been through here many times before. We should be alright under their direction."

"Make sure they do their soundings. I don't want anyone high centered waiting on the tide to rescue them," James said lastly.

"Aye, aye, Captain."

Despite Galen's wounds, the mission had to go forward as planned. At dawn the following day, the ships anchors were pulled up from their moorings and secured as the sheets were unfurled for duty. As the wind filled the sails completely, the ships groaned with the anticipation of two lovers on a secret rendezvous as wind and sail met in tender embrace. Easily and gently the mighty ships began to move through the waters as delicately as an evening waltz set to music. Each helmsman became a willing dance partner as he nudged gently this way and that to keep his ship safe and moving in the right direction.

The merchant ships all had an English flag flying along with the flag of their company's crest attached beneath it, that is all except the black ship. At the right moment, James would unfurl the black flag symbolizing death on the high seas to any pirate who dared cross it. He hoped it would add another layer of mystery to their mission, and perhaps give them an edge playing on the superstition of ignorant men.

For almost three days after passing through the straits, the ships stayed in their 'vee' formation as instructed looking out over the open Mediterranean for any sign of trouble. Within ten days they entered their first port in the city of Alexandria, Egypt. There were plenty of ships of varying sizes there from other countries, and of course small sloops rigged in colorful sails gliding about the open waters near them. However, none threatened or seemed remotely interested. For a week, the ships stayed anchored unloading their trade goods, taking on silk, sugar, grains, and tea from the Orient that had been carried overland in caravans from cities connected by the Red Sea as far away as China.

During all this time, the black ship kept its distance while the five ships were in port. Some of the local authorities were a little nervous at the presence of the mysterious ship anchored in their harbor without a flag of origin, but Henry assured them the ship was there as their bodyguard only. Henry kept James posted on all their activities once he went ashore, while the men of the ship enjoyed the foods of the Orient that were supplied each and every day for their consumption. In fact, most had never eaten the varied array of dates, raisins, fruits and nuts before, and it took some getting used to as they consumed such a rich diet. However, curious as they were, none of the sailors aboard the black ship desired to go inland for any reason, because they too had heard stories of the mistreatment of foreign sailors on these shores.

At week's end, the five ships pulled up anchor and headed for the port city of Naples off the Italian coast for a load of wines and other exotic goods, stopping by Greece, Cypress and Malta along the way to deliver the wonderfully manufactured trade goods of English craftsmen for their use. The industrial revolution was well underway in England, but it would be a long time before these isolated countries would catch up to modern civilization. The English produced fine farm machinery and tools for helping these mostly agricultural states, and that made for good trading among partners using what they came with for barter.

As far as it went, a sailor couldn't have asked for a better tour of duty as they basked in the sun most days, and swam in the Mediterranean at will. The question in everyone's mind was, could all this effort and expense have been for naught? Amid their daily runs around the ship, the sailors were growing restless, whispering among themselves, 'If there were no battles, could our pardons also be revoked?'

Amid the downtime of loading and unloading trade goods, Galen Sims persisted in trying to make a full recovery as he inhaled the fresh sea air, and the rich Mediterranean diet to its fullest. Galen had actually been here before when he was more pirate than sailor, and he regaled his fellow sailors with plenty of his stories and sage advice.

"On the African continent, be careful with whom you do business with. One day they're your best friend, and the next day they're trying to kill you because you looked at one of their females. I like the Italians and Greeks better because they want you to look at their females. If things go well, they marry off their women hoping to bring the wealth of some rich unsuspecting landlubber into the family. Either way you go it's a dangerous crapshoot."

Collectively, the ships were in different ports more than a month and were once again ready to sail back to England glutted with their rich bounty without a sign of trouble. As they were preparing to make sail, a merchant met privately with Henry to give him a warning.

"We have enjoyed our business relationship with Mrs. Boles and the others in her consortium for many years now, and hope we can continue forever. However, you have been watched very closely since your arrival, so do not be surprised if you head into trouble once you leave. We still have pirates from the other side of the Mediterranean who like to plunder what they can," the merchant almost whispered as he spun his head around looking for treacherous eyes in the room.

"Don't worry friend, we came here looking for trouble. If it comes, we're going to send a message that everyone in this region will clearly understand. Our governments may have failed to come to an understanding concerning the act of piracy, but we're here to make our own deals. Thanks for the heads up. With any luck we'll see you again in the fall."

"Be careful young man and give Mrs. Boles my best regards. She and her husband were very good to us when we got started so many years ago, and I don't wish any harm upon her or her enterprises while you're here. God speed to you Mr. Boles," the man said as he shook the captain's hand.

Henry got word to all the captains to be ready for anything as they lifted anchors and prepared for the open seas. James always felt this would be the time for trouble because the ships were heavy with goods making a fat prize. As they left Italy and trimmed their sails for home, they noticed the complete absence of vessels on the water. Coming in, there were plenty of vessels plying their trade, but going out, there were none. A day later, they noticed on the horizon dozens of small sloops laying in a parallel course alongside theirs. This was it, the moment they had prepared so hard for.

From a tactical standpoint, these small, sloops were no match for them, but there were so many of them, and so many men ready to crawl up their sides. It was purely and simply a numbers game.

A hundred miles from the straits, the first of the sloops made their move attacking the last ship in the 'vee' formation on the starboard side. They probably knew of the black ship's purpose by now and James suspected this was done to draw he and his crew away so the ship in the front of the formation could be attacked in force. What the pirates hadn't counted on was the merchant ships themselves being armed to the teeth. James stayed his course as the ship being attacked began sending volleys into the attacking sloops wrecking unexpected havoc and mayhem upon the boats. The pirates had bargained for some rifle fire from the ship, but instead received a plate full of cannon balls that sunk many of their lightly built sailing crafts in short order.

The roar of the cannon started up on the port side far ahead just as James had speculated. His lookout in the crow's nest saw a larger vessel approaching on the horizon to assist the smaller sloops and it was formidably armed. This was their call to action.

"Man your guns men and run up the black flag of death, because this is what we came for!" James shouted as everyone scuttled about making preparations for battle like ants in an angry mound. "Helmsman, heave to port and take us to the front of the line."

James could tell the ship was fairly old and of Dutch design, but she was heavily armed with plenty of guns making quite a threat.

"Mr. Keye, standby on the bow guns and shoot for the mast when you come into range," James commanded. Although the guns where small, they still were plenty deadly. He had hoped to send volleys through the mast and rigging creating havoc on deck before they got into fighting range for broadsides. "Turn them loose Mr. Keye!"

"Ka-booom!" went the roar of the four small guns and true as it gets, Mr. Keye scored a direct hit on the forward mast up about half way. It was a wretched sight as the mast and rigging tumbled forward onto the deck below doing a fair amount of damage to guns and pirates.

"Keep hammering away Mr. Keyes, we need a little more time before we're in line for a broadside. Keep ripping away her rigging so we can slow her down some."

What the other ship didn't know was that Mr. Keye had made himself a very special sight of his own design that aided him in his tasks. Over and over again the little guns roared to life doing harm all the way out from a thousand yards as the sail and rigging continued to fall down upon the main deck crews. Soon the gun crews on the second deck were the only ones firing on the merchant ships as they came alongside, because those on the upper deck spent their time clearing away debris. Though heavily damaged, the merchant ship kept returning fire as best it could, but they were no match for such a heavily armed vessel.

"Hang on for a few more minutes", James kept repeating to himself as his black ship sailed into position to rake the bow of the Dutch pirate ship with a broadside aided by Mr. Keye's marvelous new sight. At the right moment, James yelled to his helmsman to heave to port forcing the great ship over on its left side.

"As your guns come to bear, fire at will!" he shouted and men on both decks followed their orders without hesitation. As the black ship righted itself for a split second, they opened fire.

"Ka-booom!" roared the twenty-pound guns on the main deck as their new sights lined up on the bow of the Dutch ship. The same went for the thirty-two pound guns on the second deck as each roared to life with authority. Not all the shells hit the Dutch ship, but enough of them did to generate pandemonium among the crew and her captain on all decks. No one expected thirty two pound cannonballs from that distance to rip into the second floor gun deck and bounce off their cannons and men with such fierce gusto, but here they came none the less destroying everything in their deadly path.

"Heave us to starboard now Mr. Duggan," James yelled to his helmsman so the other guns could come to bear on the ship as quickly as possible. That first volley had done considerable damage from seven hundred yards out as the pirate ship flashed big gaping holes in the bow forcing it to take on water. "I want this ship sunk as quick as possible in case there's another surprise over the horizon. Keep at her rigging if you can!"

The captain of the Dutch pirate ship knew he was in big trouble as he began moving away from the first merchant ship to his starboard trying to escape as fast as he could. He was also making one last attempt to give the incoming black ship a little taste of their own medicine with a broadside of his own before succumbing. However, it was not to be as his shots went wild. The huge gaping holes in the bow were scooping up huge amounts of sea water making it impossible for steady sight alignment. Without much of its sail and rigging, it couldn't turn as agilely as before giving the black ship every possibility at another barrage. James Temple took the shot.

"Fire as your guns come to bear. We got them right where we want them!" he yelled.

"Ka-booom!" roared the big guns over and over again as each gunner saw his opportunity to make a difference in the fight. Somewhere about half way through the barrage, a hot shell hit a magazine of gunpowder and the Dutch ship exploded at its center sending death and destruction to everyone on the second floor. Pieces of exploding shrapnel flew towards the first merchant ship it had engaged raking it with debris and creating small fires. The concussion of the blast blew plenty of pirates out into the open water including the ship's captain who was now cursing the day he was born.

There was no shortage of colorful sloops with single and double masts who were racing to their rescue, trying to collect the living and the dead as best they could. The ship itself was a ablaze from stem to stern with the occasional black powder stores exploding as the fire reached epic proportions. However, amid all the destruction, the pirates only seemed to redouble their efforts to board any and all of the merchant ships during this time of chaos. They seemed particularly fascinated with the black ship.

James turned every cannon loose on the little rigs blasting them from five hundred yards out as they closed the distance. They didn't score direct hits on very many, but cannon balls even at close range can upset a small boat tossing men and material over the side. Meanwhile, the other ships were doing a yeoman's job of destroying the smaller vessels allowing no pirate to board a single ship without paying a heavy price, and for that he was very pleased. After a time, all the remaining pirate vessels fanned out, turning their attention on the black ship. By now only a handful of small sloops remained in the battle, and they determined to come at him in single file from the front. It appeared their play was to make him turn to and fro firing his cannon again and again as he had done to the big ship earlier. They knew something at this stage of the game that he was uncertain of, the depth of the water and the hidden reefs. If they could force him onto one of those as the tide went out, he might soon be at their mercy. Even American warships had gotten hung up on those shoals years earlier, and on occasion had to abandon ship because of the reefs.

Wallace Keye came forward coated in black powder soot with one of his men.

"Captain, Mr. Wiggins has traveled these waters for years and he says we're in big trouble if we get caught on a reef. He said he knows where they are, and how to avoid them."

"Spill it man, tell me what you know," James pleaded.

"Aye Captain, I will. What they're doing is one of their oldest tricks to get a big ship to veer to the left or right and end up on the reefs. I reckon we're approaching the mouth of the trench, and anything that drafts more than fifteen feet could easily run aground the way we're going. We have to remain in the trench and don't move this way or that too much. I say stay the course and head straight at them."

"What's their strategy Mr. Wiggins? They surely are no match for a ship of this size and strength," James continued.

"They'll come straight at us and split at the last minute to come up under the guns and then try to board us on all sides with grappling hooks. The loss of their big ship hurt them some, but they were robbing big ships this way long before they ever got that monstrosity, to be sure. They play a numbers game Captain in hopes plenty will make it to the upper decks for hand to hand combat. They shouldn't be a match for this ship or her crew, but don't take anything for granted," he said.

"Thank you Mr. Wiggins. If you went forward, could you see the shoals you spoke of?"

"I need to go up high Captain. The water is clear enough and things are easy to see on a fine day like this. It's the cloudy days, and nights that gets sailors in trouble."

"Make it so Mr. Wiggins, and thanks for the heads up," James said patting him on the back. "Helmsman, keep a sharp eye out for Mr. Wiggins hand signals. He's going to be your eyes for the next few hours."

"Aye, aye, Captain."

"Mr. Keye, you've done us a fine service by giving us the perspective of a man like Mr. Wiggins. He'll be our ace in the hole as we go forward," James commended. "Now get up on the bow and give those little cannons a real workout. I want them to remember us."

Mr. Keye quickly had men at the bow firing the little nine pounders in earnest. The sloops and other smaller vessels were no match for the power of a nine pound cannon ball ripping through their hulls and soon the damaged vessels began moving to one side or the other as predicted.

"Prepare for a boarding party Mr. Potts!" James yelled as grappling hooks came up over the sides. "Men, grab your blades and pistols and do your duty."

Young Mr. Potts had accumulated a fine bunch of scrappers together to receive any boarders. They held the high ground, but only as long as they could keep it. With boarding pikes and cutlass, they began slicing and hacking at the ropes as pirates clung to them screaming 'Allahu Akbar' as they fell back into the sea to be sucked under the ship and drowned. Though no one aboard understood a single thing they were saying, everyone knew it didn't sound much like they were going to tea at a church social. James had placed a few sharpshooters in the rigging to help with the sneaky ones, because it's hard to see what's happening all over the ship when you're occupied with only one small piece of it.

A few remaining small boats still in the line of fire decided not to run, but instead offered themselves up as an obstacle in hopes it would slow the great vessel. As pirates jumped from their sloops at the last minute, they realized they had underestimated their quarry and now they were adrift in the sea a long way from land. For one thing, they hadn't counted on bouncing off twenty inches of hard, seasoned English oak and a hull plated with copper meant to withstand cannon balls. As the big ship rammed into one after the other of the smaller vessels, they were crushed like so many twigs under the foot of an elephant. They were debris and nothing more.

During all the fracas at the front and sides, one of the last remaining sloops had managed to sail in behind them without being noticed and a dozen or so desperate pirates crawled up their backside without so much as a whimper. They weren't screaming and clucking their tongues as they came over the rails either like so many of the others had done. As two of them fired a shot at James from behind striking him in the leg and shoulder, heads turned from the black ship's gun crews and they ran to meet them head on. One of the gunners ran to the aft deck's rear cannon and blasted their little ship with a round through the hull, and then added the other gun for good measure. It didn't take the crew terribly long to subdue the handful of pirates in their futile attempt at a covert takeover. Though James was down and out of the fray, he told his men to take them alive, and they were quickly bound.

In the span of half an hour, all the fighting was over and James called for the ship to pull up sails and drop anchor while he attempted to interrogate his captured quarry on deck. He had never seen Muslim pirates before as they stood dressed in the colorful loose fitting clothes of the region, but these were not a gay bunch. Their faces were hard as flint as they looked steely eyed at Captain Temple, knowing their fates were sealed.

"Is there one among you who can speak English?" he asked.

When no one responded, James gave further instructions.

"Alright then, take them and castrate the lot of them," he said in hopes of eliciting a response. "Maybe that'll take some of the meanness out of them when we throw them back into the sea."

Immediately one in the group had a moment of clarity as his eyes widened and he turned his head to spit, indicating to James he might have understood more than he let on.

"Hold up there. Bring that man with the gold earring forward," James directed. Eventually, he came forward with the assistance of a knife at his back. "Do you understand our language?"

"Your English language is the language of pigs infidel, but I have learned enough to grunt," he answered. "What is it you want?"

"First, I want to offer condolences for the loss of all your men and ships. I suppose there will be much weeping and wailing in your houses tonight without men to feed their families," James implied.

"Do not worry Captain, Allah will take care of our women and children for us," the man stated matter of fact.

"You mean like he did for all those dead men floating out there in the Mediterranean?" James pressed him.

The Barbary pirate spat on James for insulting his god, and it took all of the Captain's restraint to keep from cutting out his tongue and nailing it to the mast, but that would have defeated his purpose. At the moment, he needed the man's silver tongue to deliver a message. As he wiped off the spittle, he spoke sarcastically to the man.

"My,...that was very brave. Looks as though you have reduced yourself to the level of a child spitting on a playmate. Is that what they teach you boys in pirate school these days? If so, you must be a real terror among little children back where you came from," James queried evoking much laughter from his crew.

"You are no more than dung beneath my feet Captain Temple. I merely spat on the ground," he said smugly.

James was taken aback by the fact he knew his name. No one was supposed to know who he was, or why he was here. He thought of Galen Sims and the warning he gave, and knew there was must be a network of spies operating all over England at the highest levels. They would have to be rooted out once he returned. It was also immediately obvious this man was no small fish, but suspected he was a lot higher up the food chain than he let on to have access to that kind of information.

"You have me at a disadvantage. You seem to know my name, but I don't know yours. Do you have a name hero?" James questioned.

The man stood silent trying to intimidate his captor. That may have worked in the past on some of his victims, but not so much today.

"My name is of no importance infidel. Kill me and I go to Allah and the virgins will care for me as he promised. I will go down in history as a man who died in battle against the great Satan. My family will be rewarded and respected above all families in my village because of your great act of kindness in killing me," the pirate gloated looking around.

"Virgins huh? If I castrate you before I kill you, could your virgins tell the difference?"

The man's eyes widened as he shifted them away giving James a little satisfaction that he may have finally hit a nerve concerning the man's sexual prowess in the afterlife. Then he went on.

"Well, I have bad news for you Sinbad. I'm not going to kill you, but I am going to strip you naked and put you in one of my little skiffs so you can find your way back to whatever rock you crawled out from under. The idea of castrating you still has a certain appeal to me at some guttural level, because the last thing these waters need is more of your offspring floating around in it," James continued. "I'm also going to fly your fancy striped bloomers beneath our flag all the way back to England so the whole world can see how we deal with pirates on the open seas."

"Now look who is acting so brave against an unarmed man with so many men at his back. Give me back my cutlass, and we'll see how brave you really are Captain," the pirate said trying to tempt James into swordplay. With two very deep wounds to contend with thanks to the pirate crew, James knew he would be at a great disadvantage.

"Ordinarily, I would love to play, but since I have two bullets in me thanks to your back shooters, I'm going to pass. You see, I don't want to kill you, I want your leaders back home to know out how many men and ships you lost today. Go straight to whoever it is you answer to, and tell them the English merchants are not going to pay any more ransom for trying to do honest trade in these waters regardless of what any government may officially or unofficially say about it. We have just as much right here as anyone else does and we plan to stay," James instructed. "Tell them we are going to root out all their spies in England too, and hang them high for all the world to see. From now on, every English ship that comes into these waters will be fully armed and have an escort following in their wake. Take a long, hard look at that black flag on your way out and remember it well. The time for civilized discourse is over. We're not the great Satan you make us out to be, but we'll certainly bring death and destruction to anyone who wants some. Go back and tell them what I've said."

Having said his peace, James had the man stripped naked as promised and placed in one of the ships dinghy's bound hand and foot. He was then lowered over the side to the jeers and laughter of the crew. The handful of men with him who were left alive from the boarding party were also stripped naked and thrown forcefully overboard behind the dingy. Perhaps some quality time on the water would help them reflect on their career choices as they floated home in undignified disgrace.

As the captain and crew watched them disappear from sight, James took to the high deck to brag on his crew.

"From the looks of things men, you certainly earned your freedom today. The ship had very little damage as such, and we didn't lose a single man. Mr. Keye, your gunnery crews showed extraordinary talent in wiping out the enemy from great distance with your new sight. I assure you, the pirates didn't see that coming. Who knows, there might even be a commission in the Royal Navy for a man with your talent and experience, if you were to want it. Mr. Potts, you and your men handled the boarding party's with aplomb and great skill as I expected. Please give my regards to your trainer when you set foot back on land again. I see a bright future for you and all the men under your command. As a reward for victory, there will be an extra ration of rum all around tonight for every man aboard. Let's hoist the anchors and head for home, what do you say!"

"Three cheers for Captain Temple, the best captain we ever served under!" Mr. Keye yelled to the top of his lungs. "Hip, hip, hooray! Hip, hip, hooray! Hip, hip, hooray!"

James was sincerely moved by the sentiment of the crew. He knew the only reason any of this worked, was that two hundred and seventy five former prisoners made a rational, conscious decision to fight for something bigger than themselves. They understood better than anyone how precious freedom really was.

"Mr. Potts, please inform the cook I want some kind of pudding with our rum tonight. I got a sweet tooth that's acting up."

"Aye, aye Captain."

"Helmsman, give us a heading of west by northwest after we slip through the straits and get under way. Hoist the anchors men and get us out of here. Mr. Wiggins, go topside and guide us home sir."

"Aye, Captain," said he as he scampered back up to the crow's nest to keep a steady lookout for the reefs.

"Mr. Keye, you have the watch. I'm going to my quarters and tend my wounds. You know where I am if you need me."

"As you wish Captain. Mr. Potts, please find the ship's surgeon to tend the Captain's wounds," Mr. Keye commanded.

As James eased along the handrails down to his quarters, he could feel the soreness really begin to settle in. Even though he claimed the wounds were superficial, they still did damage to skin and tissue and hurt like blazes. He didn't wish to appear weak in front of the men, but he was certainly feeling it as he opened the door to his quarters. The adrenaline was slowing as his body returned to normal, and so the pain began rearing its ugly head. As he eased to the bed and lay down, he heard a knock at the door.

"Who is it?"

"It's me Captain, Gilley McDougall. I come to tend your wounds."

"Come in Mr. McDougall and close the door," James instructed. "I don't want anyone else to see me like this. We wouldn't want the men to find out I'm flesh and blood, now would we?"

"I reckon not Captain," Gilley answered respectfully.

"That's a fine Southern accent you have son. Where do you hail from?" James asked.

"Savannah, Georgia," Gilley answered with pride. "My daddy still owns a small cotton gin there."

As Gilley rolled James over for a look at his leg and shoulder, James continued to press him about how he came to be in a prison so far from home.

"I ran away from home when I turned sixteen and worked on my first packet ship. Then I joined the English Navy because the uniforms attracted pretty girls," Gilley began his story as he probed for bullets. "Everything was going along pretty well after a few years until I got into a fight with a superior officer over one of my girls. I never was much for sharing the spoils, if you get my meaning."

"How long did you get?" James asked concerning his sentence.

"I got two years at hard labor. I was about half way through it too when you came along Captain. As soon as I can, I'm packing my bags and heading back to Georgia. I've had enough of the British Navy to last me a lifetime," he answered as he continued to work on James' wounds. "You got much pain yet?"

"It's starting to hurt plenty. Do you have anything in your little bag of tricks for that?" James asked unsure of the young man's skills.

"I have some morphine tablets, but I'd rather not use them unless the pain is unbearable. I've known a few people who came to depend on them, and it really messed with their heads. I suggest after we extract the bullets, we try some warm compresses first to ease the stiffness. Then we'll make a poultice of extracted willow bark to help keep the infection at bay. That should do the trick."

"If you don't mind me asking, where did you get your medical training? You seem to really understand what you're doing."

"The British Navy put me with the ship's surgeon on my first tour, and I've pretty much stayed with it from there. I'm fascinated with all of the healing arts and some are pretty bazaar. I went to a Chinaman's shop once at a port of call to buy some herbs and he showed me how he used little needles to deaden arthritis pain and other minor ailments. If I could have stayed a little longer with him, I believe I could have learned lots of things that would help me relieve suffering without the use of so many opiates. Those opiates are bad for you," Gilley said.

"Why don't you stay in England and go to medical school?"

"Not on your life Captain. It's Georgia for me or bust. I can find a school in America when I get back home, or I'll just keep reading and learning to do it on my own," he answered matter of fact.

"That's a good plan son. I had a teacher once who taught me how to learn for myself too. Chart your course and stay with it, I always say," he winked at his young physician.

"Where are you from Captain? I can tell you're not British," Gilley asked as he continued wrapping.

"From somewhere in Virginia, or so I'm told," James answered.

Gilley's look and wrinkled brow told James he didn't quite understand he was discussing his orphaned status, but the young man persevered on with his work just the same. In a few minutes of digging, he had extracted the two round balls and placed them in a pan. After cleaning the wounds with carbolic acid, he spent some time working with the warm compresses and poultices. Mr. McDougal was satisfied with his work and decided to leave the Captain alone to rest.

"I'll come back in an hour or so, and see how you're doing. If the pain is worse, I'll give you something for it then."

"Fine work seaman, I'll see you in an hour," James said as he closed his eyes to rest.

As the black ship sailed casually through the straits and out into open waters, they came upon the other five merchant ships who were waiting patiently for them to arrive. Henry was beside himself not knowing what had happened to James. The standing orders were that no ship goes back once they were through the straits for fear of getting tangled up in something they couldn't get clear of. At the sight of the black ship, the five captains fired their small cannons in celebration of their victory. In a little while, all the ships captains had gathered back aboard the black ship to report to James about their damages. Captain Brooks began first reporting his vessel was the one who received the worst damage from the Dutch pirate ship.

"I lost a dozen men of good report Captain Temple. Had it not been for your long distant volleys that distracted her, I'm afraid I would have lost the ship altogether and many more lives. We were certainly no match for the frigate's cannons as she wailed away with those big guns. My crews are still trying to patch the hull so we can get back to England. With any luck at all, we'll be sea worthy again by tomorrow afternoon."

"Anyone else lose men?" James asked.

"I lost two men in the first wave, but they lost a lot more," Captain Vance piped up. "How many do you think they lost in total Captain Temple?"

"I venture a guess of six hundred or more, and dozens of smaller vessels, not including their frigate. They knew we were coming, but they didn't know how well armed and prepared we were for them. We caught them with their pants down so to speak, and gave them a spanking they won't forget. I say well done to all of you gentlemen."

"Speaking of pants, what's with the fancy striped bloomers flying beneath your flag?" Captain Hines dared ask.

James snickered as he began explaining how he had come by them. In a few moments of retelling the story, everyone of the captains was snickering some too. It certainly helped to lighten the mood from what could have been a more tragic affair. Each captain there knew it could have been their bloomers instead hanging from some pirate's jib.

"I for one hope they take your message seriously Captain Temple, because I don't look forward to fighting my way in and out every time we come into these waters. I might have trouble one day finding a crew willing to come," Captain Darcy explained.

"When we get back to England, our first order of business will be to start rooting out the spy network inside our own ranks," James explained as.

"I'm quite sure Captain Edgerton was in cahoots somehow with the Turk that Galen Sims spoke of," Henry stated as Captain Darcy worried whether his relationship with the Turk might also be found out.

"That's a good place to start. We'll need to look closer at the good Captain's finances once we get back, and see if we can't find some bread crumbs that'll lead us back to the brains of the operation. Again I say well done gentlemen. In a few weeks, we'll be back in England with our fat bounty. I hope you all get a bonus for the heroic way you dealt with the cutthroats. Sometimes, force is the only thing a bully understands."

"Here, here, Captain Temple," the captains cheered.

****

In the comfort of his bed, James Temple began fomenting a plan to root out the network that had so intertwined itself into the fabric of merchant life on the high seas. It would be risky and dangerous, but should produce the results he needed. After several nights of thought on the subject, he felt it was time to bring Henry into the loop concerning his idea. As Henry was summoned to the black ship, he entered the Captain's quarters with a quizzical look on his face. There sitting before him was a strange looking man that remotely resembled the captain.

"James old boy, is that you?"

"Arrrgh, it tis!" James replied in a raspy voice. His reddish, brown hair was mussed terribly so, and he wore a patch over one eye helping to make his disguise complete. He didn't look much like a captain anymore, but rather like a wharf rat used to working the rough end of the docks. "What do you think of me 'el Capitan.'"

"What are you doing in that disguise James?" Henry asked perplexed by a game he didn't yet understand. He knew James well enough to know there was always a reason for anything he does.

"I need to disappear into the midst of the working class to find the answers I'm seeking. Somewhere along the docks, someone knows something about who's the conduit to the Muslim spies. I want them."

"Alright, when we get back, you can dress up and play detective. I might even join you, cause it sounds like it could be fun," Henry smiled. They always played well together as kids.

"Not this time Henry," James began. "Do you remember the man Keely Potts killed at the warehouse?"

"Yes, poor man, what of it?"

"Well, I'm going to become Bob Kitchens for a few weeks and see if I can't catch a fly. It's the perfect disguise," James smirked.

"You better let me pass this by Aunt Mamie before you disembark on such a dangerous excursion. Have you forgotten you're married now and have a ten year old son. They will need to know," Henry chided.

"No Henry, the fewer people who know of this, the better."

"Oh no you're not! You're not putting that on me," Henry declared flatly with dead pan seriousness.

"Don't you see it's the only way Henry? You're going to bury me at sea a day before we enter port, and you got to make it look real," James instructed. He knew this was going to make trouble for Henry back home, but he felt it was the only way to penetrate the network of spies working in England.

"You have got to be out of your ever loving mind James Temple! I'm not going back to the estate and spin such a yarn. Anne would skin me and that boy of yours would cook me over an open fire and feed my carcass to the dogs," Henry bellowed.

"It has to be this way Henry, don't you see. If I go back as a hero, the pirate connection in England could find and execute me for what happened to their forces in the Mediterranean. This ploy could keep my family safe until I'm able to weed them out. In the meantime, I want you to bring Keely Potts up to the house for duty as a body guard to my family. He's an excellent carpenter, so work won't be hard to find to justify his stay there. Make accommodations for his family too."

"You've got it all figured out haven't you?" Henry chided. "Who else will be in our little inner circle of deceit?"

"Gilley McDougal, the ship's doctor will have to know because he has to pronounce me dead, and of course Galen will be in on it. He already knows one of the spies. Mr. Potts will have to know since he'll be needed to help wrap the dead body for burial. Galen will be my eyes and ears down on the docks and pubs. No one else can know," he stated.

"You trust those two men that much?"

"With my life Henry. Oh by the way, make sure that Mr. Keye does a yeomen's job over my body. I wouldn't want the men to think he was sloughing off cause I was laying down on the job."

"You're a funny man. Anything else Captain?"

"Yes, please send Galen to me tomorrow so he and I can talk. On your way out, send for Mr. Potts and Mr. McDougal. Remember, on our last day at sea before entering port, we'll have a burial at dawn with cannons blasting and everything. You must keep our secret safe," James stated matter of fact.

"Aye, Aye, Captain Temple," Henry said saluting his friend. "And you pray for me that I'll survive my cousin's onslaught."

"If it gets too rough Henry, you can take her aside and tell her, but not the boy. He might let it slip by accident, but she's a big girl who can take it. Tell her I love her more than my own life, and we'll be together soon. Whatever you do, don't you dare tell your aunt, cause I think her whole confederation leaks like a sieve. Now git before I change my mind," he said turning his back on his friend before he could be seen tearing up. He knew how hard this was going to be on everyone, but it had to be done, and hopefully they would forgive him.

Within minutes, Keely Potts and Gilley McDougal were in conference with the Captain. After explaining his master plan, each agreed to help and swore an oath of secrecy to keep it hid. A dummy had to be made to look like a body, so the two seaman brought in different items from the ship to help in the makeup. Once it was completed, the corpse was placed in a closet to await its grand unveiling.

Within three days of entering English waters, word had gotten around the Captain was sick with infection from his wounds. One day out from entering port, the black ship paused at dawn outside English waters to bury Captain James Temple who died at sea as he so prescribed. Henry took control of the ship and her crew as they sailed into port under cover of darkness just as she had left many months ago.

Mr. Whitaker was on hand and took the news really hard of James' death. He never meant for that to happen, but he knew the risk associated with a venture like this. However, he was pleased it had turned out so well for everyone on the whole. He was also on hand to give each man a full pardon granted by the Queen herself for services rendered to the Crown, and their services were also well compensated for. There were some who were asked to leave England and never return because of their crimes. However, if they wished to stay and serve aboard the black ship for the duration of another year, then their rights to reenter the country could be petitioned for again as long as they behaved themselves. Many chose to stay with the ship and see what the future brought.

As each of the others left, all were extremely sorrowful at losing their beloved Captain. In their minds eye, he was the greatest Captain England had ever known outside the likes of Captain James Gordon, the greatest of Admiral Nelson's officers, and he wasn't even English. It was a sorrowful day for the lot of them when they slid his body into the sea and they had to say goodbye. None the less, the men who left for parts unknown knew they had been given a reprieve based on James Temple's belief in them, and they decided then and there not to squander such a precious opportunity to honor him. Wallace Keye didn't have to, but he decided to stay aboard ship for awhile and watch over his little flock of misfits as long as they needed him. He had no home or family on land, having known only the life of the sea since he was a youth. His misspent life of sin had left him an orphan in the truest sense, but he was not alone anymore because of his faith in God.

After a long day and night, the last of the ship's crew had finally gone. James Temple waited patiently until darkness fell to slip off the ship where no one could see him, under the assumed name of Bob Kitchens. He left with pardon in hand and money in his pocket in the company of Galen Sims the quartermaster. He had a month's growth on his face by now and a head full of matted hair nestled under a sailor's cap, adorned with a customary eye patch in place. In the right light, he might have passed for the real Bob Kitchens too, especially since the man was known to wear a scruffy beard. He could easily explain the loss of an eye as having come by way of battle with the pirates. So off he went with a limp to begin the first leg of his journey of discovery.

After securing rooms at a local flophouse near the docks, Galen and James went pub hopping that evening in hopes of seeing the little rat faced Hakeem. In the meantime, poor Henry had his hands full of trouble as he dared to enter the grounds of the Boles estate for the first time since beginning their adventure together.

Anne ran to him and hugged his neck with concern on her face.

"It's good to see you Henry, but where's James?"

The one thing Henry could never do was lie to his cousin. Since no one was at home, they found a place of seclusion where they could talk without prying eyes and ears. In this private place he unloaded on her the whole story. James might get mad at him for doing this, but he just couldn't bring himself to treat her this way, and the boy of course. Aunt Mamie wouldn't be told because he knew she couldn't keep a secret that big to herself.

"I've got an idea how to prevent you and Johnny from being here when Aunt Mamie returns. I'll arrange for you and the boy to stay at a nice little country cottage I own far out in the country. Don't say anything to Johnny for now, and stay out of sight until I send for you. We've arranged for a man and his family to come live at the cottage so he can keep an eye on you. To anyone passing by, he will be nothing more than a workman mending things around the house, but he knows everything. Agreed?" Henry pleaded.

She didn't like it, but she agreed.

"Now go back inside and pack a bag for you and Johnny. Meet me at the hotel where you were married. Wait inside the lobby and someone will find you there. Act normally and don't say a word to Johnny, and avoid all contact with Auntie if you can."

"It seems cruel to leave Aunt Mamie to bear all this alone," Anne said.

"I agree with James that this is the only way. Besides, it will only be for a few weeks, and she's a tough old bird," Henry stated flatly.

That evening as planned, Anne went into the hotel lobby and waited only a few minutes. A man of courage named Keely Potts met her and Johnny and loaded them into a carriage with curtains on the windows and headed out of town. He knew the location of the cottage well and scurried them out there as quick as possible. The next day his family would arrive and take up residence with Anne and Johnny at the little cottage. Anne tried to act excited as planned so Johnny wouldn't become suspicious. Thankfully Aunt Mamie had been to Yorkshire for several days to visit friends and wasn't home at the time of their departure.

On the day she arrived home, Mr. Whitaker came to visit looking ever so dour. Once inside the library he began to explain the reason for his sad demeanor.

"I'm sorry to have to tell you this Mamie, but we've lost our brave Captain. He died from wounds received in battle so I'm told, and was buried at sea as he requested. My heart is very heavy for your loss," he said as tears formed heavily in his eyes. Mr. Whitaker had taken a real liking to the young man on so many levels and considered him an equal.

Mamie Boles broke down and cried in a very restrained fashion that only a cultured woman could. She was holding back the floodgate of raging tears and anger with a stiff upper lip at losing this great man on such a foolish journey of her own folly. How would she ever be able to look into the eyes of her niece again? She needed her at a time like this to ask for her forgiveness, but where was she? All she could assume was that she must be somewhere in mourning with the boy. Since Henry had not been seen either, perhaps he was with her too.

As Mr. Whitaker and Aunt Mamie sat in the darkness weeping and comforting one another, Anne and Johnny had long since arrived at the cottage to begin the next leg of their journey of deception. She said it was time to do some grouse hunting and Johnny went right along with it without blinking an eye. So for the next few days, they hunted birds with Keely Potts' Welsh Springer Spaniel as he watched over them and worked about the cottage. All they could do now was pray it didn't take too long for James to catch his golden snitch.

Chapter VII

Through his contacts, Galen Sims had arranged for James to hire on with a crew of sailors who often worked on Captain Edgerton's ship. Since they were shorthanded now by seven men and one poor departed captain beloved by no one, he was readily hired. Word on the dock was that the good captain wasn't feeling so good these days at the bottom of the sea. Some dared wonder out loud if the loss of a head on judgment day would make it more difficult for the dead Captain to see in which direction he was headed, provoking laughter from most. While the men didn't like the Captain or his circle of friends, James sensed that here was where he needed to start. He would need to break into the office after closing time to have a look around.

'Bob Kitchens' met up with Galen at the Peacock Tavern after work as agreed upon to begin their search. This was the very same tavern where the quartermaster had first overheard the fat Turk and Hakeem the rat faced ferret talking in hushed whispers. The tavern was well stocked tonight with sailors from all over the world swapping lies about their latest adventures on the high seas. One of them made the mistake of telling how he worked aboard this mysterious black ship that went to war with the pirates of Tripoli. According to him, his position was second only in command to the Captain of the ship. After a belly full of the man's lies, Galen could take it no longer.

"Who'd you say was the Cap 'n of that there black ship?" Galen asked.

"I didn't say," the man replied.

"You didn't say, because you don't know," Galen fired back from across the room. "I heard tell he was ten foot tall and ate cannonballs and gunpowder for breakfast with his morning gruel. If you were there, you couldn't miss a man like that walking around, now could you?"

"Go sit back down and mind your manners you old sea dog, I'm telling this story the way I remembered it," the man continued as he stumbled over to the bar and called for another round of drink.

"It's a story alright, cause you wasn't there," Galen snapped again. "Tell me about her crew. Where did they come from? Most of us here, know all the sailors hereabouts. Tell these fine gentle souls in the pub here the name of one man who served aboard that ship."

The man wouldn't dare name one for fear he'd been found out.

"Well tell us what you know, since you seem to know so much about it," the drunken man challenged. Galen didn't disappoint.

"The way I heard it told, the crew was made up of salty old sea ghosts, and Lord Nelson himself was their Cap 'n. A demon possessed gypsy woman called him forth from the grave for the express purpose of leading an unhappy band of misfit sailors into battle. It had to be this way, cause no living mortal sailors wanted to part with their souls for the privilege of sailing under the great Cap 'n again. You can hang your hat on the truth of that, cause I heard with my own ears the old gypsy woman tell the story herself."

Sailors by their very nature are a superstitious lot and these were no different. Their eyes grew large with expressive thought at the possibility of something so foreign docked on their shores.

"Doesn't anyone in the house know anything about the black ship of death more than this fool man?" Galen demanded. "I'd wager ten shillings there's not a man among you who can produce a single name of someone on that ship. Anyone?"

A little fellow over in a quiet corner of the pub stood up and raised his hand, and all eyes turned to him.

"I heard tell a chap from America was her captain, and not Lord Nelson. Now he's dead too so I hear, killed by the pirates."

"Can you tell me his name little brother?"

"Temple,...is all I know. Does that satisfy you enough for the wager?" the little man asked.

"Well done sir! Come on over here and get your money cause you've certainly earned it," Galen blasted across the room. As the man walked sheepishly and cautiously over, the two sailors knew they had a good lead and set a hook to take advantage of it.

As Galen dug in his pocket for the money, 'Bob Kitchens' took a turn to ask a question out of earshot of the other men.

"How did you come by this information? I heard it was supposed to be some kind of big secret."

"Oh my sister tells me things from time to time," the man responded. "Say, she's not in some kind of trouble cause I told you that, is she?"

"No trouble friend," 'Bob' said in a comforting tone trying not to spook the man. "How did your dear sister come by this information of the captain being dead? That's news to us too."

"She told me Hakeem mentioned it after his last visit."

Both men's ears perked up intently at the mention of his name.

"Hakeem? Who's he?"

"A friend of my sister. She knows him better than I do," he stated haltingly. "You see, Hakeem is not a very handsome man, but neither is my sister. He comes by sometimes when he has money, and she helps him with his manly urges. He came some time ago with lots of money and paid her a nice bonus for services rendered. Like I said, Hakeem is not a handsome man and that kind of attention has got to be paid for."

"When was the last time you saw him?" Galen asked.

"Yesterday."

The men were shocked, because the death of the captain was a very recent event. Apparently news travels fast in Hakeem's circle of influence. What they needed to know was who was in that circle?

"Do you know where he lives, or when perhaps his next visit might be?"

"I don't know where he lives, but I think he works for a government man as a groundskeeper or something. He may come again on Saturday or Sunday," the little man said. "Then again, who knows?"

"Do you live with your sister?"

"No, I have my own place a few blocks from here."

"Would you mind telling me where your sister lives? It'd be worth another bob to you for your trouble," Galen asked.

"Are you sure my sister hasn't done anything wrong?" he asked.

"Of course not, but I would like to talk with Hakeem about a business matter. He sounds like a man with the kind of connections I'm looking for," Galen answered slyly.

The little man held out his hand for his money as he recited her address.

"Now whatever you gents do, please don't tell her about my windfall tonight. She'd be a wanting some of it for services rendered."

Galen couldn't resist asking.

"What kind of services does she do for you little man?"

The little man grinned with the understanding of his question.

"Oh I see what you're thinking, but it's not like that. She does my laundry and fixes my shirts,...things like that, and that's all guvner," he answered. "When you see her, you'll understand better why I say she's not a very handsome woman. Go gently, because she can be a little overwhelming when you first meet her. Can I go now?"

"You've been most helpful friend. Bartender, give my companion here another round on me," 'Bob' declared waving his hand in the air for service, then he turned back to the man. "I have a small favor to ask of you."

"Yes sir?"

"Please don't tell your sister about our conversation, or I'll be forced to tell her you got three times the money you received tonight. Are we agreed?"

"Fire and brimstone upon my head if I says a word about it guvner. I ain't about to kill the golden goose on account of a slip of the tongue like that," he grinned gulping down some ale with his new friends. "I may be just a slip of a man to some, but I am a man of me word."

✱✱

Two days and nights 'Bob' and Galen loitered outside the home of Eva Langtree hoping to catch a glimpse of Hakeem's coming and goings. From this distance, the men couldn't tell what she looked like seeing only snippets of her at the door from time to time as she opened it. She did have one amazing attribute in her favor though,...a strong appetite for men. All day and into the night men came and went, and it fretted the two observers as to when she had time to sleep. It was along about midday on the third day that 'Bob' fostered an idea of how to speed the process along.

"We need to get in closer where we can ask her some questions. She's got to know how to find our mark."

"What are you suggesting Cap 'n?" Galen looked quizzically.

"I mean one of us has to go in undercover to get some answers, and I can't very well do it being the newly married man that I am," he grinned.

"It's a lot you're asking Cap 'n," Galen smirked as he took a deep breath and shook himself.

"Think of it as a duty for Queen and country," 'Bob' suggested trying to take some of the angst out of it.

"Alright, I'll do it,...but only for Queen and country."

"Here take my eye patch. That way you'll only have to see half as much of her up close as you need to," 'Bob' teased as he pulled his patch off and handed it to Galen, "but I want it back after you're done."

"You're a kind man Skipper," Galen said as he put it on.

Across the street he went in disguise and marched right up to the door. It was a big oak door with fancy brass handles and a leaded stained glass window on the top half displaying the image of a ship. It seemed appropriate since most of her business probably came from sailing men. As he pulled a chain outside, a bell clanged loudly inside. Soon he could see her clearly along the outer edges of the glass coming from a room at the back of the house. She stopped for just a moment to open her night robe and readjust what lay inside it. That's when Galen got a real eye full as she took a moment to tuck her womanly attributes back into proper position so she could answer the door. As far as she knew, Galen could have been the mailman. As she opened the door, they began a most interesting conversational dance.

"Hello madam," he said in his most polite raspy voice.

"Who says I'm a Madam?" she asked roughly not understanding that he was merely addressing her in polite conversation. "You a copper? If you are, go back and tell your bosses I ain't taking no guff from coppers sent out here to harass me. They've been well paid in advance to leave me alone. So git along with yourself!"

As she tried to close the door, Galen merely inserted his boot and continued. "I'm hardly a copper my lady. Earle said you might be able to help me with a little problem I'm having," he whispered as his reason for being there. Earle was the little man from the tavern who was her brother.

"Well,...why didn't you say so you silly man, come on in. You'll have to wait a spell, cause I'm already in session with another client. We were just getting underway when you rang the bell. Please come in."

Galen stepped inside and looked around waiting for further instructions.

"Say, you got the look of a strong, hardy sailing man. Are you a sailor?" she asked quietly.

"I've done my share of sailing, yes ma'am," he answered.

"Good. I like strong sailing men, and you look like a dandy. Why don't you go sit over there in the corner of the room till I'm finished. Be real quiet and try not to move about too much, cause I don't want my gentleman friend to know anyone else is in the house. It's been a policy of mine not to ever have two men in the house at the same time, but I'm gonna make an exception for you cause I like the looks of you. Don't worry, I shouldn't be too long."

Galen moved as instructed to a darkened corner of the room and sat down on one of the fancy high backed chairs sitting there. It must have been an expensive chair, because it was very comfortable. Earle had been mostly right about his sister. She was not exactly a handsome woman in the face with her wild hair and rough manners hindering a good first impression of her looks, but she was well put together with ample parts to hang onto if the ride was to get bumpy. It did appear she had a few missing teeth in the back, but who didn't in these parts, she was English after all. She had a good strong jaw line that supported a proper English nose, and if a fellow had just a touch of rum in him in this light, he probably wouldn't have noticed any of her imperfections. It's true, she wasn't a handsome woman in the usual sense with the batty eyes and flirty ways of the gentler sex, but it was quite obvious from his first look through the glass door, she was a lot of woman. So here he sat patiently waiting his turn to vie for her attention.

After a considerable time had passed, he heard yelling as if the two actors inside were suddenly beginning to fight over something of great importance. The sounds of furniture and glass breaking brought Galen to the bedroom door with knife in hand preparing to charge in should he hear the faintest cry for help from her lips. That's of course when he heard what sounded like crying, but it wasn't coming from her, it was coming from the man. However, he couldn't tell clearly whether he was in pain or in ecstasy? All he could hear was the man calling out her name through the muffled door.

"Oh Eva,...Eva,...Eva darling!" he cried as his voice trailed off slowly into silence. As he continued to listen, he could hear heavy sighing and moaning coming from inside, and then ultimately there was complete quiet. After a time, the man started speaking again ever so softly. "Oh Eva, I can't tell whether you're the goddess of love, or some devil sent to torment me because of what's lacking in my marriage. Right now I don't really care either way, because I'm a very,...happy,... man. I'm sorry about your things. Send me the bill for the damages, and I'll send someone by with money to pay for it."

"Oh honey, you're turning out to be a lot of fun for a banker. Now you'd better get cleaned up proper before you leave so the neighbors won't talk. I told one of the local busy bodies the other day you were a minister who come by once in a while to pay his respects and pray with me. We wouldn't want you to leave here all mussed up confusing the poor gossiping biddies, now would we?"

"Come by the bank tomorrow, and we'll begin the loan process for the addition onto your house. Your first down payment has just been duly noted in my mental ledger. After next week's final payment is complete, I was hoping you might put me on the schedule as a regular paying customer? You've made me feel like a man again Eva, and I don't wish for that to end. Will you please consider it?"

"Don't worry honey, I'll try and work you in somewhere. Come on, let's get you cleaned up and back to work. There's a mirror over there."

Galen snickered under his breath as the scene unfolded on the other side of the door. They were having fun finalizing a bit of business, and he almost burst in on them. He knew he'd best be sitting back down before he got caught snooping.

In a few minutes, a dapper dressed young man in a grey flannel business suit burst forth from the room carrying a boler hat and umbrella in one hand, heading for the front door in quick step. She followed behind him in her flowing robe trying to divert his eyes from seeing Galen sitting in the shadows. She prided herself that all the men in her life need not know others were competing in the wings for her attention. That way each man felt as if he were her one and only true love when they came a knocking. At the door, the man turned and gave Eva a quick peck on the cheek and grabbed a handful of her delicious bum with his free hand and gave it a vigorous shake. With a smile on his face that showed utter satisfaction, he spoke again.

"I look forward to seeing you again next Thursday as agreed when the Missus goes to see her sister. You've really perked up my marriage since my lady lost interest in such things. This may well become the perfect arrangement for us as my wife takes care of all our social affairs, and you dear Eva take care of me. You really are a goddess. Ta 'da till then my darling!"

It had started to drizzle by now as the man placed his fresh new Boler hat upon his head and opened his umbrella outside. As he stepped off her stoop, he clicked his heels together disappearing to the left down contentment lane in a fine strut. Galen was almost envious of the man, but now it was time for him to come out of the shadows.

"Well, it looks as though you're up next dearie. Since I don't have anyone scheduled for the remainder of the day and it's your first time, you can stay as long as you like. Go on in and wait for me while I freshen up a little. Would you like a pint of ale while you wait?"

"No I'm fine thanks," he answered as he stepped cautiously inside the bedroom. It had plenty of broken furniture laying about making it hard to find a proper place to sit down. He moved over reluctantly to the side of the bed and sat down on the edge looking around. It was an odd sort of room lacking the frilly scenery of drapes and bedding that a more cultured woman of the evening might have enjoyed. He just assumed it was hard to decorate to please all her clients, so she left it rather bare on the assumption they were more interested in the scenery she offered than the room. Soon Eva reentered the room with a small hand towel drying the back of her neck.

"If you'd like to go ahead and get comfortable sweetie, this would be the time for it. You can lay your things over there on the chest so they don't get under foot," she said easily as she began the simple act of undressing. With her back to him, the unattractive robe fell to the floor in a heap revealing to Galen's startled eyes a perfectly nice round bum and strong, perfectly shaped legs. As she fluffed her wild untamed hair, Galen couldn't help but notice her fine broad shoulders and sturdy arms, as she squirted perfume on herself. When she turned around, she was wearing nothing but a mischievous smile on her face, startling even Galen's blackened heart with the expectations of her next move. Aware he hadn't undressed yet, she spoke simply. "Oh I get it, you're wanting to make a little game of it. I can see right now we're going to get along fine."

Galen jumped off the bed and stood up just as she grabbed him around the waist. Soon she had him pinned back against the wall with her massive breasts and began tearing at his clothes.

"Oh, I can tell you're going to be a lusty handful. It's true what they say about big girls liking big men. I can tell you got strong muscles and the right kind of temperament for a woman with my peculiar appetites. You got big hands too honey, and you know what they say about a man with big hands. Come on now, show Eva what kind of treasure you got hiding down there. I've been waiting a long time for a man like you to bed me, and you got the makings of the man who could do it too," she spoke boldly as she pulled roughly at his belt attempting to pull down his pants. Galen knew he'd better speak up before he was completely undressed and undone, as he stood helpless against her assault fighting for air.

It was at this moment he thought of poor Nurse Dickens, and how helpless she must have felt as he pawed over her that night in the hospital. He had never been on the receiving end of such a mauling before and as it turns out to his shame and disgrace, he didn't like it very much. From this time forward, he would mend his ways and cultivate new ways of dealing with the fairer sex, that is if he survived Eva's adventurous onslaught.

"Madam, could we please stop for just a moment. I need to talk with you about something of great importance before this goes any further," he spoke sharply trying to push her away, but she wasn't having it. She was a strong woman and very resistant to the idea. She couldn't help herself, because she was captivated by the prospect of a real man like Galen Sims sharing her bed for a change. He showed real promise at the door when she sized him up, cause he appeared as wild and untamed as she was. His rugged face wasn't all that handsome, but looks aren't everything.

"What do you mean talk about something important? Ain't this important enough for you! I tell you what, you go ahead and talk sweetie and I'll do the undressing. It'll be a lot quicker that way," she snickered as her hands continued their work.

"I'll pay you double your normal fee, if you can tell me where to find Hakeem," he blurted out finally still struggling to fend her off. "It's very important I get in touch with him and deliver a message and money to him from one of his foreign contacts. It really is that important."

Upon hearing that, she relinquished her grip on him and eased backwards a ways to study him with a curious look in her eyes.

"You mean you didn't come here for a session dearie?" she asked.

"I'm afraid not dear lady. We got off on the wrong foot from the get go and I do apologize. I must find Hakeem, and your brother Earle said you might know how to locate him. It's very urgent," he lied.

"Well this sure is a fine kettle of fish you've brought me today," she fumed as she stepped back further resting powerful hands on perfectly formed naked hips. "Here you are about to dash all my hopes. I was really looking forward to having a good romp around the house with you, cause you look like the kind of man who could make a girl's dreams come true. I tell you what, why don't we have some fun first and then we'll talk about Hakeem later. It's on the house, what do you say?"

Galen took deep breaths trying to gather his wits about him so he could talk again. It's true she wasn't a bouquet of roses to look at in the face, but she was a veritable feast of plenty as she stood before him naked and unashamed. He was tempted to lift his eye patch in order to take it all in with both eyes. This poor woman had been cruelly tricked by nature, having been blessed with an overflowing abundance in so many areas, yet offered so little help in others. He paused to think that with a bit of grooming, perhaps even that one glaring deficit could be managed down to a more reasonable level. It was for certain he had plundered much worse among the English pubs.

"I'm sorry my lady, but I'm on a tight schedule and I don't have time right now to play. My ship leaves for Algiers tonight, so I must hurry. Perhaps when I return in the winter, you and I could spend some time cozyed up around your fireplace. I'd like to believe in time, I could make a real woman of you. Now can we talk about Hakeem?" he asked trying every sweet talking thing he knew to get her to open up.

As she reached for her cotton robe to put it back on, Galen's heart sank. He did so enjoy the view.

"If that's how it's gonna be, then you might as well try this place first," she finally conceded. Taking pen in hand, she began writing down the address of the little ferret faced man, "but don't you dare tell him I sent you. He always pays good for what he gets here, and I can't afford to lose such a valuable customer."

Grateful for the address, Galen began rummaging in his vest pocket for money to leave her. He felt he owed her that much at least.

"Put your money away silly man. I'm the one who stepped in it," she said plainly. "I mistook your intentions, and it was my own danged fault for jumping in so fast. I hope I didn't embarrass you too much."

"Don't worry, I'll recover. You're a fine woman Eva, but the timing is all wrong and the pressure I'm under to find Hakeem is enormous," he said trying to soothe her feelings.

"Well, if you're ever up this way again, I wish you would stop by and see me, even if it is just a social visit," she offered. "I have a feeling you have the makings of something I've never seen in a man before, and that intrigues me. Would you come by and see me again?"

"If I do, it's because I want to know Eva the woman first. I don't think I'm quite ready for this other version of you just yet. I also think you have the makings for something pretty special too, but you'd have to give me a chance apart from all this."

"That's a very honest answer sailor. Most people don't come here to know me, all they want is what they want. I'll remember what you said for next time," she said plainly.

"Have you ever felt fine Oriental silk next to your skin Miss Eva?" Galen asked as she handed the folded paper to him.

"No I can't say that I have," she answered. "Why do you ask?"

"When I come back from my trip , I'll bring you a nice silk robe for helping me. A woman as fine as you would enjoy the way the fabric clings and moves about on her body," he said as he placed a big gentle hand under her chin and gazed into her big brown eyes. As their eyes connected, he could feel the magnetic pull of a kindred spirit. She was as wild a thing as he once was in the not so distant past. There was a time he wasn't sure if he was some kind of dangerous animal, or a full born pirate for the blood lust he carried in his heart. With the help of men like Captain Temple and Captain Boles, he had come to grips with the horror filled acts he had committed in his sinful life. Soon, even the heavy drinking he needed to function ceased and with their help and the good Lord's, he found a new purpose for living. In the right hands, he felt Eva could easily do the same, that is if she would concede the need for taming. Upon releasing her face, he took the high road out while he still had the courage of his convictions. "If you'll excuse me now Miss Eva, I'll show myself out lest I too find myself tempted to squeeze on something I shouldn't. My thanks to you again dear lady."

Galen stepped quickly from her bedroom while he still had the presence of mind and the willpower to do so. Crossing the large living room in big strides, he stopped suddenly at the front door to contemplate something clever to say in leaving. Just then she stepped from her bedroom chamber still smiling from his playful reference to how her last client had left the premises with a lusty handful of happy thoughts. At he turned to say goodbye, she leaned back against the doorway and opened her robe slightly one last time allowing him to feast his eye on what might have been. He stood there for a moment taking it all in and shuddered at the thought of seeing such plenteous bounty going unrequited. He smiled and blew her a token kiss, because the words wouldn't come. Stepping through the door, he felt almost the same euphoric high the last man had enjoyed on his way out. It wasn't the same mind you, but almost.

He crossed the street in the drizzling rain to meet up with 'Bob' who stood patiently waiting in the alley with his collar pulled up.

"Well, it sure took you long enough. Were you sampling the woman's wares while in there?"

"No Skipper, but it was all on full display if I had wanted to. I understand now why so many men come here, because it's worth a week's wage to see the full show. However, because of duty, I persevered in spite of overwhelming temptation to get what we were after," he said.

"Are you quite certain you didn't sample just a little forbidden fruit while you were in there. You do look a little flush up around the cheekbones," 'Bob' teased as he pointed at Galen's face.

"It's not like that Cap 'n. I think she's a real nice lady who just got lost somewhere along the way like so many of us do. I suspect she had a man in her past who dumped her for a pretty face. I can tell you for true, it was his loss. If she could just manage to tame that wild head of hair and maybe primp up a little, she wouldn't be nearly as scary as she comes off," he stated flatly.

"I didn't take you for such a soft touch Galen," 'Bob' declared.

"In our own way, we're all looking for love Cap 'n. Judging by your cheekbones that night you came to the hospital, I gathered you had found what you were looking for too," Galen smiled as he handed the instructional note to his friend. "You are in so many ways, a very different man than the one I came to Liverpool with four months ago, and I like this version of you even better."

"We are all men who can be changed for good or ill. It all comes down to what influences the change, don't you see? Now let's get going, cause we have a far piece to travel before morning."

****

After locating two good riding horses, 'Bob' and Galen rode all day and night until sunup when their horses tired. After securing two more from a local farmer and riding another four hours, they finally came upon the address Eva Langtree had given them. According to her, this is where Hakeem said he worked as a groundskeeper. The estate was huge and well guarded with gated walls and sentries all around it. Since Galen was the only one that had seen him, they felt it wasn't prudent to just march up to the front door and announce they were here for Hakeem. What they decided on doing was a little reconnaissance first, then develop a plan of action. So they went and found a livery to stable their horses, and then a place of rest for themselves at the Cavendish Inn located directly across the street from the estate.

After checking in, the men took time for a well deserved rest. Later that evening after a good nap, they went downstairs to eat in the dining hall. Whoever the man was that lived there, he must be very important. Around four o'clock, a carriage rode past the sentries at the gate and swiftly up to the front door. As the occupants disembarked, James took his glass from the coat he wore to venture a peek through the glass window.

"Do you see anyone you know sir?" Galen asked.

"I'm not sure, here take a look," he said handing the glass to Galen.

"That's Hakeem Cap 'n, big as you please, but he ain't dressed like no groundskeeper. He's the one carrying the fancy satchel," he said as he handed the glass back to James for a quick look before he disappeared into the great house.

"We have to find out who lives there," James stated flatly.

"Allow me sir," Galen said as he held up his big hand for service. In a moment, a perky young lass with a bouncing pony tail stood before them with a cheery smile on her face. "Good afternoon missy. Who might I have the pleasure of addressing this fine evening?"

"My name's Matilda Cavendish, and my grandma and granddad own the inn. I'll be your waitress today." she smiled.

"Could you tell me Matilda darling who lives in that big fine house yonder? We're strangers here and have never seen such a fine estate."

"Oh that sir is the home of Lord Thomas Denman, a very famous politician. He used to be the Chancellor of the Exchequer many years ago in his youth, and for a time he served as Lord Chief Justice of the Kings Bench. Now he's back in private practice as a solicitor in his old age. I heard tell he now serves as the Queens Council once in a while when she needs him," she beamed proudly.

"You are indeed a very bright child. Now tell me one more thing if you can, could a private citizen visit with the famous solicitor by knocking on the door?" Galen queried.

"I don't rightly know," she replied honestly. "You might wish to walk across the street to visit with the gate guards. I'm sure they could be of help to you. Now what can I get you gentlemen to eat?"

After a light meal of fish and chips, the men sat scheming as to whether they should visit with the guards, or try and catch Hakeem away from the grounds. From this vantage point, it was hard to tell who was coming and going, and they actually weren't sure if Hakeem was living within the great house or merely working there. And more frustratingly than that, who the dickens was this mysterious Hakeem?

Finally they decided to go ask the guards about trying to secure an audience with the great man himself. Once they were almost there, James looked down at his clothes.

"We don't look much like party guests dressed in these, do we?"

"Don't fret Cap 'n, I've come through worse trials," he laughed thinking back to his encounter with Eva Langtree. "Why don't you let me do the talking 'Bob.'"

At the gate, two men in a little guard house came forth to meet them, and they didn't seem none too pleased to see them either.

"How do gentlemen. We'd like an audience with Lord Denman if you please," Galen began with bluster.

"His Lordship is receiving no guests today, so move along," the guard spoke roughly to him.

"Could you at least let him know it's a matter of great importance. We've come a long way to see him," Galen continued with his reasoned assault.

"Move along there, or I'll have you arrested and charged for trespassing," the guard declared with more force in his voice this time.

"Well do this for me then, go inside and tell Hakeem, that I wish to see him concerning a little matter of money he's got coming from Tripoli. That ought to put a bee under his bonnet," he replied thinking that would force Hakeem out into the open.

"There is no one here by that name," the guard said plainly.

"Oh he's here alright sir, because I seen him get out of that black carriage yonder not more than a half hour ago. He's a skinny little man with a face like a rat. Surely you know who I'm talking about," Galen bantered back.

The two guards looked warily at one another. He had just described Richard Havilland to a tee, but he was not known as Hakeem to them or anyone else here as far as they knew. They were not about to tell these two seafaring scabs Mr. Havilland's real name either out of privacy concerns.

"Come back tomorrow after you've sobered up and had a bath. Maybe then we'll look into the matter for you. In the meantime, you're not getting in here today."

"Well tell me this before we go, does the rat faced man live here with his Lordship?" 'Bob' asked. If he didn't live here and he left during the night, there would be no way of ever finding him away from here. The guards didn't recognize the name, so perhaps their mark was using another.

"That is none of your concern. Now for the last time move along, before we call the coppers on you."

The two sailors looked at each other knowing the direct approach wasn't going to work.

"Let's go, they can't help us," 'Bob' said to his partner and they eased back across the street to the safety of the shadows. 'Bob' looked at Galen and spoke. "I don't want to wait till morning, so we'll have to sneak in when it gets dark. I just hope they don't have dogs on patrol."

"According to the girl, the old gent's basically retired. Maybe no one thinks he's very important anymore," Galen suggested.

Around seven o'clock the sun went down and the mists rolled in almost as if they had been summoned. The two men eased across the road to the fence and waited for the right time to climb it when no one was coming. Up and over they went and landed with little fanfare on the other side. From their vantage point they could see plenty of activity going on inside through the huge windows. As they got closer to the house, they could see Hakeem at a desk with others discussing something or other, and it looked as if he was in charge. The mystery only deepened with the revelation he was no mere groundskeeper.

As the two men sat silently trying to figure out their next move, they knew they were in a pickle. They couldn't very well barge in on men at this level of government without severe consequences, even if their cause seemed just, and especially since they didn't yet understand the mysterious rat faced man's role here. Maybe this is a matter best handled by someone like Albert Whitaker through his contacts. So as they prepared to leave and chart another course of action, the worst of luck happened upon them. Having been so intent on their mission at the window, they neglected to watch behind, and that's when the lights went out.

****

"Mr. Potts, can I come up there and help you," Johnny asked. Being an inquisitive boy he wanted to learn things.

"You'll have to ask Mrs. Anne," Keely Potts answered. "A roof can be a dangerous place for a child."

"I'm not a child Mr. Potts, I'm a sailor," he said flaunting his status confidently.

"You'll still need to ask the lady of the house. If she says yes, then bring me some more nails and shingles when you come."

Soon Anne and Johnny appeared outside together. As she looked things over, she called out to Keely.

"If you need things, Johnny can come up for that. Please keep an eye on him so he doesn't fall," she said as she turned to Johnny. "And you do what Mr. Potts tells you."

"Yes Ma'am!" Johnny shouted excitedly as he climbed the ladder with more nails and shingles in hand.

"Easy does it son," Keely said as he assisted him around the ladder onto the roof. "Now sit there and I'll show you how to fix a roof using wood shingles."

"How come some of the houses hereabouts have grass on the roof?" Johnny asked.

"It's not really grass, but a thatch made of cereal straw or water reeds. Sometimes, if the roof is very old, mold and mosses grow on the roof making it look green like grass," Keely answered.

"You know a lot of things Mr. Keely. You might even be as smart as my father. Do you know my father?" Johnny asked.

Keely didn't wish to lie, so he answered the only way he could.

"I have certainly heard of your father. Mrs. Anne has told me a lot about him, and I'm sure he is a great man."

Johnny beamed at hearing such kind sentiment from his new friend.

"When my father shows up in a few days, I'll introduce you. I think you two will get along just fine."

"I look forward to it, now hand me some more nails so we can finish and get down. My belly says it's time for dinner, what does yours say little sailor?"

"Mine's been growling for an hour Mr. Potts. Your wife sure can cook, that's for sure. What do you reckon she's come up with for dinner today?" Johnny quizzed.

"I wouldn't be surprised if chicken and dumplings weren't on the menu, cause I plucked a couple of big fat hens this morning. Quick, hand me those shingles behind you so we can get down."

****

It may have only been hours, but it felt like days before the two men revived back to consciousness locked inside their separate cells. Their heads were swollen and bleeding from where the rifle butts had been administered with authority. James kicked himself for losing focus with his surroundings allowing the patrol guards to slip up behind them. With the light from the windows in their eyes, they couldn't very well see what was lurking in the darkness behind them. It was a rookie mistake that had cost them dearly. Soon he heard voices and stood to listen to understand whose they were. He couldn't see out because the little opening in his door was closed, but what he heard terrified him.

"That's the man alright who killed the Ottoman's Ambassador," the rat faced man said as he leaned in to have a look at Galen Sims laying semiconscious on his bunk. "I remember the drunken lout well sitting next to us while we were in conference at the Peacock Tavern. I should have known he was up to no good, and I can't help but feel responsible for the Ambassador's death. I should have stayed with him until he returned to his residence. It was a real tragedy to lose such a great man. I hope they hang the scoundrel quickly.'"

The rat faced man backed away from the opening in the door as it was slammed shut.

"What about the other man, could you identify him too?" the big guard asked.

"I don't know, let me see him," the man answered.

As the guard turned and walked to the door, he unlatched a small opening allowing the rat faced man to peer into the darkness for a quick look around. He wasn't expecting James to ease up so close to the opening and look straight at him.

"Hello Hakeem," James said eerily.

The man jumped back and squealed at the mention of his covert name and began going off on James in terrible fashion.

"That man was certainly with the other one, and I want them both charged and hanged as soon as possible as traitors to the crown. I'll swear out a warrant to that effect, just get proceedings under way as soon as possible. I have no doubt they came as assassins to kill Lord Denman last night. Why else would they have been snooping around under cover of darkness. Don't let anyone come near them, lest they meet with others co-conspirators waiting to finish their work. Be careful, for I fear they have spies everywhere."

As the guard went to close the little door opening, James called out to the man once again.

"We know who you are Hakeem. You can run, but you cannot hide from the long arms of justice. You may have fooled these people with your double life, but you haven't fooled us. We'll meet again very soon when we go into open court. The whole world's gonna know who you really are."

"Close it up guard, quickly!" the man said as sweat formed on his brow. Even the guard noticed his sudden nervousness.

"You alright Mr. Havilland? You don't look well," he said.

"Shut up you fool and get me out of here!" he cried out in panic. He didn't know how much the man in the cell knew for sure because he kept calling him Hakeem. One thing was for certain now, the man inside the cell now knew his last name too as it was blurted out by the blundering guard.

"Goodbye Mr. Havilland," James called out to him as he ran from the cells.

After the man and the guard left, James sat down in a corner of the room to ponder. He knew that Hakeem would never let this case go to court for fear of being exposed. James felt a case could possibly be made against Galen putting him the hangman's noose, because the man's story was close enough to the truth to persuade a jury or a judge. Even if Galen revealed the actual conversation he overheard between Hakeem and the Turkish ambassador, who would a jury be more prone to believe considering who the rat faced man is, or at least represents.

However, there was no way that same harness could fit the both of them, especially in open court. He had been miles away with verifiable witnesses when the death of the Turk happened. As James saw it, that left only one option open to Mr. Havilland, the rat. Someone would have to come and kill them before a court could be convened to try them. The rat could not afford the truth of discovery to come out in open court revealing who he was. From this time forward, he knew they would have to be on guard twenty four seven, cause he knew an attack was imminent.

"Galen," James whispered across the hall. "You awake yet?"

"Is that what we're calling it now?" Galen responded sarcastically as he rubbed his sore head. "I thought I must be in purgatory, since I'm neither dead or alive. There is a purgatory Cap 'n, isn't there?"

"No Galen, there's no such place. Now get up close to the door and listen to me. Our man's last name is Havilland, and he's some kind of a player in the court system I think. He said he could swear out a warrant, and that takes someone with some moxie. I think they're going to try and kill us first before we have our day in court, so be on guard," James declared.

"Heaven's be Cap 'n, I should have stayed at Eva's," Galen declared as he rubbed his sore head and thought of her in a much better light. "What time do you think it is?"

"I don't know, and stop calling me Captain unless I tell you too."

"Okay,...does Bob know the time?" Galen blurted out trying to bring a little humor to the front.

"Bob says he thinks it's late afternoon, cause he's plenty hungry."

"I hope they feed us well in this place, cause I could eat a horse about now," Galen mused.

"Well, I hate to break it to you old friend, but you can't eat until we meet with a solicitor. I'm afraid to eat the food in here for fear of it being poisoned by the rat. I have a sense that he's gonna have people everywhere watching our every move," James explained.

In an hour, someone came down the hall rolling a cart full of food on small trays. As the cart stopped in front of his cell door, he noticed the tray had a written note attached with the name of Bob Kitchens on the cover. Galen Sims had his name on one as well, but none of the other prisoners did. This had to be it.

As the little man opened a door down low to slide the tray in, James slid it back out. Once again the man slid it back in, and James pushed it back out once again.

"Say, what's the matter with you. Aren't you hungry? The cook got orders to make this up special for you," the little man said as he opened the tray to reveal a big juicy steak and all the trimmings.

"Give mine back to the cook and tell him he can eat it. Give me one of them off the bottom," James instructed the jailor.

"Alright if that's what you want, but it's only a sandwich."

"I'd rather have it than a steak right now," James countered. "My heads hurts too much for anything that heavy on my stomach."

From across the hall, Galen screamed for the same. As the little man complied and rolled on down the hall, he thought the two men were daft. The occupants in the last two cells had been released earlier, so it appeared the little man would have rich victuals to take home to the missus tonight. It's not too often the Mumford household ate steak.

"Galen, you okay," James asked after a half hour of time had passed. And just for the record, the sandwich tasted almost as good as a steak as hungry as he was.

"Doing fine 'Bob'," Galen retorted.

"Good, it's time now to put on our acting face. I have a feeling someone will be along soon to check on us."

"How should we act?" Galen quizzed.

"Like dead men. If they happen to open both doors at the same time, we may have a chance at escape. Do your best impression of a dead man. I've already died once so I got the routine down pat," James instructed. "From here on out, it's got to be silence lest we're discovered."

"Aye, aye," Galen answered.

So an hour later footsteps came quietly down the hall. It wasn't the same guard but another who came to investigate his handiwork. Looking into the cells revealed two apparently dead men, one lying on the floor and the other across a bunk. Soon a key was heard to unlock James' door as he lay still. The man crossed the floor and took his wrist to measure for a pulse. That's when James grabbed the man and kicked his feet out from under him, bouncing his head off the floor as he landed upside down. Up on his feet, James edged to the door and looked discretely out. There was no one else coming so he eased over and let Galen out of his cell. Once outside, he closed the door locking it. That ought to have them scratching their heads for a while.

Then they took the man down to the last cell and locked him in there bound and gagged. Since he was still unconscious, they slid him under the bunk making it hard to see his body in the darkness. Easing back over to James' cell, they locked it and began plotting their escape. Now the trick was how to get out undetected. Galen had an idea of some merit cross his mind.

"If I put the guard's coat and hat on, I think we could walk right on out of here as if I was a guard. I could put the handcuffs on you and make it look real convincing," he offered.

"Do you think you can get in the man's coat? He did look a mite small," James asked.

"I won't know until I try it."

Galen put the coat on and it was plenty tight. He couldn't button the front, but that would be okay if he kept the prisoner at the right angle to the desk sergeant as they walked out. With handcuffs in place and the guard's hat on, they opened the door leading from the cells to the outer offices. It was a busy night with drunks and street women making trouble all up and down the halls. Amid all this mayhem, the two men walked casually out. They bumped into one rookie policeman along the way who had his hands full with two fighting women, and Galen merely shook his head from side to side acknowledging the chaos. Then he rough talked James as if he were some kind of a drunk, and they walked safely outside. Quickly they turned into the shadows giving Galen time enough to peel away the bobbies' clothes. As they disappeared into the night a far piece from the police station, James came up with a plan that shocked Galen. As they rested for a moment, he spoke of it.

"Well Galen old friend, this is turning out to be a lot more than you bargained for isn't? The black ship may be our undoing if we don't figure out a way to swim out of this mess with our skins intact."

"I've rode out gale forces winds that I've enjoyed more. What you think we ought to do now 'Bob'?" Galen teased remembering his captain's instructions.

"We have to go back to the house and confront what's inside."

"Cap 'n, they have me and you pegged as wanted men now. They can shoot us on sight and then hang us later," the quartermaster warned as he put his hand to his throat and twisted his neck to show he wasn't too pleased with the idea.

"I know we got a raw deal the last time we tried to get in, but I have a better idea how to do it this time," he said as he scratched the hair on his chin. "First we need to find a telegraph office."

"What for?"

"It's time to summon our back up forces for an assault on the fort," James declared.

After some time, they located one and went inside.

"Yes sir, can I help you?" the young man with the visor asked.

"Does your system go to Liverpool?" James asked.

"Yes sir," he boasted proudly. "We go all over England."

"Splendid. I need to send a wire to Mr. Albert Whitaker in Liverpool marked urgent. How long will that take?" James quizzed the lad.

"To send a wire will take an hour to get there. Getting a response back could take several more hours depending on how fast they locate your man."

"Do you know the Cavendish Inn over by where Lord Denman lives in his great house?" James asked.

"Yes sir."

"If it comes within the hour, send the response there and ask for Matilda Cavendish. If it's later than that and I suspect it will be, wait until tomorrow morning to send it over. She'll know how to reach us."

"What is the message sir?"

James laid out the message and signed Galen's name to it. He still didn't want anyone to know he was alive just yet. Once they finished, they lit out for the Cavendish Inn and the comfort of the inn's amazing cooks.

"The fish and chips were good last time Captain, but I'm hoping for a leg of lamb or something more substantial," Galen complained.

"For Heaven's sake man, you had a roast beef sandwich not more than five hours ago," James teased back.

"Yeah, and mine could have used some more seasoning too," he bantered back. "I swear Cap 'n, that meat was so thin you could have strained tea grounds through it. If you took the time to fold it over a couple of times, it would still only have one side to it. I don't think it actually qualified as food to be perfectly honest. Come to think of it, I might have ate the paper it was wrapped in thinking that was the sandwich."

"Next time we're over that way, you can complain to the kitchen staff. Maybe they'll cook you another steak," James teased.

"Never mind Captain, I'm smelling the Cavendish Inn from here and it smells like venison stew."

"You always had a nose for food and trouble. Eat hearty, because it might be a while before we eat again. If you got extra pockets, you might want to pack us a few extra biscuits away," James laughed.

"There she is Skipper. Ain't she a sight for sore eyes?" Galen spoke upon seeing the quaint little inn. It did have plenty of charm.

"You were right Galen, there's the inn straight away. Can you tell what kind of pudding they're having from here?"

"Can't rightly say, but I think bread pudding would be my choice if I was cooking up the stew."

"I didn't know you were a cook too," James declared stunned by the revelation.

"My mum taught me how to cook at an early age. She said I was gonna have a hard time finding a mate cause of the way I looked. She said she didn't want me to starve to death in case she passed on. That was my mum alright, always thinking ahead."

"Mr. Sims, you are a wonder. Just about the time I think I have you figured out, you show me a new wrinkle in the fabric of your life. I'm impressed," James declared proudly.

"Oh, it twern't nothing really. When life throws you lemons, mum says you learn to make lemon pies and be happy about it."

"Like I said, I'm impressed," James said opening the front door of the inn to his friend.

Chapter VIII

James and Galen slept the sleep of kings after a hearty meal of venison stew and bread pudding within the confines of the little inn. The thumping sounds in their bruised heads had finally quieted as they woke to the promise of a new day. As they dressed and walked down to the dining area, they walked in on the same two gate guards from the other night having their breakfast. They might have gotten away without being detected had it not been for Matilda calling out Galen's name merrily across the room to tell him of his telegram's arrival.

The two guards put down their forks and slowly picked up their rifles leaning against the table. They knew they were supposed to be locked up in jail after being caught last night.

"Thank you Matilda darling," Galen said as he paid her a tip for keeping it close. He wasn't upset by her innocent gesture, cause she had no way of knowing the trouble she had just created for the two of them. "Now go about your business while I visit with my friends there."

"It's best you two buggers come with us so there won't be any more charges added than you've already earned," one of the guards stated matter of fact as he stood and addressed the two sailors.

"Where are you going to take us?" 'Bob' asked.

"Back to jail, where else?" the guard answered.

"If you'll take us to the big house like we asked the other day to see Lord Denman, we'll go willing with you, but we are not going back to jail at any price. So what shall it be gentlemen, jail or pandemonium upon your heads?"

"We don't take kindly to threats from sea rats," the guard bounced back. "You're going back to jail and that's the sum total of it."

James looked at Galen and nodded. Holding up their hands to let them get closer gave them the advantage they needed as the guards closed in with their bayoneted rifles. The long guns were unwieldy in such tight quarters as the men grabbed the barrels in one quick move to disarm the guards.

Pointing the guns up in a safe direction forced them to fire, and that's when the two sailors struck with some real authority of their own. Lucky for the Cavendish's there was no one else in the building who might have been alarmed by the sound of gunfire. As the Cavendish's came running from the kitchen, they discovered the two guards laying on the floor unconscious, and it alarmed them.

"I hate to ask, but do you have a place where we can store these two poor fella's for a couple of hours?" Galen asked. "I know it looks bad, but I promise you it's a matter of great importance, or we wouldn't be asking."

"Are you men criminals? If you are, we won't help you," Pop Cavendish muttered out defiantly.

"We are not criminals sir," James spoke bluntly, "but we are being chased by the authorities as though we were. Men have already tried to kill us, and we have been denied our day in court. So we have come here to see Lord Denman, because he is the key to clearing our name. If we were truly criminals, would we come back here and take such a chance at recapture? You must decide quickly whether you'll help us or not, because time is of the essence."

Pop looked over at Mom and then at Matilda to gauge their reaction. Matilda just beamed because she was young and innocent, and grandma had not yet taught her to be suspicious of strange men.

"What do you think Mum?" he asked.

"They look like good men to me. I'm willing to take a chance on them if you are. Are you going to tie us up too?" she asked.

"No ma'am, all we need do is put these gents someplace where they can't get free for a couple of hours. After that time you can cut them loose so they can run for help," James instructed. "Give us those two hours to complete our business, then help them escape. You can tell them we had you tied up in another room if you'd like, and they won't know the difference."

"Very well gentlemen, you can hide them out back in the storage building. If they screamed their heads off, no one would be able to hear them from out there. I just hope I'm doing the right thing," Pop muttered under his breath as James and Galen took the two men out to the buildings draped over their shoulder.

Before tying them up and gagging them sufficiently, they stripped them of their clothing and locked the door. After dressing in the soldiers uniforms, they spoke to the Cavendish's again with final instructions.

"Put your closed sign out after we leave till our time is up and you will have helped us and England more than you know. If we are successful, it could mean a lot of people will go to jail instead of us, and maybe even save some lives including our own. Oh,...and stay out of sight for the time being."

Pop Cavendish spoke simply to the two men before they left.

"I hope you men know what you're doing?"

"We do too!" they sang out together.

"Have you read the telegram yet?" Galen inquired as they left.

"Just about to," James said as he pulled it from his pocket.

"Is it good news?"

"Mr. Whitaker is on his way here by train. Said he would meet us at Lord Denman's about noontime," James read from the telegram.

"It's almost noontime now 'Bob'. If we hurry across the road, we might accidentally catch the man when he rides through," Galen exclaimed.

Off they scurried across the road to the guard shack to give new instructions to the guards currently stationed there. They looked good too, just like real soldiers with their freshly pressed uniforms and fancy caps. Lucky for them, the two original guards were close enough in size to pull off their disguise.

"Good day corporal, we've been sent here to assist you," Galen stated plainly.

The guards looked puzzled, cause it wasn't their normal routine.

"What do you mean assist us? With what?" the corporal dared to question.

"Lord Denman has a very special guest arriving here at any minute to visit on a matter of great urgency. We were ordered to ride in with him and act as his bodyguards for the duration of his visit. Seems there may be some sort of threat hanging over his head," Galen said without blinking an eye. This wasn't a time for uncertainty in tone.

"See here, this all seems very irregular. Where are the other two men who normally relieve us?" the corporal asked skeptically.

"The last time I looked Corporal, a Sergeant still outranked a Corporal. Do you want to go on report for disobeying a direct order from a superior? I can make it happen if that's what you're a wanting."

162

"Sorry sir. It just all seems so irregular."

"These are irregular times Corporal. Suck it up."

"What are your orders sir?" the Corporal finally conceded taking a load off Galen shoulders.

"Man the gates as usual. When Mr. Albert Whitaker arrives, call out to us. We shall be standing on the backside of the guard house awaiting his arrival. You have your orders, and we have ours. Now snap to like the fine soldiers you are."

"Yes Sergeant," the Corporal said as he saluted and went back to his duty.

Within the half hour, Albert Whitaker's coach pulled to the gate, and the Corporal whistled out.

"Your man is here Sergeant!"

'Bob' and Galen stepped from behind the guard houses and entered the coach on either side startling Mr. Whitaker.

"See here, what's the meaning of this?"

"Begging your pardon sir, can we just drive along a ways? We'll explain it to you out of earshot of our two friendly guards, if you please," Galen whispered.

"Very well," he said as he bumped the top of the cab.

As they eased away, the guards closed the gates behind the carriage.

"Do you not recognize me sir? I'm Galen Sims," Galen said as he pulled down his collar to show a fine fresh scar alongside his neck. "You saved my life some nights ago by carrying me to the hospital, and I'm still beholding to you."

Mr. Whitaker's mouth flew open in response.

"It's been months since I've seen you. I apologize for not recognizing you right off," he said as he eyed the other guard with suspicion. There was something about him that seemed out of place. "Can you tell me why I've been summoned. I'm not used to being in the dark about important matters."

"Do you remember Hakeem, the rat faced man I said was a spy the night you rescued me?" Galen persevered. He had to hurry, they were almost to the front door.

"Yes, what of him?"

"We followed him to this house last night," Galen continued.

"I don't believe it. Lord Denman is an honorable man without question or peer. I can't go in there and accuse him of being part of something like that without heavy weight proof. Who do you think came here last night?" the old gentleman questioned. He was being put in a very bad spot.

"The man's last name is Havilland. My friend and I spent the night in jail last night because of him, and he tried to have us killed by poisoning our food. He knows we're on to him," Galen finished.

"I find all of this completely preposterous and full of poppy cock. Lord Denman couldn't be so easily duped. Whoever this man is, he must have the utmost loyalty and trust of the solicitor to even be here. If this turns into a bust, I'll assure you jail will look like paradise compared to what I'm prepared to do to you. And who is this man here? Is he mixed up in all this too?" Mr. Whitaker complained.

"All in good time guvner, all in good time," the other guard said.

"Alright Mr. Sims, what do you want me to do?" Mr. Whitaker asked. His neck was certainly on the block.

"After the pleasantries are out of the way, ask Lord Denman if it's possible to have a word with Mr. Havilland on a matter of some importance. We'll be just outside the door hearing everything. If he's here, he'll no doubt react when we step through the door cause he would have thought we were dead by now. It should be quite a show," Galen continued.

"How do I explain your presence?" the old man wondered aloud.

"Threats upon your life is what we told the gate guards, and they bought it."

As the carriage slowed to a stop, servants of the house came and opened the door expecting one man to exit. They were startled upon seeing the two soldiers also inside. As Mr. Whitaker emerged, he called back to the soldiers.

"Stay close gentlemen and keep a sharp eye out. I've had a bit of trouble in getting here," he responded to the soldiers and the servants moved aside allowing them to follow him inside and stand guard outside the room he entered. Galen cracked the door just a little so they could hear as Mr. Whitaker entered.

"Albert old friend, it's good to see you. How have you been these many months. Would you like something to drink before we begin?"

"Yes please Thomas, some scotch if you have it. You might as well have one too, because what I'm about to tell you may cause your knees to buckle," Mr. Whitaker declared.

"Well, you've certainly piqued my interest old friend. Your cable did say it was very urgent. Is it news about the adventure of our black ship?" Lord Denman asked with genuine curiosity as he poured.

"The black ship docked six days ago. I've been slow about updating you because we've been in a state of mourning over the loss of our beloved American captain, James Temple. You remember him Thomas, we met him that first day on the docks."

"Yes I remember him. Fine lad he was too," his Lordship lamented. "Was he buried at sea or on land?"

"At sea I'm afraid, so closure has been rather difficult to deal with for the family. His wife has gone into hiding with his son for now," Albert continued speaking bringing his friend up to speed on part of his reason for coming.

"How was the trip? Did it pay off as we hoped?" Thomas asked.

"Yes, the trip was very successful thanks to him, but they knew we were coming Thomas, and who the captain was aboard our 'secret' black ship. That disturbed me to my core when I heard it from one of the other captains. I planned to come in a few days anyway and lay it all out for you, but something extraordinary has been revealed to me about the possibilities of spies from foreign governments operating right here under our very noses."

"That is disturbing if it's true. Do you have any proof?"

"Yes, I'm afraid so."

"Well spit it out man. Don't keep me standing here in suspense, or my hair might catch on fire," Lord Denman declared most urgently.

"Do you have someone working here by the name of Havilland?"

"Yes, Richard Havilland, what of it?"

"He's involved Thomas, I'm pretty sure of it."

"Preposterous, he's one of my brightest protégés on the bench. Surely, you don't suspect him?" his Lordship asked nervously.

"He is also known to us as Hakeem the rat," Mr. Whitaker stated plainly. Well there it was, all out in the open. All he wondered about now was whether he would leave in one piece or many after this powerful accusation.

Lord Denman drank all his scotch down in one big swallow and poured himself another. After downing that one too, he poured yet another but halted trying to wrap his analytical mind around it all. He was not a man known for making swift jumps to judgment, but this one had him stumped. It just couldn't be possible, because Richard Havilland was the one man in all of England he would have trusted with his life and his biggest secrets. Suddenly, as if emerging from a dark cave, he could see it all as clear as day! When he needed help in securing the ship, supplies and men, Richard Havilland became his legs and backdoor liaison on so many occasions running errands between himself and the Queen. All the secrecy was done this way to help keep the waters particularly mudded in order to keep the Monarchy out of it officially. Finally, he spoke.

"I don't want to believe it Albert. I've known this man for years."

"There's only one way to find out, send for him," Albert said plainly.

Lord Denman walked over to a long silken chord behind his desk and pulled it summoning one of the servants. In a moment, the young servant girl entered the room from a side door.

"Yes, your Lordship?" she curtsied.

"Do you know if Mr. Havilland has arrived yet?" he asked.

"He's not coming in today sir. He sent word that he had a family matter to take care of," she said simply.

"Thank you Phoebe. That will be all."

"Do you know where the man lives Thomas?" Albert Whitaker asked. "This has got to be looked into now. If he is our man, he could be on the run. We need him in order to find out the depth of their organizational structure."

"Yes, yes, of course," his Lordship said as he fumbled through his desk trying to retrieve his address book. Flipping through the pages, he found what he was looking for. "This is all so unbelievable. I'm going with you to confront this head on. I'll have to see it with my own eyes before I believe it."

"Very well, I still have a coach and two body guards standing just outside the door that we can take. Do you have a pistol?" Albert asked. "This might get sticky."

"I have two pocket pistols, but I haven't fired them in ages. I might better recharge them." Taking the two pistols from a desk drawer, he walked over to a window, opened it and fired off each pistol at a tree standing nearby. The first one fired, but the second was a dud. "Glad I did that. It could have put us in a pickle barrel had it not fired when I needed it to. Just like old times, eh Albert?"

"Yes Thomas, just like old times. Only we were a lot younger then as I remember it. Has it really been so long ago? I would have sworn it had only been a few weeks ago since our swashbuckling days," Mr. Whitaker recited.

Suddenly, the servant girl reentered the room full of fear.

"Are you alright sir? I heard a gunshot."

"Yes child, I'm fine. Go on about your duties. I was merely testing an old pistol, no need for alarm," his Lordship declared. "Now where did I put that ball and powder? Oh yes, on top of the hearth. It keeps the powder dry you see. I'll recharge the guns before we go."

Stepping through the door, the two men inside met the two guards standing outside. Mr. Whitaker introduced Galen Sims, but didn't mention the other man because it didn't seem important at the time. As they entered the carriage, Galen Simms was asked again to retell the whole story of seeing Richard Havilland with the fat Turk at the Peacock. It was unfortunate, but his story seemed believable. The part about him possibly being a Muslim troubled him because he had seen no sign of it in his life. In fact, he had even remembered seeing him in church on rare occasions. Time would certainly tell.

Arriving at the home of Richard Havilland, they were met by a kindly housekeeper who let them in with the soldiers standing close by.

"I'm looking for Mr. Havilland, is he in today?" Lord Denman asked. She certainly knew who the great man was, and there was no pretext of treachery or deceit in her voice.

"No my Lord. He received a message from someone early this morning and had to go to the precinct jail. It appears there was a breakout of some kind there last night and it seemed to trouble him ever so much. Also, a jailor and his wife died mysteriously of some kind of food poisoning at their home late yesterday, and he thought it might be connected somehow," she said.

Galen and 'Bob' rolled their eyes. They didn't know the poor man was going to take the steaks home and share them with his wife.

"How long has he been gone?"

"He's been gone since around eight o'clock this morning sir," she answered.

"Where is Mr. Havilland's office?" the solicitor asked thinking there may be a clue or something left behind for them to follow.

"No one is allowed in there sir. It is strictly forbidden. I've worked here eight years, and even I have never been in there. I'm sorry sir," she answered trying to defend the man's privacy.

"Which room would that be?" he asked again nicely.

"Oh sir, you mustn't," she said almost in tears as she pointed to the door at the end of the hall.

It was a massive door with sturdy locks, but with the determined help of two strong soldiers at his disposal, it was soon opened. After opening the blinds to let the light in, the men felt like they had stepped off a boat in Tunisia directly into the heart of the Middle East. There was a prayer rug and shawl that faced toward Mecca and multiple copies of the Koran on his desk next to plans of the black ship. There was also row after row of history from the region laid out in books. Richard Havilland might have been born English, but he had sold his soul to Allah and kept it well hidden for years. So, after becoming a Muslim convert, the burning question was why?

"Why this big charade Albert? We English are a tolerant people. If the man wanted to be a Muslim, I wouldn't have cared one wit. It doesn't lessen my admiration for his skills as a litigator, but why would he betray us?" Lord Denman asked over and over again.

"I think the black ship made the difference," 'Bob' the soldier finally spoke up. "The ship was being sent to fight Muslims, and it didn't matter if they were pirates or not. There may also be other reasons we don't know about yet, but that's my best guess. "

"I didn't catch your name soldier?" his Lordship asked.

"I didn't give it," 'Bob' said.

"But why man? You seem to understand a lot about what's going on here better than any of us, and you've offered an opinion that actually has some merit. Who are you sir?" Thomas Denman asked.

"Don't you recognize me from our first meeting on the docks the day I came aboard the black ship. I'm James Temple, the ship's captain," he said as he removed his soldier's hat and eye patch.

"Oh My Lord! It's Resurrection Morning as sure as I live and breathe!!!" cried Mr. Whitaker in a loud voice as he grabbed James' hand and began pumping it up and down with tremendous vigor. "Is that really you my boy under all that scruff?"

James stood grinning from ear to ear as Galen and Lord Denman looked on in great excitement.

"Yes sir, it's really me, and it feels like resurrection morning for me too in more ways than you can know. For the first time in years, I feel like a man again with a purpose."

"You truly are a man with a purpose, but why the disguise my boy?" Mr. Whitaker asked unclear of his mission.

"I felt it best this way in order to find our man. When I interrogated one of the pirate's aboard ship who knew my name, I was immediately concerned. I knew they could come and kill me and my family at any moment of their choosing once I got back. Since they knew who I was and where to find me, I had to weed them out, and this was the only way I knew to do it."

"Captain Temple, I was saddened when I learned of your death this very day, but I'm certainly glad to see you have overcome it. You appear to be in fine health, can you continue your work sir?" Lord Denman asked.

"We're going to see this through to the bitter end, you can count on that," James answered with clenched jaw.

"I can't wait to send Mamie a cable and tell her the good news," Albert Whitaker stated excitedly.

"We can't do that just yet Mr. Whitaker. We have to find Richard Havilland first before he sets the hounds loose upon us," James declared sharply, "and I will still need my disguise for a little longer. Right now, I'm traveling under the name of Bob Kitchens, a man who died aboard ship." He might have technically stretched the truth a little.

"Where do we look?" Mr. Whitaker prompted. "He could be anywhere?"

"Judging by the fact he's emptied his wall safe, I think he's making a run to the Middle East somewhere," James stated matter of fact. "For some strange reason, I have a suspicion he's gonna sail on the same ship that Captain Edgerton used to pilot. I still believe there's a connection to something going on at the docks. We had planned early on to break in and look over some of the manifests from that shipping line, but we got side tracked with a hot lead that brought us here instead."

"I have another idea Cap 'n,...I can call you Cap 'n now, can't I?" Galen asked.

"Yes Galen, the cat's out of the bag. What's your idea?"

"I wouldn't be a bit surprised if our man didn't go by Eva's house one last time before leaving, cause she was kind of special to him. We could send a wire asking for help in detaining him as long as possible until we got there. What do you say Skipper, is it worth a shot?"

"At this stage of the game, I say let's try it," James stated. "We'll need to find a telegraph office and get a wire off."

As the housekeeper stood nearby, she was becoming more and more anxious. She had no idea of what was going on, or what the men were talking about concerning her employer, but it didn't sound good. Lord Denman saw her anxiety, and went to talk with her.

"Do you live in this house with Mr. Havilland?" he asked.

"No my Lord. I come every morning and leave after his evening meal," she answered.

"Does he have many visitors?"

"Not really my Lord. His last visitor was a heavy set foreigner who came here a year ago, but I didn't catch his name," she answered not realizing she was an indirect witness to the collusion of he and the fat Turk.

"Write your name and address down for me so we can find you, then give me your key and go home. Your are not to return here until I say so, because Scotland Yard will be combing the house over in their investigation. It would be best for your sake if you didn't tell anyone about any of this for now. If you need references for other work, have them contact me. From what I see, you keep a very proper house," he instructed.

"Thank you my Lord, that would be very kind of you. Am I in any sort of trouble?" she asked before leaving.

"No dear lady, you're not in any trouble. Now go home and remember my instructions. Someone will be in touch with you soon. Good day."

After writing down her name and address and handing it to Lord Denman along with the key, Agnes Gladstone left the house and went home. She would keep his instructions faithfully as she was told until further notice. She wasn't sure what Mr. Havilland was mixed up in, but she wanted no part of it. The only good thing to come from all this was his Lordship Thomas Denman said he would stand in reference for her in a new job. Her status and pay in the service just went way up.

"Well gentlemen, where do we go from here?" his Lordship asked.

James answered with a plan of his own.

"Now that I know who you are Mr. Denman, I think you should stay here until Scotland Yard arrives and follow the investigation. You may stumble into something that will need your delicate touch concerning the people you answer to. Mr. Whitaker, Galen and I will go back to the docks to follow my hunch about a certain ship sailing with our man aboard. Are we agreed?"

"It's a good plan Captain," Lord Denman agreed. "You have done us all a great service by what you have uncovered, and we are indebted to you. Henry Boles is to be commended too for bringing us such a good man to help us in our hour of need. Thank you Captain Temple, and happy resurrection morning to you once again."

"Thank you Lord Denman. That means a lot coming from you," James said as he shook the man's hand firmly. "Will you be alright here till we get reinforcements to you?"

"Yes I believe so. I still have my two pistols and plenty of powder, cap and ball. I haven't shot a skunk since my youth, but I learned a valuable lesson from the experience. If need be, I believe I can deal with the stench one more time for England's sake," he laughed. "Keep me posted Albert. It has been good seeing you again old friend."

"Same here Thomas," Mr. Whitaker said as he shook his friend's hand. "We'll go directly and find a Bobbie to help you stand guard till Scotland Yard arrives."

"Tell them to hurry, I'm getting hungry," Thomas replied.

Galen interjected with something of interest to his Lordship.

"If you wouldn't be offended sir, I have two extra breakfast biscuits filled with bacon from this morning that are still wrapped and ready to eat, if you'd like them. They're from the Cavendish Inn, and I assure you they are delicious."

"Ah yes indeed," he said as he held out a grateful hand. "I remember the Cavendish's well, and I know they are delicious. I need to visit there more often and refresh our friendship. During our swashbuckling days, Albert and I used to recuperate from some of our more daring adventures in the comfort of those marvelous people and their magical inn. Do you remember those days Albert?"

"Yes Thomas, I certainly do," Albert snickered under his breath.

"Thank you Mr. Sims for your generosity. Now the three of you best be off before I start recalling too much of our ancient history. We wouldn't want anything to slip out that might reflect badly on us, now would we Albert?"

"See you soon Thomas," Albert snickered understanding the full meaning of his words. "We'll send a Bobby along shortly."

∗∗

"When do you think father is coming home? It's been so long now," Johnny Temple asked of his step mother. Anne didn't have an answer, because like Johnny she missed her husband too.

"All I can say is, any day now he'll come up that road and cart us off. In the meantime, we need to practice patience. Maybe, you can help Mr. Potts repair the fence today," Anne answered hoping the work would take his mind off his father. "Mrs. Ginger said if you two are good today, she'd make us a delicious plum pudding to go with our supper."

"Tell Mrs. Potts for me that I'm going to be on my best behavior all day, and I'll make sure her husband is too," Johnny said as he hugged Anne and took off in search of the fence building Mr. Potts.

Not too far away, Johnny found Keely and asked him a question.

"Mr. Potts, why do you work so hard on this house and property since it doesn't belong to you?"

"This is how I make my living. If people see my work and like it, they will hire me. If they don't like my work, then I go hungry as do my wife and child. A man should take pride in what he does for a living and also with his life. I'm sure your father must have taught you this by now," Keely said.

"I guess he has in his own way. He has spent so much time at sea, that most everything he teaches revolves around sailing. What you're doing is what someone would do who loves the land as much as he loves the sea. I know I'm proud to be a sailor alongside my father, whether we are on land or sea," Johnny beamed with pride.

"I grew up not too far from here, and I hope one day to own a place like this. Everyone needs a place to come home to, even if he is just a sailor. Wouldn't you agree?" Keely asked.

"I see your point Mr. Potts. I hope you can find a home like this one someday. It would a fine place for your boy to grow up for sure."

"It is a fine place isn't it? There's plenty here to keep a youngster busy. Who knows, maybe I'll figure out how to do it in time," Keely said.

"I hope so Mr. Potts. I'd love to come visit sometimes and teach your boy how to fish, since it's apparent you don't know how."

"Why would you say I can't fish?"

"We haven't gone fishing one time since we got here. I just figured you didn't know how," Johnny teased under his breath.

"Help me get this fence up young man, and then I'll give you a real lesson on how to fish," Keely teased back.

"Now that's more like it Mr. Potts. The way I got it figured, we can't get in any real trouble if we're out catching fish."

✶✶

Riding the train back to Liverpool was a delight compared to their first night going on horseback. They were sore for two days because of that experience. James and Galen relaxed and ate inside the food car in comfort, and enjoyed the warmth of the English countryside which was a veritable smorgasbord of farms and small ranches laid out like a patchwork quilt on both sides of the tracks. Thatched roofs and clay cottages dotted the region in a comforting sort of way that made him feel very much at home.

Since leaving Virginia, he had spent very little time on land. He enjoyed the scenery, forcing him to realize there was still some land lubber lurking deep inside after all these years at sea. Eventually, he would have to settle somewhere cause he had a wife now, and not just any wife, an English wife. That's when he realized how much he missed and longed for this woman, his beautiful and unexpected English wife. He certainly hoped all this intrigue would end soon, because he was ready for life to return to normal or some semblance thereof. He also knew that she and Johnny were the reason he was still pursuing the intrigue, so they could live in peace without fear of reprisal from some unknown, faceless evil. It had to stop here.

"We're coming into the station Cap 'n," Galen said as he shook James from his sweet slumber. Thoughts of Anne had restored his sense of purpose and gave him new vigor.

"While we're here, try to avoid calling me Captain for a little while longer. James will do just fine unless 'Bob' needs to take over, got it," James directed.

"Aye sir."

"Where do we go first?" Mr. Whitaker asked.

"To find some proper clothes for a dock worker; I'm tired of playing soldier. Mr. Whitaker, I would like for you to go see the local constabulary in case we need backup. We're going to need a place to put our pigeon once we clip his wings. If Scotland Yard has a branch here, it might be worthwhile to bring them in. The more eyes the better, I say," James instructed.

"How are you fixed for money?" Mr. Whitaker asked knowing they must have spent plenty chasing this lead from one side of the country to the other. "Here, I have a few pounds on me, take this. Where shall I meet you later?"

"At the Peacock Tavern. We'll be sitting in the back around ten o'clock tonight if we haven't found anything. After making contact with the law, you should go home and wait."

"Once we get new clothes, can we go see if Eva has any information for us?" Galen asked.

From the look in his eye, James could tell there was more than duty on his mind concerning her.

"Why don't we go in our uniforms. You know how women love uniforms. I'll just wait outside the door to keep down the flow of traffic while you investigate the premises," James teased unmercifully.

Within the hour, the two maverick soldiers were standing on Eva Langtree's stoop about to enter when they heard someone cry out. Ordinarily, this would have been reason enough to break the door in and investigate, but Galen was an old hand at interpreting sounds coming from Eva's home.

"Come on, let's get in there," James pleaded.

"Hold up Cap 'n. These waters should be tested using a measure of delicate diplomacy," Galen said uneasily. "Trust me sir, I know what I'm doing. Let me ring the bell instead."

James stood firm as Galen took the lead and rang the bell.

Through the glass edges, Galen could clearly see someone moving around inside the living room coming to the door, but something was off. Eventually the door opened, and there standing before him was a far different woman than Eva. The woman's hair was platted in an elegant French braid down her back, and her face appeared fresh with just a hint of pink flushing in her cheeks. Her lips had a tint of color about them that made them very appealing. The lady was dressed in a nice blue business suit that a woman of purpose might have worn professionally, and she cut quite a figure. There was yet however, an air of familiarity about her, but who was she? Perhaps Eva had taken sick and this was a sister or family member come to tend her. Galen only hoped she was okay.

"Begging your pardon Madam. I'm needing to have a word with Miss Eva Langtree if she's home," Galen blurted out.

The woman looked oddly at him and smiled.

"It's me sailor, Eva," she said looking him up and down, "or should I say soldier." Her tone had changed from wild and unrestrained to something bordering on refined civilization. What a difference a few days and a different set of clothes have made on her.

"Eva?" Galen questioned. "You're Eva Langtree? You look so different. Why, you're simply amazing! What,...?"

"When I got your cable about looking out for Hakeem, I knew then you were coming back. I spent the day thinking about my life and decided to make a few changes. I asked what would it hurt to try out something different and see if it appealed to you. Do you like the new look?" she asked.

"I'm speechless. I wasn't sure you were the same woman, no offense meant," he said.

"None taken. Won't you and your friend please come in?"

"First things first Eva. Have you seen Hakeem? It's a matter of great importance."

"Yes, he came by earlier asking for a little special consideration since he was leaving town on business," she answered coyly.

"How long has he been gone? And did he say by any chance where he was heading?"

"Oh, he hasn't left yet."

"You mean he's still here in the house, right now?" Galen whispered.

"Yes, come see," she answered nonchalantly.

Into her bedroom the two men went, one behind the other. There on the four poster bed lay Hakeem the rat, tied at all four corners of the massive bed with leather straps, fully naked and terrified for his life. He made noises but the heavy gag over his mouth kept the insane terror emanating from his black heart quite subdued.

"Is that your man?" Eva asked with a grin on her transformed face.

"Like I said Eva, you are amazing. Isn't she amazing 'Bob'?" Galen beamed as he turned to introduce this new and improved version of Eva Langtree.

"Yes, I believe she certainly is. It appears as though everything our sailor has told me about you is absolutely true. You are amazing," James spoke proudly. "If you two will excuse me, I'm going to step out and find a copper. We need a caged paddy wagon to come pick up our pigeon so he don't fly away. Will you two be alright here while I'm gone?"

"Yes sir," Galen said unable to take his eyes off Eva, "I think we're going to be just fine."

"Be back soon," James said disappearing out the front door.

Hakeem recognized Galen and James from the jail, and he really began to act up again trying to get loose from his bonds. Before Galen took measures in his own hands to shut him up, Eva held up a butcher's knife to where Hakeem could see it.

"If you don't settle down, I'm going to cut something off and stuff it in your mouth. Can't you see I'm trying to talk here," she blasted.

Hakeem settled down immediately, because he knew Eva meant every word she said. To the rat faced man, there was only one thing more terrifying than death, and she was standing in this room with a big knife in her hand. So here he would sit in humiliation and disgrace waiting for the wagon. Who knows, maybe Lord Denman would find someone to defend him. Then again, maybe not.

"What's with the soldier's uniform?" Eva asked as she traced his buttons with her finger.

"It's a very long story," Galen answered smiling back at her.

"I think I have the time," she said. "Why don't we step into the other room and you can tell me all about it. You're allowed to do that aren't you?"

"Talking is allowed," Galen said as they went and sat down in the parlor on the nice chairs and began a conversation. He couldn't tell her everything just yet, but he could make small talk and stare. She was after all, amazing.

Within the hour, James returned with some coppers and a paddy wagon filled with three drunks, one of which had just thrown up.

"Too bad we didn't have time to paint your picture in that pose, because where you're going, it would've been a good means of introduction to your new cell mates. Maybe after they hang you, one of them will paint a different pose of you for old time's sake," James said as Hakeem passed by him on his way to the wagon with his pants held tightly in front of his private parts.

"They will find you Bob Kitchens and your family and kill you. You will regret the day you ever crossed my path," Hakeem threatened.

"Yeah, and I think you're going to regret the day you crawled into the back of this wagon with three happy drunks. Watch your step," James chided. That's when he fully comprehended that Hakeem had just called him Bob Kitchens. If Hakeem's people go looking for Bob

Kitchens and his family, they're going to be mighty confused for a long time. First off, he's been dead for a while, and second, he had no family. This could actually work to his advantage if Hakeem could manage to get a message from prison to one of his supposed assassins. What a twist of irony that 'Bob' could give his life so freely in the first unselfish act of his miserable life in order to save a fellow sailor. His death might yet be noted in the national archives as one of England's most heroic merchant seaman.

All the way down the road until out of sight, James could hear Hakeem screaming as the drunks sang their favorite bar songs in an effort to drown him out. If there was such a thing as poetic justice, then it was on display here in perfect three part harmony. They weren't half bad either.

"Galen, where are you? We have to go," James called out.

"Be right with you," he answered as he was attempting to say goodbye to Eva.

"Will you come back and see me again?" she asked.

"You can count on it. I'll send a telegram first so I don't come up on something unexpected," he answered.

"Could I tell you something before you go sailor?" she asked.

"Of course Eva. You can tell me anything."

"I haven't always played the part of a wicked woman. You may find this hard to believe, but I was once a teacher in a very exclusive private school. The way I met you at the door was how I used to dress every day for work. Luckily, I could still fit in one of my old outfits. The thing is, I made the mistake of falling in love with a fellow teacher who happened to be married. Once we were found out, it seemed a scandal was imminent, so I left school in the middle of the night to spare him the humiliation. As far as I know, he and his wife are still married," she began. "I even changed my name from Sarah Langley to Eva Langtree."

Galen held up his hand cutting her off.

"I don't care about your past, all I'm interested in right now is you and what kind of future you want for yourself. It's true you have a lot to overcome, but you haven't heard my story yet. You might not be so interested in me after you hear it all."

"Well, it does look like another visit would be in order. Maybe we could sort it all out then. Will you really come back?" she asked.

"Of course I will Eva, as soon as this mess is cleaned up."

"There is one other thing before you go," she began. "I want you to know I never had any sexual relations with Hakeem. He was an odd duck who always loved to come here and play act, and that's how I captured him. My role today was to dress like a schoolteacher and tie him up, which I did. Sometimes, I would just whip him with a leather strap till he found his sexual release, and that would be the end of it till next time. I think he must have had something pretty dark hidden in his past that drove him to do such strange things. In fact, most of the men who come here, come to play. I made it safe for them to act out their fantasies without fear of discovery or humiliation. That's why I began calling them sessions, because I felt more like a doctor treating sick men than a harlot."

"That does bring me some comfort Eva, if that was your intent. Right now I have to go because our business is not yet finished," Galen said plainly. He knew James was getting impatient.

"Will you really come again sailor?" Eva asked once more as they stood up , still unsure of Galen's intentions. Her lifestyle had been a lot to take in.

"The answer is still yes," Galen whispered as he kissed her cheek.

****

At the waterfront, 'Bob' and Galen fumbled with the lock on the back door leading into the office of the company Captain Edgerton once sailed for. They had to know for sure whether Hakeem ran an organization of spies, or was it just a handful of greedy men who owned Hakeem. He was after all a very high placed mole with plenty of valuable information sticking to his fingertips on a daily basis. Lord Denman was probably still kicking himself for not seeing it. Once they were in, James spoke softly as he lit a couple of candles.

"Pull down the shades."

"What are we looking for exactly Cap 'n?"

"I believe Scotland Yard calls them clues," James answered. "I believe there has got be something here that will give us some insight. We just have to figure out what it is."

Slowly they began rummaging through drawers and boxes looking for clues. It had to be something out of the ordinary or they might never find it.

"Look behind those wall paintings to see if there is a wall safe," James instructed Galen as he continued to dig. In a moment he heard Galen snap his fingers together to get his attention.

"Well, hello there. What do you reckon these are for?" Galen wondered aloud as he handed James his find. It appeared to be several daguerreotype pictures containing the group images of young females in various poses and sundry levels of disrobement.

James took one of the pictures and studied on it. They all appeared to be English or European girls between the ages of twelve and eighteen. Turning the first picture over, he found a single inscription on the back that read: 'Group fifteen, ten girls, Tunisia.' The second picture had: 'Group sixteen, twelve girls, Algeria.' The third plate had: 'Group seventeen, nine girls, Tripoli.' Suddenly, Galen broke James' concentration with a further revelation of something he found.

"Skipper, you need to see this!" Galen said excitedly as he held up a small ledger he found next to the pictures. "It may help to explain some things."

James took the little ledger and opened it. On the left side of the page was a reference to eighteen girls who had been bracketed as group one. It had the first name and last name of a girl and her age. On the right side of the column across from it were sums of money posted in pounds sterling by that girls name, and each was a princely sum. Also listed was the shipping date of each group. As he studied on the pictures and ledger, he began to understand everything. This shipping line was not only dealing in lawful goods of commerce on the surface, but someone was running the very unlawful practice of selling young females into servitude as concubines or worse. The way the girls were posed, it appeared they were showing off their assets so a client could see what he was getting for his money. There was probably only one buyer in each port who purchased the lot and distributed them as he saw fit just as the American slave traders did. Nasty business all the way around.

The question still remaining was who ran this particular endeavor? Was it one of the owners inside the consortium who did so with full knowledge of the operation, or was it someone from inside the working office here on the dock who stood to profit. He certainly had enough evidence to give Scotland Yard something to work with and so they decided to leave. After placing the pictures and the ledger in a small canvas bag they found, they walked to the door intending to leave. As James touched the knob, he felt it turning slowly in his hand startling him. He knew they had been found out so he turned to Galen motioning him to step to one side in preparation for what was coming through the door. Quickly they snuffed the candles and prepared for battle.

As the door opened, a pistol barrel came forward through the crack as the man wielding it stepped in. Quick as a Virginia rattler, James grabbed the man's hand and pulled him into the darkened room forcing the gun to fire. With the flash of gunfire lighting the room for a millisecond, James struck his man with a firm blow across the left side of his jaw sending him across the room. He dove in after him to make sure he would stay down, but the man was still moving. As they grappled on the floor for dominance, a second man came in with two pistols in hand. Galen slammed the door on him forcing one pistol to fire and punched the man in the gut with all his might. The man doubled over and Galen hit him behind the head with another massive fist sending him down to the floor. Taking the one pistol in hand that hadn't been fired, he turned his attention back to the door to see who else might be lurking behind it. It took only a second for Galen to grasp these two were not alone. It was hard to tell for sure, but he sensed there were possibly five or six more on the outside.

As James finished his man off with an ivory paperweight from the desk, he stood to his feet assuming a defensive posture. It was still plenty dark in the room, but he could hear the men on the outside. He whispered to Galen checking on his status.

"Galen you still with me?"

"Right as rain, but we got ourselves a mess of trouble. I heard one of them call for some lantern oil. I think they're going to burn the place with us in it. Any ideas?" Galen queried trying not to get to anxious.

James looked around as best he could in the darkness, cause he had an idea. This office was built over the water on wooden piers. What if it had a trap door of some kind that led below?

"Quick, prop a chair against the door handle to keep them from rushing us. Then get down on your knees and help me see if the floor has a trap door," James instructed.

181

In a moment, both men were moving things around try to find a doorway leading out of here. Rugs were lifted as the two men rolled everything around in their efforts to escape. The only place they hadn't looked yet was under the desk.

"Help me push this back," James said. As they heaved on the heavy desk, it slid forward. Down on their hands and knees again they went in search of hope.

Suddenly, James called out.

"I think I have it,...yes here it is," he said as he grabbed the iron loop and pulled up on it. "Do you still have the pistol?"

"Yes Cap 'n."

"Hand it to me. I have a suspicious feeling they know about the door too. You pull and I'll shoot if there is anyone down there waiting for us. Ready, set, go!" James said as Galen lifted the door.

As their moment of escape seemed eminent, the fire on the outside of the office was beginning to burn with serious intensity. James hesitated waiting to see or hear something stirring below him in the darkness. As the flames got higher, it began to illuminate the whole area including the walking deck directly below the office. There on the catwalk was a man with a rifle positioned to fire on anyone trying to escape through the trap door. At the moment, he was more engaged in watching the fire than in watching for them which was to their advantage. The only thing they couldn't tell for sure was whether or not he was alone.

"Here Galen, hang onto this bag. I'm going down to get our man. If there are more of them, I want you to get out of here and get this to the authorities," James commanded.

"Begging the Cap 'n's pardon, I'm not going anywhere without you," Galen said plainly. "So take your best shot."

James grinned back at his stubborn friend as he steadied his aim. Luckily for James, the pistol Galen had handed him was a Weiss Brothers fifty caliber over and under made in London. Smooth bore guns were notorious for not being very accurate beyond fifty feet, so he had the benefit of a second round in case he missed. The man on the catwalk looked up at just the right moment to notice James bearing down on him with his pistol. As he raised his rifle to shoot, James fired, hitting him dead on in the chest. As the man fell to one side into the water, bad luck dictated there had to be two of them. Quickly the second man slipped behind a massive pillar awaiting a clear shot at James. If James missed, he and Galen were dead men.

They could certainly feel the intense heat from the fire as it began to roar around them. James quickly came up with an idea how to draw his fire. Turning to Galen he spoke.

"Slide one of those men over here to me."

Galen crawled around on the floor in the flickering light till he found one of the men, pulling him to the opening. James tried to move the man into position making it appear as if he was the person coming down the stair. There was only one chance at this deception, or their goose was literally cooked.

Positioning the man ever closer to the opening, he made him an easy target for the rifleman as he animated his limp arms to draw his fire. He and Galen moved back to keep out of the line of fire. If the rifleman hit his mark, there was a good chance the bullet could pass through and hit one of them. Soon the rifleman slipped to one side of the pier and took his shot, hitting the man straight on. The bullet passed through and hit the wall behind them. As the body fell to the catwalk for dead, the rifleman cheered and stepped back behind the pier to reload. Reloading takes about a minute to complete giving James ample time to scurry down and tag him. If there were a third man, James figured he could shoot him and still get to his man before he could finish reloading.

Down he went like a cat squirrel and ran to the nearby pillar where the man was hiding. The rifleman heard him and turned to face James as he was ramming the bullet home, but it was too late. James struck him across the head with his pistol knocking him into the water without a shot being fired. He reached out and grabbed the man's rifle before it went in, giving them two effective shots to fight with.

"Come on," James signaled.

Galen and James scurried across the poorly lit catwalk to freedom. Finding a small skiff tied to the dock, they crawled in and paddled away into the night leaving the main offices of Wilson and Sons Shipping L.T.D., to burn down to the waterline.

"Do you still have the bag Galen?"

"Aye Skipper, it's held fast."

"Good, we'll need it to sort all this out. I wonder if Mr. Wilson is in on any of this?" James queried.

"I have a righteous feeling that Hakeem will spill the beans before long. He doesn't appear to be a man who's accustomed to hard life behind bars or worse," Galen replied.

"I never dreamed we would stumble into human trafficking before we set out tonight. This adventure has got more twists and turns that a garter snake. We still don't know who is behind it all, but I believe we are closer than ever to finding out. With any luck at all, Albert might be able to shed some light on what we've discovered."

"I bet you didn't know when you signed on for this little adventure, that it was gonna turn itself into a real stem winder. One thing is for sure, a fellow might get hisself killed following you around, but he won't die of boredom," Galen chuckled.

"I'm glad you're having so much fun. Now paddle hard you lusty old pirate, or I'll tell Eva about how her brave sailor is afraid of spiders."

"Aye Cap 'n, I'm paddling, I'm paddling."

Chapter IX

James and Galen met with Mr. Whitaker at the Peacock Tavern a little after ten p.m. in a very disheveled state. The elder gentleman was mighty glad to see them, having feared they had met with foul play somewhere along the way. From their vantage point they could see the immense fire lighting up the night skies on the horizon. Mr. Whitaker felt compelled to comment on it.

"Did you fellows notice the fire on your way in? It looks to be a bad one."

"Yes sir, we couldn't help but see it, we were right in the middle of it," James explained, lighting Mr. Whitakers eyes up with the news.

"Tell me everything," he pleaded.

So from the beginning, James and Galen regaled him of their exploits bringing his expressive face to life. Finally they showed him the satchel with the ledger and photographs in it.

"This is why they tried to burn the place down Mr. Whitaker. They needed to destroy all the witnesses and the evidence we have for a conviction. The only thing we don't know yet, is whether or not the owner knew about any of this, or if it was a side line for someone on the docks. I'm hoping the book still has some clues in it," James said.

"Come gentlemen, let's get out of here," Mr. Whitaker declared. "I have a safe place for us to stay tonight. Tomorrow we'll meet with Scotland Yard, and then we'll see where the facts lead us."

"Does this safe place have anything to eat?" Galen asked about the time his belly growled like a hungry lion on the prowl.

The other men laughed.

"Yes, Mr. Sims, I believe we can accommodate your appetites," Mr. Whitaker laughed. "Come gentlemen, my carriage is out back."

****

The next day at Scotland Yard almost turned out to be a fiasco as the chief of detectives practically refused to believe their report. Mr. Whitaker finally took all he was going to and asked to see the police commissioner. Happily, the detective moved the whole affair from his office over into the hands of the commissioner and disappeared. After retelling their story, the commissioner shook his head in disbelief.

"Let's just say for the moment I believe you. How should I approach Mr. Wilson with this information? He is not merely a wealthy business man, he is also a magistrate in this district. I do believe he would bring charges of harassment against me and the entire department for trying to besmirch his good name during his reelection. The man has higher ambitions, if you haven't heard. This could be a serious house of cards that comes crashing down around our ears should something go wrong," the commissioner bellowed in despair.

Mr. Whitaker finally had enough of the whining concerning the merits of political correctness.

"My good fellow, if you do not do your duty after what I've presented you, I will be forced to contact Lord Thomas Denman himself and report this whole sorry affair. He is well aware of everything I've just told you, and I assure you sir, I am not without political capitol of my own to rival that of Mr. Wilson. Bring the man in so we can find out where the facts lead us. He is part of my trading consortium and I assure you, he is a reasonable man. You ask him to come, he will most assuredly come."

"Oh very well,...Sergeant, call Chief Detective Fields back into my office!" he yelled to the man in the outer office. In a matter of minutes, a frustrated Chief Detective Fields was standing front and center.

"Chief Detective, I want you to go find Magistrate Wilson and ask him to come down to the station for a sit down conference with us. Tell him it's concerning a case and his presence is required. Are we clear?" the commissioner asked knowing how difficult this was going to be for his Chief Detective. The Detective was retiring at week's end and his plan was to work as a constable in Magistrate Wilson's court. He was hoping in a year to have a nice little nest egg built up in order to purchase a sail boat with his two salaries. Sometimes duty is a difficult mistress.

"Yes Commissioner, as you wish," the perplexed Chief Detective answered.

"Can I get you gentlemen some refreshments while we wait?" the Commissioner asked trying to be a gracious host.

"Tea would be nice," Mr. Whitaker answered.

Galen looked over at James and spoke his peace.

"I need something stronger than tea. There's a pub across the street if anyone cares to join me."

"I believe I'll go with you Galen. If you gentlemen will excuse us," James said standing to his feet. Then Mr. Whitaker shocked them with a request.

"Would you fellows mind terribly if an old fuddy duddy like me joined you? My backbone needs a little stiffening for this occasion and tea just won't cut it. Care to join us commissioner?"

"As long as one of you jokers is buying. If I go down in flames because of this, I can at least go home with my own money still in my pocket," he laughed. As they stepped through the door he spoke instructions to the sergeant. "When Chief Detective Fields gets back, send someone to O'Grady's across the street to fetch us. We'll be in conference there till then."

"Yes sir."

****

Bill B. Blankenship stepped up to the door and pulled the chain ringing the bell inside. It was Thursday and he had a business appointment with the woman inside concerning a loan of some importance. Today he was to receive his final payment of collateral towards the loan she had requested, and he couldn't wait to get under way with the details of final closure. As the door opened, he had just finished wiping the top surface of his shoe on the back of his britches leg to make it shine.

"Oh, good day madam. I'm here to see Miss Eva Langtree. Would you please tell her that Bill Blankenship is here to see her. I have an appointment."

"Yes, my sister told me you were coming. I'm afraid I have bad news for you Mr. Blankenship," the woman began. "Eva has taken ill, and I'm not sure if she'll make it through the night."

"What do you mean?" the man questioned with serious intensity.

"It appears she picked up something contagious from one of her clients last week. Are you a client, or merely here on business as you propose?" the woman asked knowingly. "Don't worry, I know what my sister does here. I've been trying to help her stop for some time now, but it looks like death has stepped up to offer a helping hand."

Bill Blankenship's thirty year old face turned ashen white with the news. Could he possibly be next?

"What's that honey?" the woman turned as if listening to a voice coming from the bedroom. "Just one minute please sir, I'll be right back. Eva's calling me." In a moment, the distinguished looking woman reemerged from the bedroom with her head down. "Mr. Blankenship, Eva said to give you a message."

"What kind of message?" he asked

"She said you should go back to the church where you once were a choir boy and take hold of your forgotten faith. She apologizes for any corrupting influence she may have had in leading you down this sinful path. She asks for your forgiveness."

"Tell her I forgive her, and I hope she makes a full recovery for a whole host of reasons. Good day madam," he said as he turned and ran down the street in a terrified state of mind.

As the woman closed the door, she leaned back against it and sighed deeply with real sadness for the life Eva Langtree had lived. Her final thought before leaving to prepare tea was, 'Welcome back Sarah darling. I've been missing you.'

∗∗

An hour and a half passed before someone finally came to retrieve the men at O'Grady's pub. The three men had been very constrained as they spoon fed the commissioner all their information again. He seemed to take it better after loosening up with a few belts, and that plied well for their cause. Finally, he spoke in defense of his first meeting with them.

"I'm sorry about the way I treated the lot of you when you first came in. No hard feelings I hope. Oops, I'm not Hope, that's my daughter's name; how shrilly of me," he giggled. "Whew, it's getting hot in here. Are you men hot? Oh my, I find police work so stressful at times, don't you agree Mr. Whippleker," he laughed and giggled all the more. Of course, that made the men laugh too because they sensed the commissioner was beginning to slip into his happy place.

Galen noticed it first and ordered black coffee for the table.

"Come on fella's, we gotta have just one more for the road," the commissioner belched out. "Why don't we go get the whole bunch and bring them over here to sort it out. What do you say Gayle ole' boy?"

"More coffee please," was all Gayle ole' boy had to say.

Another twenty minutes passed before they could leave in good conscience. The poor commissioner hadn't eaten anything that morning, and the alcohol hit him like a ton of bricks. The walk, fresh air and the acquisition of a couple of muffins really helped in lifting the fog of silliness clouding his head. So by the time they reached the top of the stairs, Commissioner Ragsdale was mostly back in the game and looking for a toilet to accommodate his full bladder.

"Be right with you," he said as he disappeared inside the loo.

Meanwhile the other men went inside the commissioner's office and found the magistrate and Chief Detective Fields waiting.

"Brian, it's good to see you. I'm so sorry about the fire and the loss of your offices last night," Mr. Whitaker spoke first.

"It's a bloody mess Albert. One of the night watchmen told me it was a couple of heavily armed hooligans who broke in. They killed four men once they were discovered and torched the place on their way out to cover up their crimes. It left a bloody mess all the way around. I don't keep any money there, so I don't know what in the world they were after," Brian Wilson answered very disheartened.

"Maybe they were after records of some kind to slander you with. Do you keep anything there that could have been of a sensitive nature if it got out?" Mr. Whitaker asked trying to guide the conversation.

"The only thing I kept there was ship's business. All bills of laden, ship manifests and crew records are there, but nothing I would deem scandalous," Brian explained. "Oh, there were a few trinkets from the early years that I valued from our travels, but they would have no meaning or value to anyone else."

"What about these?" Mr. Whittaker asked as he handed the three daguerreotypes to his friend.

As the men fastened their eyes onto Mr. Wilson's face for signs of guilt or exposure, they weren't disappointed. Looking up from the pictures, he stared squarely at his colleague and the other men with a troubled look in his eyes.

"What's it all about Albert? Who are these young people and why are they dressed like that? I've known you long enough to know there must be something more to this," he said. "Where did you get these?"

"You sure you've never seen these?" Albert asked.

"No, of course not. Why would you ask such a thing? I have grandchildren the same age as some of those children. Who would take such disgusting pictures? If you think this has something to do with me, then spit it out. Otherwise our business here will be done gentlemen," he fumed as he stood to leave.

"Brian, hold up. I'm not accusing you of anything. It's just that these pictures were found in your offices that burned on the docks," Albert declared.

"Preposterous! I would never have owned such filth, and I would have seen them had they been there," he answered.

"Not where these were hid," 'Bob' spoke up.

"What do you mean by that? How do you know they came from there?" an agitated Mr. Wilson queried as he turned to look at the scruffy man who made the statement.

"Because we took them from your office," 'Bob' answered for he and Galen. "And just for the record, we didn't burn your building. That came from the dozen or so other armed thugs outside your offices who were there trying to kill us. We did get four of them on our way out using their own weapons against them."

Magistrate Wilson looked flabbergasted. Were these really the two men who caused so much destruction to his business and the loss of four lives? If so, why hadn't they been arrested? Turning to the commissioner, he asked a simple question.

"Do you know anything about this George?" he asked of the commissioner. This whole affair was starting to make his head hurt.

"I know a lot about it Brian, that's why you're here. You had better sit back down while these men tell you a little story. Judging by your reaction to the pictures, I'm confident at this stage you were not part of this. Are you gentlemen satisfied he's not a part of this?" the commissioner asked the three other men.

The three men nodded their head in agreement.

"Albert, why don't you start and go slow. Sometimes it takes a while for unbelievable things like this soak in," the commissioner stated flatly. "Mr. Whitaker, you have the floor."

"Alright, but I don't see any way I can do this delicately, so I'll just jump in. Brian, it looks as though someone has been stealing our children and selling them to markets in the Middle East. They have been doing it through your shipping line and on your ships for some time now," Mr. Whitaker began.

Brian Wilson liked to have popped a cork with this accusation.

"That's impossible!" he screamed. "I don't believe a word of it."

'Bob' handed the man the ledger with the names and ages of the girls. As he opened the book and began to read the columns, he saw the sums paid for each child and almost screamed in despair. This couldn't be true.

"We found the ledger and the pictures hidden in a cubby hole behind a painting on the wall behind your big desk. I have suspected for some time something was going on through those offices, but I wasn't sure what it was. Believe it or not Mr. Wilson, someone is selling English children as sex slaves through your respectable business right under your nose to markets all over the Middle East."

After looking through the ledger, Mr. Wilson's demeanor was shaken to the core. He closed the book and tears welled up in his eyes. Finally, he looked up with a new awareness in his eyes.

"I recognized two of those names on the roster that lived in my neighborhood. The girls grew up playing with my two grandchildren and stayed in my home on many occasions when we had birthday parties. They went missing more than a year ago and it tore our hearts out. I loved those girls as my own. Who would do such a thing?"

"Mr. Wilson, who runs your day to day operations?" 'Bob' asked.

"Well, I hired a man three years ago to help me when I went into the legal service. He came to me with a long list of credentials and has kept things running smoothly ever since. In so many ways, he has been a godsend by taking the load of operations off my shoulders. I can hardly believe he would be involved in a thing like this," Mr. Wilson spoke in despair.

"Who is he?" 'Bob' asked once again.

"His name is Able Puckett, a former sea captain in his own right, but I just don't believe he could be involved. He has become almost like a son to me."

'Bob' and Galen gasped out loud as they turned to look at each other, because now they knew with certainty who the head of the snake was. Everyone in the room watched the two men with blank expressions on their faces knowing something was amiss. Mr. Whitaker spoke first in anticipation.

"What is it gentlemen? What do you know?"

"Mr. Whitaker, do you remember my file?" 'Bob' asked.

"Yes, I read every word," he answered unsure where this was going.

"The man who had me drummed from the Navy on charges of interfering in lawful commerce and scourged in the public square was none other than Captain,...Able,...Puckett. Only a slave trader could have a soul this dark. To a man like him, this is nothing more than an another act of commerce."

Brian Wilson sat flabbergasted unable to speak. Could it be true?

"Magistrate, where does this man live?" Commissioner Ragsdale asked. He thought it might be wise to detain him for questioning.

"I have his records at my home. I always keep a separate set of books there just in case of a fire. I'll need to go and unlock the safe to retrieve them," the magistrate answered with a great amount of inward pain.

"We'll all go with you sir," the commissioner said as he placed his hand on the magistrate's shoulder. "Chief Detective, assemble a squad of men and arm them with weapons. Find out the status of our paddy wagons while you're at it, cause I think we may need them all before this day is done."

****

Two hours later, a squad of policemen, Commissioner Ragsdale, Chief Detective Fields, Mr. Whitaker, 'Bob' and Galen, and poor distraught Mr. Wilson arrived at Captain Puckett's house to arrest him. The commissioner deployed his men around the block as the five men marched up to the massive front door. Mr. Wilson was certain the good captain would come along peaceably if he saw him standing in the midst, and cautiously stepped up the door to test his theory.

As he rang the ship's bell to announce their presence, two shots rang out through the heavy door hitting Mr. Wilson squarely in the gut. Lucky for him, the hard oak door took the brunt of the blow, but it still hurt like a good punch in the gut. Puckett had seen the commissioner and the string of police officers lining the street through the glass window, and assumed they were there for him concerning the fire and other things. Had he not come back for a few things he valued after the fire, he might have gotten away scot free.

"That's our cue," James remarked as he and Galen commenced to battering the door in. It took four good heaves to shake it loose from its moorings, but it finally gave way frame and all.

As the men landed in the center of the opulent and expensively furnished room, Puckett ran to the fireplace to grab a sword from the mantle. The commissioner stepped through the doorway about this time with pistol in hand intent on shooting this foul bird and be done with it. James stopped him.

"We want him alive to tell us where the girls went and were the ones are he was about to ship. Dead men can't talk."

"I see your point Bob, and I concede it. Since he's not going anywhere, how do you plan on disarming him?" the commissioner queried.

Looking around the room, 'Bob' saw plenty of ways to distract the good captain. "Watch and learn commissioner," was all he said.

Rushing headlong at the captain, 'Bob' began throwing books, pillows, vases, chairs and finally a small statue that was commissioned by Puckett of himself. All the items had the desired effect of distracting Puckett long enough so 'Bob' could deflect the sword from harm's way and strike him across the face. Tossing the sword to one side gave them equal footing, and now it was time to settle an old score. The only thing was, Puckett didn't know who was smashing his brains in.

"Who are you people, and why are you here?" Puckett screamed out from the corner of the room where he had landed on his buttocks.

"We're here about the girls," 'Bob' said as he slapped the man.

"The girls were all Captain Edgerton's idea," Puckett stammered out trying to deflect blame onto a dead man.

"Throw me your knife Galen. I'm going to castrate this feral dog with the next wrong answer he gives me," 'Bob' said plainly. This particular strategy had worked before, so why not try it again.

Galen threw 'Bob' his knife and Puckett began to sing like a canary.

"Alright, alright,...the girls are in an abandoned warehouses along the waterfront. The three groups were being stored there until time to sail. They were supposed to sail last night with Richard Havilland on board, but the fire created so much havoc he failed to materialize."

"Don't worry your head none about Mr. Havilland, we have him in custody too. How was he involved in all this?" Chief Detective Fields questioned.

"He took over from the Turk once he died. He's the only one who knew the contact information once they reached their destination. The girls here haven't been harmed, because the new owners wanted virgins."

"What about the other girls you've already sent over. Do you have information on them?" the commissioner asked.

"Yes, yes, the files are in my desk in the other room, but you will never find them. They have probably been bought and sold many times since then," he sneered causing 'Bob' to strike him in the mouth with a broken chair leg knocking out his front teeth. Through the blood and pain he cried out, "Who are you tormentor?"

"You don't recognize me Captain Puckett? You should, cause I put you in chains one night in the middle of the Atlantic ocean ten years ago," James said loudly barely able to contain his fury.

Puckett's eyes went wild in disbelief.

"It's impossible! They told me you were dead Captain Temple!"

"That's what everybody keeps saying, but as you can tell, I'm very much alive and standing here before you as your accuser."

Galen came back into the room with good news.

"The Chief Detective found his books Cap 'n. It tells us everything including who's on his payroll and who's been bribed to look the other way. It goes pretty high up and should make for some interesting late night reading. I imagine some of the fellows from last night are in there too. Judging by how fired up the Detective is, it shouldn't take too long to round them all up and hang the lot of them."

"Are you Quartermaster Sims?" Puckett asked in disbelief as his sordid past came hurtling back to haunt him.

"Aye Cap 'n Puckett, tis your old shipmate."

"I almost didn't recognize you. Why are you working to help this man? You almost beat him to death once. How is this possible?"

"All things are possible to him who believes. Since they're going to hang you in the not too distant future, I'd like to offer you a piece of advice. Find someone who can explain the eternal penalty of sin to you before it's too late. You got a lot to answer for Cap 'n Puckett when you stand before the great Judge for all those poor black souls you had us throw overboard off your ship," the Quartermaster stated matter of fact. Galen knew well the heavy weight of guilt a blackened heart lays on a man, because he once had one too. Since those days, he had been reconciled with his Maker in due course, and now lives with a new and different kind of heart. Strangely enough, James Temple, the man he almost killed with the whip, showed him mercy and how to do it. It was quite a moment for both of them as they were reconciled to each other to become friends. As Galen left the room, Puckett began calling after him with cursing and rage.

"I'll see you burn in Hell you black hearted traitor for turning your back on your old captain!"

Galen stopped for a moment and turned back to look at his former shipmate one last time with real sadness.

"I won't be seeing you in Hell Cap 'n, cause I ain't going that way. I hope you get it figured out before they hang you. I heard tell they always send someone around before they put the noose around your neck to explain what's going to happen to you in the afterlife. If I was you, I'd listen real close to what he has to say."

Outside, the men stopped to check on Mr. Wilson's condition as he lay on a litter. James knelt down to visit with him.

"Tell me your name again sir. I want to remember what you've done for me today as long as I live," the Magistrate implored of 'Bob'.

"Well sir, I've been traveling incognito under the name of Bob Kitchens for the last couple of weeks while chasing a hunch. You and I have never met that I recall, but I work for you indirectly. You probably know me better as James Temple, captain of the black ship."

Mr. Wilson's eyes opened wide in disbelief.

"I was told you died at sea Captain Temple."

"Everybody keeps telling me that," James laughed. "That was part of the deception to give me freedom to move about. It worked too, because that's how we ended up here. I would appreciate it very much if you kept our little secret for right now. I want to make sure these skunks can't get back at me or my family until I know they're all hanged."

"Your secret is safe with me Captain Temple. I want you to know, I was on board from the beginning of our little experiment with money and resources, but I was always too busy to meet with you as the other's did. Henry Boles always said you were the right man for the job, and by golly he was right. I'm privileged to finally make your acquaintance my boy. You've done us a great service today by rooting out this evil scourge from among us. Do you think we have any hope of getting our children back?" he asked. Mr. Whitaker spoke up before James could answer.

"I think once the Queen is apprised of our discovery, the entire Royal Navy will probably be sent to the region to ask for them back. Now let's get you to the hospital and tend your wounds."

"Before I go, I want to say one thing more to you Captain Temple. When the Navy goes back, I hope the Black Ship will tag along too as a little reminder of what happened the last time it visited the region. I heard what happened from some of the other captains who were there. The legendary exploits of the ship and her Captain are growing by leaps and bounds every day."

"I can't take all the credit sir. I had the finest crew of sailors any captain could hope to sail with, and had it not been for my friend Galen Sims accidentally overhearing a conversation one night, all this might never have been discovered. We all owe him a real debt of gratitude for his service," James said humbly as he watched Galen squirm from the praise.

"I was just doing my duty to the Cap 'n," Galen smiled.

"I assure both of you men, you will find us a generous and grateful nation for what you've done on behalf of our consortium and for the families of England who have missing loved ones. God bless and keep you both my heroic friends. Let the legend grow Captain Temple, England needs her heroes."

"As you wish sir," James smiled understanding his meaning.

As they watched Mr. Wilson being placed in the ambulance, Mr. Whitaker asked them what their next move was.

"I'm going home Mr. Whitaker," James stated matter of fact. "I forgot to tell you I got married since I've been here?"

"What?" he asked in disbelief. "When did you have the time, and for Heaven's sake who is she?"

"I married Ann Boles four days after arriving. Things got rushed a little, but I think she's worth it."

"I agree with you Mr. Temple, she's a real catch. How did Aunt Mamie take it?" Mr. Whitaker asked.

"She fainted," James laughed causing Mr. Whitaker to laugh too.

"I wish I could have been there to see it. Well, welcome to the family Captain Temple. I believe you're going to add another level of interest to an already interesting family," Mr. Whitaker exclaimed. "Now if you'll excuse me, I'm going to the hospital with my friend. He and I have some catching up to do."

"Goodbye Mr. Whitaker. Whenever things have settled down some, I'll bring the consortium up to speed on the exploits of our little adventure. It'll make for good reading," James called out to him as he rode away.

"I look forward to it," the old gentleman said as he disappeared from sight.

"Well Galen, what's your plans?" James asked suspecting his answer.

"I'm off to chase a hunch of my own Skipper," Galen offered.

"You mean Eva?" James queried.

"Yes sir, and I know she's going to be a handful. I never had any desire to settle down until I met her, and Lord help me, I can't help but like the woman," he snickered. "I'll let you know how it all works out."

"Come out to the Boles estate when you're free and meet my new wife, and please bring Eva along too. I would be very pleased to introduce you to some of the people who put this adventure together," James stated casually trying to show Galen his acceptance of Eva as a friend and an equal. Her past was just that as far as he was concerned, and the future was looking more promising with each passing day.

"Do you know where Captain Boles is staying?" Galen asked.

"I think so. Once I'm back at the hotel, I'm sure I can find him. He told me he was going to disappear once he delivered the news of my death to everyone to keep from spilling the beans," James said.

"Do you think one of these coppers would give us a ride back to our side of town?" Galen wondered aloud.

"I'm not sure. You reckon they would come after us if we stole a carriage?" James reciprocated. "Maybe we better ask Chief Detective Fields before we go too far afield."

After procuring a ride back into town, the two men split up at evening time and went their separate ways. It was a bittersweet moment because they had been together off and on for months now and had built a stronger friendship. In the meantime, it would be a long night and day before Henry finally swaggered back into the hotel. James heard him the moment the door opened into his room.

"Where can a sailor get something to eat around here?" James asked as he leaned back against the door jamb. Henry turned upon hearing his friend's voice and reacted appropriately.

"Well looks whose back from the dead, you salty old sea biscuit!" he shouted with joy as he ran across the hall and grabbed James.

"Hi Henry, you look pretty darn good too," James grinned as he pushed back his arms to really look at his friend, his brother. It was true enough, because no two men of purpose were ever more closely bonded in their undeniable trust and love for one another. After a few moments, James asked after Anne and Johnny.

"How did they take the news of my death? Do you think they will be too angry when I show?" That's when Henry revealed what he had done.

"I just couldn't do it James. So I took 'em out to a little cottage where I used to stay when I was in port before connecting up with the Boles family. They're safe with Keely Potts and his family. I'll take you there when you're ready."

"Let me grab my hat and coat."

After procuring two horses, they rode out of Liverpool into the countryside to Henry's picturesque cottage getaway. After coming upon a little rise, they could see the house clearly and the bustling activity around it. As their horses slowed, Henry couldn't help but admire the way the little rundown cottage was starting to shape up.

Mr. Potts was indeed a fine carpenter and had done a lot of fine work on the place, and especially to the rundown split rail fencing. They found a place to tie their horses so they could walk across the field in the tall grass and be upon the house before anyone saw them. They had walked about half way across when their plan was accidentally discovered. As Ginger Potts stepped through the door to feed the chickens, she called out to Anne upon seeing the two men.

"Mrs. Anne, we have strangers coming across the field. Should I call for Keely?"

Anne stepped to the door for a better look. It didn't take but a glance and she was off like a shot racing across the field to see her sailor and cousin. Within five or six feet, she stopped suddenly to drink in their essence. As she walked slowly in a circle around them, she wanted to be sure they were the same two men. James was much thinner than she remembered and freshly groomed, but he was just as handsome and desirable as the first night they met.

"Hi Henry," she said as the two men stood in formation as the mock inspection continued around them.

"Hi cousin," he answered. "I brought you a man home for supper. Do you like?"

"He's got potential, but so did the last one who got himself killed off on a fool's errand," she chided.

"That couldn't be helped cousin, he was just doing his duty as a good sailor," Henry rebutted.

"Well this one better not be a sailor, cause some sailors sure know how to keep a girl guessing," she replied.

Henry reached out and took James' jaw in his hand.

"Ain't he pretty cousin?"

"The prettiest thing I ever seen," Anne said as she jumped and wrapped her arms around James neck kissing him all over his face.

"Please cousin, show a little restraint. You're not at the hotel," Henry chided in good fun.

Around and around James swung her as they kissed. That's when he felt something out of place. Setting her back down, he moved his hand slowly down her belly to feel a slight bulge that wasn't there when he left almost four months ago. All she knew to do was smile weakly.

"I haven't told anyone yet," she said.

"You won't have to in a couple more months," he teased.

"You're not unhappy about this are you?"

"I guess not. I was just hoping to have you all to myself for a little while longer is all," he answered sweetly.

"We still have a little time before it becomes an issue. I promise to make it worth your while till then," she said kissing him as sweetly as honey dripping from the comb.

"I'm sorry it's taken so long to get home. I'll tell you all about it as we walk up to the house. Where's Johnny?"

"He and Keely are fishing. They should be home in a little while," she answered. "That young man has certainly missed his father."

"Well, it's been hard on all of us to be sure. I hope you'll think it was worth it when you hear the whole story," he said. "Some of this Henry doesn't yet know. Oh, I forgot to tell you I met Lord Thomas Denman. Turns out, he was the mysterious man on the ship the day I went to inspect it. He's the Queen's right hand man, so I'm told."

Anne and Henry were awed by his comment, because even they had never met the great man. James assured them, his name was still a secret within the consortium and was meant to stay that way for reasons of security and plausible deniability as requested by the Monarchy. This was one story that would never make it officially into the history books, but it would be remembered in hallowed halls for generations nonetheless by those who lived it and their offspring.

"The cottage is charming," James said as they walked slowly up to it through the tall grass.

"Mr. Potts is a wonderful craftsman. Did you know he grew up not far from here and still has family hereabouts? We've even been visited regularly by some of his brothers dropping off game for our cook pots. They are lovely people," Anne said.

Ginger Potts met them at the door with an effervescent smile and curtsied them in. She could see by Anne's expression that she was a very happy woman.

"Please come in sirs. I have hot tea ready to pour and little tea cakes fresh from the oven. Dinner should be ready in an hour or so. Be sure and wipe your feet," she smiled wanting nothing brought into her clean house except love and good cheer.

In an hour or so, Keely and Johnny came home with their basket filled with fish. Upon entering the room and seeing his dad, Johnny dropped his fishing gear and ran to his father's open arms. He tried hard not to cry, but he couldn't help the emotional tug of the heart he felt at the moment.

Ginger Potts made the men clean up, and they all sat down to dinner for the first time as a family of kindred spirits. James and Henry regaled them with some exploits of their trip, but not all. Most of the conversation about the sex trade of young women would wait until young ears went to bed, and even then all might not be told.

At the conclusion of the evening, all parties seemed anxious to find time for more normal pursuits, and James Temple for one couldn't wait to return there. Ever since he hired on with Henry back in America, nothing about this particular tour of duty had been normal, and most assuredly his unexpected marriage to Anne Boles.

Henry and Johnny took the high road and slept out under the stars with Keely Potts hunting dog nestled between them allowing James and Anne to share a bedroom for the first time in many months. James and Anne weren't too noisy, showing great restraint on behalf of the Potts family sleeping soundly in the next room. Tomorrow the foursome would head back home to the Boles estate and the fire and dread of Aunt Mamie's fury as she finds out firsthand her captain is still alive after all the tears shed on his behalf. However, tonight would be a time for lovers to reunite and dream of their futures as lightening bugs danced like fairy tale pixies in the country darkness.

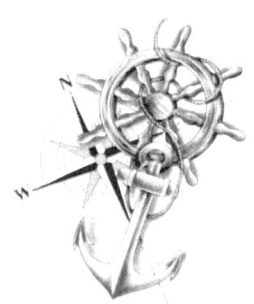

Epilogue

Early the next morning after breakfast, James and Henry walked the land the cottage sat on and talked of many things the way good friends do who enjoy each other's company. Suddenly James turned the conversation in an odd direction.

"Who owns this cottage Henry?"

"Why, I do," Henry responded, curious where this conversation might be headed. "Why do you ask?"

"I'd like to buy it," he responded.

"James, you don't seriously want to live this far out in the country, do you?" Henry asked curiously.

"Just so you know, I happen to like the open country. If you remember, I'm from rural Virginia where cotton and tobacco were king," James said casually. "I used to love riding in the wagons by the big plantations and wonder what it must be like to live in one of those fine houses. It kindled a desire to have a place of my own one day."

"I don't think Anne will like living this far out, but I could be wrong. One thing's for sure, the pace is a lot slower," Henry replied.

"It's not for her, nor is it a summer cottage like some of the upper class have for their little getaways," James stated matter of fact.

"Then what's it for?"

"I wish to give it as a gift to someone very special," James answered casually.

"Oh,...if not for Anne, then who's it for my good Captain?" Henry demanded in his best stage voice reminiscent of a Shakespearean play he had seen recently.

"It's for Keely Potts and his wife."

"Whoa,...I didn't see that coming," Henry replied. "Why?"

"He and Ginger belong here among his family and friends. Look what he's done to this place in the short time he's been here. Think what it might look like in a year or two under his care. Besides, even with a pardon, there might be difficulties finding work at first. They'll have to start over somewhere, and I ask why not here among his own people? After I was drummed out of the Navy, I couldn't get ten cents on credit at the bank and I don't want that to happen to him. Tell me how much you want for it, and I'll find some way to pay it out over time. Surely we'll have more sailing to do in the future."

"What if I gave it to you as a wedding gift to do with as you will. Would that suffice?" Henry grinned.

"I'm not comfortable with such a generous endowment on behalf of my happy marriage to your cousin. I would rather pay for it if you please," James responded not wishing to take anyone's charity.

"Alright then, I'll take fifty pounds for it just as it stands," Henry said holding out his hand to shake.

"I say it's worth a hundred pounds," James stated flatly startling Henry, "and not a penny more."

"But I only paid fifty pounds for it two years ago James. I just never got around to fixing it up. So it'll be fifty pounds and not a shilling more back to you, or there's no deal," Henry insisted.

"It's a hard bargain you drive Henry Boles, but I accept your terms," James laughed shaking Henry's hand. "When Mrs. Boles pays me for services rendered, I should be able to pay for most of it then."

Henry looked at James oddly.

"What do you mean, you should have most it then?"

"Well, I don't yet know what I'm going to be paid in regards to my short tour of duty as Captain of the black ship. When I find out, I'll pay you from the proceeds of that."

"James old boy, I think you're in for the surprise of your life," Henry rebuffed him. "You're still talking like an employee of the Boles Shipping Line."

"But that's what I am, unless I've been fired while I was away."

"My goodness dear cousin; you don't mind if I call you cousin do you, since you're officially in the family now?"

"Of course not. In fact, I kind of like the sound of it."

"Well, here's the thing dear cousin James, I suspect that by the end of this great adventure, you will probably not only end up being executive head of Boles Shipping, but probably head of the entire Consortium as well. Your net worth today at Lloyd's of London stands at five thousand pounds from Aunt Mamie's account alone, not to mention two dozen others who agreed to back you with equal amounts. So you see cousin James, you are a man rich beyond your wildest dreams, and could buy a dozen plantations if you like."

James' mouth flew open in disbelief.

"I don't understand."

"Surely you don't think I brought you all the way over here because I was desperate for a top rigger, do you? Better yet, do you think I seduced you into coming along for a dangerous suicide mission because there was pocket change in it for you?" Henry asked. "If you thought that, then you got mush for brains."

"Alright, I'll bite. Why did you really bring me over here?" James queried. He still didn't see the big picture the way Henry did, but hoped he could fill him in on the details.

"I brought you over here cousin so you could take your place among the great sailors and business men of our times. You have an opportunity now to make your own mark in history and restore your good name as it should be. The success of the black ship may have anchored you a spot in the unofficial history books of the Royal Naval Academy, but it was your last great adventure which landed you a spot in the hearts of all English men and women everywhere. Going the extra mile to uncover the sex trade of their children and breaking the backs of some high ranking people along the way will probably get you a knighthood, if I'm any judge of royal character."

"Hold up just a minute there fast talker, I'm just a sailor. I didn't sign up for any of this. I merely did what was asked of me," James replied overwhelmed by all this talk of a knighthood and large bank accounts. What had he gotten himself into? "Is all this because I married Anne? If it is, I'm not interested."

"Hardly James, Anne's marrying you was just her good fortune. However, I did without your knowledge entice you over to run in a race where the odds of winning where a thousand to one, and you won big for a whole lot of people." Henry stated flatly as he patted his friend gently on the back. "Don't you see, you were made for this. Most men would still be crowing from the rooftops about the impossible things they'd just done, but not you. Being the humble man you are, you haven't uttered a word or a peep about anything. You're certainly not political material because of that one weakness, but you are the right man for getting a job done when there's something important to do. I believe in you sailor as do a lot of others, so like it or not, you're going to have to adjust to being an important man once again. You'll just walk the deck of a different kind of ship in order to sail it."

James didn't know what to say. It all seemed so unreal that Henry's voice started to sound faraway like it was coming from one of those open ended barrels they used to play in as kids. For the moment, he wasn't going to give it any more thought, forcing it from his head and hoping instead to move on with Anne where ever that took him. The idea of living at the Boles estate never occurred to him either, but wealthy people do that here in merry old England as they surround themselves with family. Thankfully, all the right people living in this particular house got along great.

"James, the idea always was to bring you into the company and the consortium as a partner on some level. As you can tell from the age of most of the current players, they are not a young lot. Some of their children are just now stepping up to take their rightful place, but they will need guidance from a man with a strong sense of purpose and a moral compass. You James Temple will be their compass"

"What if I don't want the job?" James roared back. "It seems like everyone went to a lot of trouble in their long range planning without discussing any of this with me. I'm not sure I'm even qualified."

Henry laughed.

"If anything, you are probably over qualified. What this group needs is a leader with a backbone who's smart enough to hold a course without running her aground. Sounds like Captain's work to me."

"But, I don't know anything about running a business like this Henry."

"In six months, you'll know more about this business than anyone here, cause that's how your mind works. Like I said, it's nothing but Captain's work on a different kind of ship. You're a smart man James and a natural for the job. You'll figure it out."

"Then why don't you do it Henry? I haven't had any complaints working under you."

"If I was only half as smart as you, I would do it," Henry replied honestly, "but you have something I don't have."

"What's that Henry? You are every bit my equal and then some."

"You have something to prove and the drive to follow it through. You have been granted a genuine 'Resurrection Moment' by the hand of Providence to make up for what the American Navy took from you in drumming you from their ranks. Even when we were kids, you were always a driven lad with your sense of honor and duty oozing from every pore. Your whole life has been in training for this job. America will one day see you rise above your circumstance and take your place among the great leaders of the world. Sadly, it will be their loss and England's gain. That's the truth of it, and like it or not James, that is where your story is headed," Henry conceded.

"Whew, you almost had me there for a moment Henry," James teased as he stepped back to catch his breath. He'd had enough praise heaped on him to make his head swell like yeast rolls at a Sunday picnic. "Why don't we stop talking about how important I am and go back to the house where the really important people are. I need time to figure out what I'm going to do with the rest of my life, especially since I find myself with a new English wife thanks to you."

"Just so you know, I'm not the one who's going to do the asking. That will come later when the time is right, and you've had time to adapt and learn. And like it or not, you're still going to be a very rich man. You can run from responsibility here in England, or stay and help make it a better place for everyone. I think the consortium and the country could use the touch of a real Virginia man to help sharpen things up a bit, don't you?" Henry asked not taking any pressure off his friend. He knew some men weren't good under pressure, but James Temple thrived in that environment because of his strong moral compass and commitment to duty. He was after all, a real Virginia man of quality through and through despite the rough road he'd been forced to travel his whole life. Like it or not, James Temple was that rare breed of man the consortium needed desperately, and Henry knew it.

"Enough of this kind of talk Henry," James said placing both hands over his ears. "Let's go back to the cottage and give Keely the good news about becoming a new homeowner. It's time we made someone else happy for a change. Who knows, maybe Ginger will feed us some more of her delicious plum pudding before we go."

"I'm glad we met as kids James, and had the opportunity to grow up together," Henry said as they walked along. "I don't care where life takes you or how big you become, you'll always be my best friend. The English are big on titles and placement in polite society, but we are not bound by that because of where we came from. We had some tough times together growing up, but all that only made us better men."

As they walked along, James placed a strong hand on Henry's shoulder and squeezed it in agreement, cause he understood.

"You are the best friend I ever had Henry, and for a long time after the Navy, my only friend. Thanks for believing I was worth saving."

"It was my great pleasure Captain."

✱✱

Aunt Mamie fainted upon seeing the bodily remains of James Temple walk through her library door as he entered with Anne and Johnny in tow. Henry laughed and laughed as he ran to lift her up on the divan. As her eyes fluttered open again, she cried tears of joy at the sight of her beloved Captain, knowing everything was back on track.

"Well,...you have certainly surprised an old woman today Captain Temple. I just hope I didn't embarrass myself too much when I landed on the floor," she said.

"You didn't embarrass us, but you scared us almost to death. I hope you don't keep doing that," James countered.

"And I hope you don't keep dying on me either young man. I expect a full explanation when we're all in our right minds again, cause I'm assuming there must be a reason for all the secret drama," she said.

Henry answered for James before he could respond.

"Auntie, you better hold on tight when you hear it. Virginians have a word they use when someone tells a tall tale; it's called a whopper, and honey this one is a whopper!"

"Give me your hand Henry," Aunt Mamie said bluntly. Upon taking it, she kissed the inside of it, and then turned it over and smacked the back of it firmly causing poor Henry to withdraw in pain.

"What was that for?" he cried out like he didn't know.

"The kiss is because I love you, and the smack is because you left me alone during all these trying times. It was not a good trick to play on your Auntie. Now help me stand up so I can kiss all of you good and proper. My day of sorrow is past, and my time of rejoicing is at hand. Come here to me, all of you," she said as she reached out kissing the lot of them one at a time, including Johnny. He remembered what his father had said once about English women and wanted no part of it. Like it or not, Johnny got kissed just the same.

"I also have some news for you Aunt Mamie," Anne began eagerly. "James and I are going to have a child."

Aunt Mamie was thrilled as she extended her hand to Anne.

"Oh my dear, I hope you have a house full. This old place has been like a mausoleum for far too long, and before I die, I would like to live with grandchildren gathered at my feet. You wouldn't mind too much if I thought of them in that way, would you? You've been as dear to me as any daughter could be," Aunt Mamie said as tears formed in her eyes with the happy news.

"Of course not Auntie, you are as dear to me as my own mother. If we have a girl, I wish to name her after you and my own mother of course. We'll call her Haley after my mother, and Grace after you if that's okay?"

"Haley Grace," Mamie said softly as she rolled the words around listening to how it sounded. "I like it. Will you call her Haley or Grace?"

"In Virginia, they use both names together as one. I like the way it rolls off the tongue, don't you?" Anne asked.

"Yes, I believe I do. Normally, I would advise using Haley's first name for when the child gets into mischief, and Grace for when she does something good, but today I'm feeling generous," she snickered. "I suspect your mother will probably take the opposite approach so you'll have to keep me informed of her decision."

As everyone sat around laughing, one of the maids entered the room with some news.

"I'm sorry to interrupt madam, but there are guests at the door."

"Who are they?"

"A Mr. Sims and a Miss Langtree. They said they were hoping to speak with Captain Temple or Captain Boles. Shall I send them in?"

"Yes of course," Aunt Mamie answered as she looked at her two wayfaring sailors with suspicion.

As the two entered the room, the two captains met the pair with great enthusiasm. Even though Henry didn't know the woman, he knew Galen well enough to know she was probably okay.

"I'm sorry to barge in on you like this Cap 'n Boles, but Cap 'n Temple told me you married him and his missus recently. Here's the thing, Sarah has agreed to marry me, and I would like it very much if you would perform the ceremony," Galen said openly with gusto.

"But of course Mr. Sims, and just who is this mysterious lady you've brought us. Have we ever met?" Henry asked innocently.

"I don't believe we have, but it's very nice to finally make your acquaintance. Galen has told me so many fine things about you and Captain Temple that I feel as though I've known you all my life," Sarah answered in that polished way the cultured English have at introductions.

"I don't know how you did it, but it sounds like you've found yourself a real lady of class and distinction Mr. Sims. How did you two meet?" Henry inquired knowing nothing of their story.

"We accidentally met following up a lead on the trafficking case. Ten minutes alone with her and I was smitten," Galen smiled at Sarah as she blushed remembering that first encounter. He told only what was necessary, and no more. "She was very instrumental in resolving this whole affair, wouldn't you say so Cap 'n Temple?"

"Indeed she was. It's good to see you again Miss Langtree. I hope your marriage will be a happy one. You're marrying a fine man and a good friend, and I wish you many happy returns," James beamed.

"When would you like to get hitched?" Henry asked.

"Today sir, if it's not too much trouble."

"That's kind of quick, isn't it?" Henry asked.

"Well, I've known Sarah longer than Cap 'n Temple knew his wife before marrying her. Is there a time requirement for things like this?"

"I'm afraid you got me there Mr. Sims. There is no time limit on such things," Henry replied sheepishly, "but technically, I can only marry you aboard a ship. So which ship shall it be?"

"I was kind of hoping you'd marry us on the same ship the Skipper was, if she's still in port," Galen answered.

Henry was caught flat footed, and answered in the only way he could.

"I'm sorry Mr. Sims, but that particular ship has sailed," he replied looking over at Anne. "How about the Argyle?"

"Would it be too much to ask for the black ship?"

"That's kind of morbid Mr. Sims. Are you sure about this?"

"Well sir, it's because of that old ship that I met Eva...,I mean Sarah," Galen said forgetting himself.

"Then the black ship it is," Henry replied satisfied with Galen's answer. Had he asked anything more, he would not have gotten a straight answer anyway. Some secrets would just have to keep.

"How about four o'clock this afternoon. Since we have just arrived ourselves, we can have dinner first and rest some while we get better acquainted with your new bride to be. Do you have a honeymoon destination in mind?" Henry asked curiously.

"We're thinking about going to the south of France for a little getaway after we move into our new house," Galen answered.

"New house?" James asked. "When did you have time to buy a new house?"

"Oh, I forgot to tell you Skipper. Do you remember the house Hakeem owned?" Galen asked.

"Yes of course. You mean to move in there?" James asked again knowing it was an expensive house in a very exclusive neighborhood. "That's pretty tall cotton on a quartermaster's pay."

"Yes sir, I see your point, but we had a little help," Galen stated matter of fact.

"It's certainly a beautiful home. Tell us how it all came about," James asked once more delighted for his friend.

"Well, the thing is Cap'n, Lord Denman arranged to have it given to me in exchange for the price of two breakfast biscuits. He assured me the last tenant wasn't coming back, and it desperately needed a new one. I even have the same housekeeper. You'll have to come by and see us once we're settled in," the quartermaster smiled.

"Did you say you knew Lord Thomas Denman, Mr. Sims?" Aunt Mamie asked suspiciously. How was it such a common, rough sailor knew his lordship on such an intimate level, while she had only met him once at a formal dinner. To her way of thinking, something mighty queer was going on here.

"Yes Ma'am, Cap 'n Temple and I both know him well. Oh by the way, he asked for you to stop by as soon as you can and help him fill in the gaps concerning our little expedition. He said, 'you know who' was asking for her unofficial report on certain things," he said covertly.

Aunt Mamie sat befuddled with all this talk swirling around her of people in high places, and she wasn't even in the loop. What had these men been up to these many months since they left? For now it would have to wait, because they had dinner guests and a wedding in the making. It was hard for her sometimes to understand this younger generation, and she hoped she wasn't becoming obsolete.

Johnny had sat quietly with Anne as all this marriage hoopla was swirling around them. He didn't exactly understand adults all that much, but he could tolerate them when necessary. That's when he had a burning question for his father.

"Father, could Anne and I go aboard the black ship too for the wedding? I'm sure she would like to see it, wouldn't you?"

"Of course," she answered as she squeezed Johnny's hand in approval. This was a special moment between the two of them. Johnny had simply called her by her first name without the usual 'Miss' attached to it.

"Very well and after the wedding, I'll give you the grand tour. It's a fine ship with a good story to tell," James answered. "If you'd like Aunt Mamie, I could give you the whole story then as well, if you promise not to faint."

"Pish, Posh, I only faint at funerals and resurrections, both of which I am now well adjusted to. I promise to be a good girl from now on aboard your ship."

About this time, the maid reentered the room with news of yet another guest's unexpected arrival.

"Mr. Whitaker is here Mrs. Boles. Shall I show him in?"

"Yes of course."

As Albert Whitaker entered the room, he saw plenty of familiar faces and one of course he didn't know.

"Did I call at a bad time Mamie?" he asked as he shook hands with everyone there in spirited fashion happy to see them all.

"Not at all. We were about to eat dinner and then at four o'clock we were going to a wedding aboard the black ship. It seems Mr. Sims is about to marry Miss Langtree and Henry is performing the ceremony. It will be fun, would you like to come?" Mamie asked.

"Only on one condition," he said mysteriously.

"And just what would that be dear friend?" she asked.

"If you would do me the honor of marrying me on board the ship as well. It's a big deck, I think it would accommodate the four of us."

Mamie didn't faint, but she put her hand to her mouth speechless for the first time in her life. After catching her breath, she spoke.

"Are you sure this is what you want Albert? It would change everything between us," she replied.

"I would hope so! You and I have lived alone too long Mamie. It wasn't until I came to tell you of our good captain's death that I realized what a fool I've been for waiting so long to ask for your hand. I wanted so much to comfort you the way a husband might have, but couldn't because of our silly traditions. I have harbored so much affection for you these many long years since our spouses have passed, and we're not getting any younger. So what do you say old girl, give it a go?" he asked.

Mamie looked up at him with real tenderness and placed her hand alongside his distinguished face and answered.

"I believe I'll give it a go Albert. You've been a dear friend, and I'm ready for the next stage of our life together if you are," she said sweetly as she turned to look at Galen and Sarah. "Would you mind too much if we made it a double wedding? It's okay if you don't won't to, because I certainly wouldn't want to spoil your moment, if it's too much to ask."

Galen smiled at Sarah and nodded his approval.

"We would be delighted if you'd join us. Afterwards if you'd like, you could join us as the Peacock Tavern for a proper send off. Sarah's brother Earl is preparing a little something for us there, and a few more or less won't matter one wit to him."

"Thank you Mr. Sims, we would be delighted," Albert Whitaker said happily as he kissed Mamie's hand. As he looked steadfastly at her, he saw the young woman she used to be staring back at him with joy beaming from every glint and sparkle of her dazzling blue eyes.

At that moment, the door into the dining room opened and a servant announced that dinner was served. As they made their way in, James quietly asked Henry the obvious question.

"Mr. Matchmaker, did you arrange that too?"

"I was in the area and just gave it a little nudge by asking Mr. Whitaker to give her the news of your death. By not being there in her time of sorrow, she was forced to seek comfort from someone close. A blind man could see how crazy those two were for each other. They'll make a cute couple, don't you think?" Henry teased.

"I reckon so," James answered back.

"This is only the first step. Remember what I told you back at the cottage? Those two would never have done this had it not been for you being here to assume command when the time comes. She'll be leaving the estate now to live with Mr. Whitaker, and it'll be yours to manage. Remember, I'm a matchmaker, and you will soon be courted by a different kind of mistress called the 'Consortium'. Be brave my Captain and don't ever lose sight of what's important, and it'll be a match made in Heaven for all of us," Henry touted.

"Thanks for believing in me Henry. I hope I'm up to the job."

"Don't worry James, you will be. How can you lose with people like us in your life to help you along. I say let the adventure begin!"

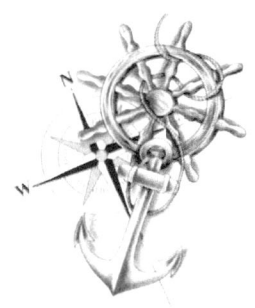

If you're interested in some good reading, I'll leave you with some of the resources I used for this book.

Marked For Death ....by Geert Wilders

Thomas Jefferson and the Tripoli Pirates ..... by Brian Kilmeade and Don Yaeger

David Farragut, Sailor ....by Ferdinand Reyher

The Bible, King James Version ....Inspired by God

Google ....Man's Best Research Friend Ever

Britain's KINGS and QUEENS .... Pitkin Pictorials Ltd.

****

Other Books by the Author:

The Texas Man .... in print

The Legend of One-Eyed Jack .... in print

Dr. Hob's Journey .... in print

Emilee's Secret .... in print

The Gunfighter's Gospel .... in print

Kiko's Honor .... in print